SMOKE OVER OWL CREEK

Small town. Dark secrets.

SMOKE
OVER OWL CREEK

CAREN HAHN

Smoke over Owl Creek by Caren Hahn

Published by Seventy-Second Press

www.carenhahn.com

Hardcover ISBN-13: 978-1-958609-01-9

Paperback ISBN-13: 978-1-7352272-3-8

Cover design by Andrew Hahn.

Edited by Midnight Owl Editors.

Printed in the USA

To my parents, Joan and Dennis,
who exemplify the best of small town life.

BOOKS BY CAREN HAHN

Find all of Caren Hahn's work on Amazon.com

CONTEMPORARY SUSPENSE:

This Side of Dark

What Comes After

THE OWL CREEK SERIES

Smoke over Owl Creek

Hunt at Owl Creek

ROMANTIC FANTASY:

THE WALLKEEPER TRILOGY

Burden of Power

Pain of Betrayal

Gleam of Crown

HATCHED

Hatched: Dragon Farmer

Hatched: Dragon Defender

Hatched: Dragon Speaker

Visit carenhahn.com to receive a free copy of *Charmed: Tales from Quarantine and Other Short Fiction.*

SMOKE OVER OWL CREEK

OWL CREEK MYSTERIES BOOK 1

CAREN HAHN

1

It wasn't a baby.

Val's head snapped up. She blinked to clear her vision, her hand limp against her book. For a single heartbeat, she tried to make sense of her surroundings. The clock on the nightstand read 1:40 am, and she vaguely realized she must have just drifted off.

The bedside lamp cast long shadows against the faded wallpaper, stained and bruised from years of use. As she reached to shut it off, the thought came again.

It wasn't a baby.

Val sat up, alert. She threw back the sheet, slipped her bare feet into a pair of flip-flops, and hurried to the door. Heart pounding, she moved down the stairs as quick as she dared, the flip-flops making a slapping sound against the aged wood. The air was sharp with the scent of smoke. Moonlight shining through a large window on the landing illuminated her way to the back of the house. The outside porch light made the small panes of stained glass in the Victorian-era door glow in tones of amber, blue, and emerald. The heavy door protested when she pulled.

A cool breeze greeted her bare arms and legs as she stepped outside; a fresh contrast to the stuffy house. With a brief glance, Val took in the yard, her eyes drawn to the shadows under the trees. Keeping one eye on the darkness, she ran to the lump on the trampoline.

Abby's hair was just visible above the blankets, the rest of her burrowed deep for warmth.

Val stroked the thin blond curls.

"Hey, sweetie," she murmured. "Let's go inside."

If Abby were smaller, Val could have scooped her up in her arms and carried her to the house. But she was seven now, and big enough that Val wouldn't have made it more than a few steps.

"Come on, baby. I need you to wake up. I want you to sleep in the house tonight."

With gentle prodding, Abby finally stirred.

"You said I could sleep on the trampoline," she accused, her words slurred with sleep.

"I know, but I changed my mind. I don't think it's a good idea." Val looked back toward the shadows where the line of trees marked the rise of the mountain behind the house.

Earlier that day, while Abby had been playing on the rusty swing set, Val had been indoors packing away some of her parents' old stuff to make room for the boxes she and Abby brought with them when they moved in. The rhythmic squeal of the swing set chain was a soothing accompaniment to the childhood memories reawakened by each book, each card, each photo she unearthed.

At some point in the afternoon, she'd heard the distant sound of a wailing baby drifting over the dry fields. The Parkers lived down the hill and across the road, and in the full foliage of summer, she could barely make out the roof of their barn through the trees. She'd assumed they had family visiting with children and hadn't thought anything of it.

Until in her sleep, she remembered the Parkers were out of town.

Yet there was something else that could sound hauntingly like a screaming child.

Would she know if a cougar watched her now? She felt a chill on her neck at the thought. Keeping an eye on the dark line of trees at the edge of the yard, Val shushed Abby's protests and helped her down from the trampoline. When her feet hit the dry grass, Abby yelped.

"I've got a sticker in my foot."

"We'll fix it in the house."

"But it really hurts."

"Let's get inside first."

Her arms full of blankets, Val helped Abby hobble across the yard, supporting her daughter's weight. She couldn't shake the feeling that something was watching her from the shadows. But the light from the porch blinded her to the darkness under the trees. The yard seemed so much bigger in the dark, the safety of the house far away.

She restrained a sigh of relief when they reached the porch. The old door squealed against the frame as she pushed it open. It stuck worse now than it used to.

She turned around as she closed the door, taking

one last look at the yard. There, under the distant trees, she saw a faint patch of…something.

She blinked, her eyes straining.

There was a smudge of something not-quite-shadow. As she watched, it dissolved into the darkness.

A gust of wind sent a fast food bag skittering across the ground as Joel parked next to Larry's sheriff-issued Yukon. Everywhere he looked was brown. The hard-packed earth that served as a parking lot behind the elementary school. The dry grass in the baseball field bordering the chain link fence. The dirty tents sprouting side by side across the playground. Even the air was tinged with a brown haze from the surrounding forest fires. The world had curled in on itself under the heat of an unrelenting sun like the last gasp of summer before the rains of September.

But it was only July. There was still a lot of summer left.

The sun baked Joel's forehead as he stepped out of his unmarked Charger and he wished for a hat. His eyes itched. Something in the air was stirring up his allergies, and he guessed it wouldn't get better until the weather shifted.

He followed the trail through the tents, passing a food cart with a line of dirty, exhausted men and women who still managed to smile and tease one another through their weariness. Most of the faces here were unfamiliar, firefighters who'd been brought in from all over the West. But on occasion someone nodded his direction or offered a wave.

Larry was waiting for him just inside the play shed, a large covered structure that allowed school recess to continue through the rainy winters. Even without the brown deputy uniform he would have stood out in this crowd just by having shaved that morning. He stood near a little gray pup tent and greeted Joel with a nod.

"Hey, Joel."

Joel frowned at the number of tents crowded in the shade of the structure. "Not a lot of breathing room here, I guess."

"They say you can tell who got Taco Bell versus Burger King based on the smell of your neighbors' farts."

"Nice." Joel grimaced as he pulled on a set of gloves. "Tell me about our missing person."

"Samuel Howser. White. Fifty-seven. His wallet and personals were all left behind."

Joel ducked into the small gray tent. The air was thick with the scent of unwashed man and campfire smoke. A black sleeping bag lay rumpled in the middle of the floor. In one corner, a worn duffle bag spilled clothes onto the floor. Joel spotted a pair of jeans with one leg inside out, a long-sleeved denim shirt, thick hiking socks, and pair of plaid boxer shorts.

A backpack lay near the door, and Joel reached for it. Wallet. Keys. Phone. A switchblade knife. A prescription bottle. Toothbrush and stick of deodorant. Another pair of crusty socks and a pocket-sized notebook with a pen sticking through the spiral binding.

Joel removed the pen and flipped through the notebook. It contained a few rough sketches and text scrawled in tiny script. Almost like a comic book, but completely unskilled. The last page held a drawing of a round symbol with some kind of swooping shape inside it.

"This mean anything to you?" he asked, showing the page to Larry who crouched in the doorway.

Larry shrugged.

Joel dropped the notebook and reached for the wallet, pulling out the license. Samuel Howser looked older than fifty-seven. His gray hair was slicked back, and heavy pouches bulged under his eyes. His pronounced cheekbones made him look gaunt and undernourished.

"How about his boots?"

"They're gone. Just these sneakers here."

Choosing boots over sneakers might not be significant, but if Joel had been a firefighter headed downtown, he would have picked the sneakers.

He also would have brought his wallet. Joel lifted it and thumbed through the contents, counting less than forty dollars in cash.

"His license says he's from Pineview," he said, emerging from the tent. "Better see if that's current."

"I've got a call in to the station there."

"And the guy who reported him missing?"

"Thomas Morrison. I told him to stay close." Larry gestured to a beefy man in short sleeves standing not far away. The man straightened as Joel walked over.

"You're the one who reported Samuel Howser missing?" Joel asked, shaking his hand. It nearly swallowed

Joel's and was rough with calluses. He smelled of smoke and sweat and tobacco.

"Yeah, that's me."

"And your name?"

"Tom. Uh, Thomas Morrison." He pulled at his coarse beard, eyeing Joel's notepad.

"How do you know Mr. Howser?"

"We're on the same crew. My tent's this one right here." He gestured to the blue tent next to Howser's.

"Are you friends?"

Tom shrugged. "Sam's all right."

"What makes you think something's happened to him?"

Tom blew out a stale breath. "Sam has his habits. Always has to do things a certain way. Eats the same thing every day. Always the first one up. It's not like him to just up and disappear during the night."

"Tell me about the last time you saw him."

Tom described coming off a 24-hour shift the previous day and going to dinner with friends at McGowan's, the only restaurant in town. He couldn't say how Howser had spent the evening and when he'd come back, Howser's tent was dark.

"I thought he'd just crashed hard, you know? It wasn't until Sam didn't get up in the morning that I realized he was missing," Tom finished. "Bruce didn't know where he was either. That ain't like Sam. He's a rule follower. Wouldn't have left without making sure he checked in."

"Who's Bruce?"

"Our crew chief."

"Thank you, Mr. Morrison. Can I get your number

in case I have more questions?" As Joel wrote down Tom's phone number, Larry approached with a man wearing a Portland Trailblazers hat.

"This is Bruce Johnson, Howser's crew chief," Larry said, his face flushed in the heat.

Joel didn't know how these firefighters could stand it. His own dress shirt clung to his back and sweat trickled down his temple behind his sunglasses.

"How can I help?" Bruce adjusted his cap, exposing dark underarm stains. His eyes were earnest but he didn't have much to add to Tom's story. The camp had been searched that morning with no sign of Howser. It seemed that Tom was the last person who'd seen him the previous night.

When Joel asked if Howser had any friends in camp, Bruce shook his head.

"Sam doesn't really hang with the rest of the crew. He keeps to himself, just him and his art."

"Art?"

"Sketches, drawings, whatever he's doing in that notebook. I don't think he likes people all that much. He'll get mad if the guys get too loud and is always kind of jumpy. Reminds me of my wife when she quit smoking. It's too bad. Maybe if he had a friend or two we'd know where he is and wouldn't have had to call you."

"Anyone in particular who doesn't like him?"

Bruce tugged at his cap. His face was lined and dirt had settled into the grooves around his eyes. "I mean… not like you're saying. He's a great worker and doesn't cause trouble. But he's the kind of guy who would have been picked last in PE when he was a kid, you know?

No one minds him much, but they also don't go out of their way to be his friend."

"How about Tom Morrison? Does he get along with Sam?"

Tom was talking to a woman with thick curly hair pulled into a ponytail. She was talking animatedly, but Tom didn't seem to be paying much attention. Instead, he kept glancing over at Joel and Bruce.

Bruce followed Joel's gaze. "They get along fine, I guess. As well as anybody. Sam likes his peace and quiet, so he and Tom may have exchanged a few words once or twice about that."

"They argued?"

"Nah. Just needed to sort things out, you know? It can be tough being in each other's space day in and day out. But Tom's a good guy. He would watch out for any member of this crew."

Joel wondered if Bruce meant to imply an unspoken *even Sam,* but didn't say so. Bruce was trying so hard to convince Joel that Sam wasn't an outcast that it only cemented Joel's impression that he was.

Visiting with the other members of the crew didn't change that. None of them had seen or heard from Sam during the night, and most of them didn't care.

"You're wasting your time, Detective. He's probably just sleeping off a hangover somewhere."

Joel hoped it was something that simple, but it was hard to get drunk without a wallet unless Sam had taken some cash with him when he left. He gave Bruce his number in case Howser wandered into camp later that day. When he headed for his parked car, someone was there waiting for him, leaning against the driver's side door.

It took a minute before he recognized Carter Millston under the baseball cap and sunglasses.

"Slow news day?"

"Apparently not." Carter grinned and rubbed the soul patch on his chin. "You wanna tell me what's going on?"

"What in our history together makes you think I'd do that?" Joel asked, but he smiled as he said it. Though Joel generally had little patience for reporters, his friendship with Carter went back a long way. Friends through high school, they'd shared lunch breaks at Stan's Market and traded bruises on the football field.

"It doesn't hurt to ask," Carter said casually. "Firefighter brawl? Jealous lovers' quarrel?"

"Possible missing person."

"Really?" Carter straightened. "Who?"

"It may turn out to be nothing. I'll give you a call if we need your help."

"I'm here to serve," Carter said with a mock salute. As a journalist, Carter was respectful and conscientious in his work. Better yet, he knew how to be discreet. Joel knew that from experience.

"I saw your piece on the news last night," Joel said. "You spend a lot of time hanging around here?"

Carter's eyes darted past Joel's black Charger to the SUV with the Wallace County Sheriff's Office shield printed on the side. "I was driving past and thought I'd check things out. Crazy how a small city can pop up almost overnight. Just the laundry alone is a massive logistical undertaking."

Joel nodded absentmindedly. He'd seen Carter's story about the fire camp and didn't need a recap. "Well, like I said, I'll call you if this turns into something." He brushed past him and reached for the door.

"Did you hear Valerie's back?"

Joel turned and squinted at him. "No kidding?"

"I guess you two aren't in touch, then."

The way he said it slid under Joel's skin like an itch.

Joel kept his tone neutral. "Nope. Haven't seen her since her dad's funeral. Do you know why she's here?"

"I guess she lost her husband a while back. Now she's taking care of the place, getting it ready to sell."

"That'll be hard in this market."

Carter grunted, and after the obligatory pause to acknowledge the struggling economy in the shrinking timber town, Joel got in his car. As he drove away—the air conditioning on full blast—Joel wondered if Carter was a busybody because he was a reporter or if it was the other way around. Chicken or egg?

Either way, it could be downright annoying.

2

"MOM?"

Abby's voice interrupted Val's reverie. She looked up, surprised to realize she was sitting on the couch with a half-folded kitchen towel on her lap. How long had it been since she'd sat down to fold the laundry?

"When are we going to have lunch? I'm hungry." Abby stretched herself out on the old shag carpet. The TV was on—showing one of two stations the old antenna could pick up—but the children's programming had moved on to Bob Ross, a sure sign it was lunchtime.

"Sorry, sweetie. I'll go make lunch now."

Val tossed the unfolded towel back in the basket, feeling a wave of shame. She'd been thinking about the house. Thinking about where she and Abby would go after it sold. Wondering whether they would stay long enough in Owl Creek that she'd have to enroll Abby in school. She was always thinking these days. But she didn't understand how hours could pass when it only felt like a few minutes. And she wasn't any closer to knowing what to do with her future than she'd been two weeks earlier when she and Abby had moved in.

The floorboards creaked underfoot as she moved through the kitchen in the well-worn pattern of a lifetime. This was the house she'd grown up in, and it had changed very little in the eleven years since she'd left home. But now her parents were gone. They'd buried her dad two years ago, and a year after that her mom had moved closer to Val's sister in Arizona. The vacant house turned into an unexpected blessing when the bottom fell out of Val's life six months ago.

"This is boring," Abby moaned from the living room. "Why can't I go outside?"

Val glanced out the kitchen window, taking in the trampoline, swing set, overgrown garden, and dead lawn. The wooded hill loomed over the back yard.

"You can go out if you stay where I can see you. But shut those windows before you go. It's too hot to keep them open now."

It must have been close to eighty degrees inside, but outside was even hotter. Val had no way of cooling the house besides box fans in the windows at night, and it was a daily challenge to balance the benefit of a breeze with the cost of welcoming the heat inside. The Rockwell home was over one hundred years old and had never been updated with central air or modern insulation. Somehow, that hadn't bothered Val when she was Abby's age, but now she wondered how they'd survived the long, hot summers.

Out of curiosity, she flipped the TV to the local noon news to hear if there were any updates on the fires, which had been the main story for the past week. Two fires were in danger of merging, and another to the south was competing for resources. Looking at the map, it seemed the whole state was on fire. It wasn't Carter reporting today, but rather a chipper woman who had a habit of punctuating each sentence as if it ended with an exclamation point.

Soon Val's attention wandered back to the window, and she smiled to herself. Abby sat in the small patch of shade cast by the trampoline. Apparently sitting outside in the crunchy grass full of dried stickers was still preferable to being cooped up inside.

If only there were kids nearby she could play with, Val reflected, turning to the task of slicing carrots for lunch. Before moving back to the mountains of rural Oregon, they'd lived in a suburban neighborhood outside Chicago with a park in walking distance and several nice kids Abby's age. But now, living in the remote hills near Owl Creek, Val knew making friends wouldn't be easy for her daughter.

What about you? a small voice inside her asked. *It's not good for you to spend so much time alone either.*

I don't need friends, she snapped in reply.

Solitude. Quiet. That's why she'd come back to Owl Creek. And if she sometimes got lost in her thoughts when she was supposed to be folding laundry, there was no shame in that.

Val set aside the carrots and glanced again out the window. Abby wasn't under the trampoline anymore. Nor was she on the swing set. Val blew her bangs out of her eyes and stretched to see the garden, but Abby wasn't there either.

She pulled up the sash of the old wooden window, letting in the hot breeze. "Abby? Abigail? Where are you?"

In a moment, Abby came running around the side of the house. "I was talking to the funny man, Mom."

Alarm ignited in Val's chest. "What funny man?" She tried to keep her voice light, hoping it was just Abby's imaginative play.

"The man in the garage."

Val was halfway to the door before thinking to snatch her phone from the counter. By the time she'd made it to the front door, the screen was active, and her thumb was poised to dial 911.

"Go on into the house, Abby," she ordered as she crossed the porch. "Lunch is about ready."

A free-standing workshop with an attached garage had been built off to the side of the dirt driveway decades earlier, but it was too far from the house to be convenient, so it had never been used to store vehicles. A red pickup truck was parked there now with its bed partly inside the garage bay. She heard the distinctive clatter of someone tossing lumber onto a pile.

"Excuse me!" Val said loudly, squinting against the sun to see inside the dark garage.

A man in a brown Stetson hat slid a 4x4 into the bed of the truck. He looked at Val and smiled, revealing a gap in his yellow teeth.

"Oh, hi there. Sorry if I bothered you."

"Can I help you?"

"No thanks. I've got it."

He loaded another 4x4 into the truck bed. He wore faded overalls that bulged over a large belly and seemed completely unperturbed about the interruption.

"I'm sorry, but who are you?" Val asked.

The man paused and took off his hat to reveal graying red hair curling over his ears, matted with sweat.

"I'm Paul Sheen," he said. "And who might you be?"

"Valerie Fisher. Er, Rockwell," she added, realizing her married name wouldn't mean anything to the stranger.

At the name Rockwell, understanding dawned. "You're one of Mary's kids?"

"Yes. I live here now."

Paul's eyes crinkled in a smile. "Ah, you must be wondering why I'm here stealing from you, then!"

"Something like that, yes."

Paul chuckled and walked around the truck to thrust out a hand. "I was a friend of your dad's. Your mom didn't know what to do with all this stuff when he died and said I was welcome to it. Sorry to surprise you. She didn't mind if I just showed up whenever I wanted."

His hand was sweaty when Val shook it, with grease and dirt embedded in the knuckles and under the nails. She resisted the urge to wipe her hand on her shorts.

"She didn't mention it to me."

"Well, I don't want to steal from you. But do you mind if I take this load?"

"I'll have to check with my mom." He seemed harmless enough, but the thought of someone rummaging through the shop made Val uneasy. "I'll give you my number so you can text me next time before you come. I'd rather not have people here without knowing about it first. I'm sure you understand."

The way he tilted his head at her suggested he didn't. She saw a look of judgment flash through his eyes. A *Who does she think she is?* kind of look.

"Well, sorry to bother you, ma'am," he said, his tone decidedly cooler. "Your dad was a good friend. And your mom was as happy to get rid of this stuff as I am to use it."

Val glanced at the pile of lumber, PVC pipe, and rebar stacked against the wall. She certainly didn't have any use for it, and it would need to be cleared out before she could sell the house.

"Go ahead and take this load. But please check with me next time before you come."

She left him loading the truck, with a plan to keep an eye on him from the house. But as she rounded the garage, she noticed a jacket draped on the handlebar of an old bicycle left to rust under the eaves.

"Is this your jacket?" she asked Paul, snatching it up. A whiff of smoke drifted toward her as she moved it.

Paul shook his head. "Not mine, ma'am."

"Are you sure?"

As if in answer, he lifted his hat and wiped his brow with a wadded orange bandana that looked even filthier than his hands. "What would I need a jacket for in this heat?"

He had a point. But then, where had the jacket come from?

With a shiver of dread, Val remembered the previous night when she'd thought she'd seen something under the trees. She'd almost convinced herself it was just her imagination. But now…

She was certain she hadn't seen the jacket the day before. And the smell of smoke was definitely fresh.

The window A/C unit was working overtime. The little pre-fab building that served as Owl Creek's substation for the county sheriff's office had windows facing both west and south, turning Joel's office into a cook oven. The blinds were drawn, an oscillating fan blew in the corner, but still his skin felt sticky as he filled out paperwork on a recent robbery at the local gas station.

Over the hum of the fans, he felt Larry coming. That was the thing about working in what amounted to a glorified trailer. Every footstep shook the floor and could be felt from the opposite side of the building. So he knew without looking up the exact moment when Larry stopped in his doorway.

"I've found an ex-wife!"

"I thought most men were happy to lose theirs."

Larry snorted. "No, I mean for Sam Howser. Turns out he was married. Not for long, but she still lives here in Owl Creek. I thought maybe she might know where he could've gone."

"Was she helpful?" Joel imagined his ex-wife being questioned about his habits and guessing his motives. It wasn't a pleasant thought.

"Not really. She doesn't know where he is. She didn't even know he was out of prison."

"Prison?" Joel looked up with interest. Howser

hadn't returned to the fire camp and the prescription medication he'd left behind nagged at Joel. It had taken a quick Google search to learn that it was a psychotropic and skipping doses could be a problem. Howser was going on two days now without it.

Larry handed Joel a printout from the state's database. "I checked it out, and sure enough, he got released in February."

"No kidding." Joel glanced over it, thoughts of the robbery dissolving when he saw the conviction. A drug charge was pretty common in this area. But this? "Accessory to murder? Where was this?"

"Salmon Ridge, about seven years ago. And get this," Larry added, his blue eyes shining beneath heavy eyebrows. "The murder victim? None other than Ryan Moyer."

Joel frowned as the words settled over him. Ryan Moyer was a seventeen-year-old kid who'd been beaten to death by his girlfriend's father after she went missing. It was before Joel had joined the force, but it had been the biggest news story for months all across Oregon.

"I don't remember the name Sam Howser."

"That's because everyone only cared about the dad and the uncle. Sam made a deal and didn't go to trial. I don't know how he was involved in the first place, but I've requested the case file."

Joel nodded. "It seems awfully suspicious that someone connected with the Ryan Moyer murder would disappear less than six months after getting out of prison."

The floor creaked as Larry shifted his weight. "Should we issue a press release?"

Joel clicked a ball point pen as he considered. "Give me everything you have on Howser's conviction and I'll talk to Carter. I don't want the connection to Ryan Moyer to come out just yet. The last thing people need around here is to get worked up about that whole mess."

But Carter disagreed.

Joel didn't mention Ryan Moyer or Eliza Bellingham, but not ninety seconds into their phone conversation, Carter had Googled enough information to figure out Howser's connection.

"This is important, Joel," Carter protested. "I don't feel right about holding this back. The public deserves to know if a convicted murderer is on the loose."

"He's not 'on the loose.' He served his time and was released on parole. And besides, he didn't kill that boy. He was charged as an accessory because he drove the car. But he turned himself in the next day and helped police catch the others. That hardly sounds like a threat to public safety."

Joel heard faint typing on Carter's end.

"What more can you tell me about him?"

"Just share the hotline in case anyone saw anything the night he disappeared. We don't have a reason to suspect foul play, but we're covering our bases."

"Do you think the public is in danger?"

"If I did, you'd be the first to know."

Carter snorted. "Thanks. I'll get this to my producer and see if we can put it out on the evening broadcast. We've still got all that footage from the fire camp we can use."

"Sounds good. And Carter?"

"Yeah?"

"Remember this is a real person. He's already been through hell. Let's not do that to him again."

"Agree to disagree. I'll bet there are people in this town who would revere him as a saint."

"Maybe. But I'd rather not test your theory. No mention of Ryan Moyer or Eliza Bellingham. We're trying to find a missing person, not dredge up ghosts from the past."

"You aren't any fun, Joel. Tell you what, I'll give you twenty-four hours. If this guy—what's his name? uh…Samuel Howser—wanders back into town in one piece, I'll keep quiet about his connection to the Moyer murder. But if he hasn't turned up by then, I make no promises."

"I'll take it." Joel knew this was more than he could reasonably expect. Eliza's disappearance and Ryan's subsequent murder were both a matter of public record, and Carter was plugged into the rumor mill of this town well enough to bypass Joel's investigation without too much effort. Joel could have sworn Carter was related to half of Wallace County and treated like an adopted son by the other half.

After a pause, Carter asked, "Off the record, do you have any idea what really happened to Eliza Bellingham? Do the police think Ryan killed her?"

"I can't say. That was before my time. But even if I knew, I couldn't tell you."

"I know, I know. Friendly with the press when it suits you. You'd better offer to buy me a drink sometime to prove you're not just using me until the next reporter comes along."

Joel laughed. "Tell you what, let me know the next time you have a night off and I'll meet you at McGowan's."

He ended the call and turned back to the notes he'd started on Sam Howser's disappearance. A part of Joel was surprised anyone had bothered to report him missing. No known family. No close friends. Even before his prison time, the man had lived on the fringes. It might be worth visiting with Tom Morrison to learn more about the disagreement Bruce had mentioned. The little Joel had pieced together about Sam's life so far wasn't particularly inspiring. He couldn't help but wonder how a man like that got caught up in the most infamous murder in Wallace County history.

3

"ARE YOU EATING?"

Val's phone was warm against her ear. She watched a stray crossing the yard, a beautiful calico Abby had taken to calling Creampuff. The cat paused, looking toward the garage with her ears perked up.

"Val?"

"It's fine."

Now it was Gina's turn to pause. "What does that mean?"

Val thought about the toast she'd eaten that morning and how hard it had been to swallow each bite. How the stress of the move had made keeping to her routine harder, and the daily pressure she felt to restrict what she ate.

"I'm eating. It's...I'd be lying if I said it wasn't tough, but I'm doing okay."

"Are you sure?"

Val could picture her sister on the other end of the

line, pinching at her lower lip the way she did when she was concentrating.

"I'm okay, I promise. And if I stop being okay, I'll go see someone."

"Okay," Gina said, but she didn't sound convinced.

Val wasn't convinced either. Now that she was back in Owl Creek, she was remembering how hard it was to get access to the things a person needed. Like a good therapist. Or high speed internet. Or a grocery store that was open past 10 pm.

She tried to bring the conversation back to her point. "But you can see why I wanted to talk to you about this. Is it all in my head? Am I getting worked up over nothing?"

"Well, I'm not there, so I can't say. But I know what a junk heap that garage is. How can you know for sure it's not one of Dad's old jackets?"

"I asked Mom about it. I didn't tell her why, of course. I didn't want her to worry. But when I called her up to ask about Paul, I described it to her. She didn't know what I was talking about."

"Well, it's been a long time. You can't expect her to remember—"

"Gina, it's not Dad's. Have you ever seen signs of squatters when you came to check on the place?"

The cat settled into the shade of a walnut tree, patches of white murky from the pinkish haze of a smoke-filled sky.

"I've never seen anything like that. No damage, no vandalism. But I wouldn't be surprised if local kids visit the property sometimes. It was probably left months ago by someone looking for a place to get drunk."

"And then they came back for it?"

"What do you mean?"

"I put it back on the bike where I found it. This morning it was gone."

"Hmm, that is weird," Gina said. "If some kid is snooping around at night, I can see why you'd be nervous. But it's just a jacket. Maybe Abby found it in the garage."

She hadn't. Val had asked. But anything else she could say would sound paranoid. And maybe Gina was right. Val couldn't trust herself to know when she was overreacting anymore.

Still…

"Do you know what Dad did with his guns? The ones he wanted to give to me?" Val hadn't been interested in the rifles except as sentimental pieces. But Jordan had talked her out of accepting them. At the time, his mom had been behind a big push for increased gun control legislation, and he'd been appalled when Val suggested they take them. Now, she wished she hadn't listened.

Gina hesitated, just a brief pause of discomfort. "You didn't want them, so he let me take what I wanted and sold the rest. Are you looking at getting a gun?"

"I don't know. Maybe. I hate the idea of having one in the house with Abby, and I'm not even sure what I would get."

"A revolver would be best if you're looking for self-defense. I don't know what a concealed carry permit costs there, but here it's less than a hundred dollars. You could probably find a good revolver for under four hundred."

"Whew. Guess I'd better start saving my pennies." She said it lightly to disguise the fact that it might as well have been ten times that amount for as long as it would take to save. Since the move, Val's bank account was shockingly low.

"How's work going?" Gina asked, as if guessing her train of thought.

"It's fine. They don't have a lot for me to do right now because so many doctors are out for the summer. But it's probably about all I can handle right now anyway."

"I'm glad you have a little something to get by. Have you thought about full-time work yet?"

Yeah, that's number forty-seven of the hundred and twelve things that keep me up at night, Val thought. But she didn't want to sound more pathetic than she already did.

"I've given it some thought. We'll see. Not a lot of options around here, you know."

"It might be a nice way for you to meet some people. Make some friends."

Val grimaced. It was the same advice Val would have given if the roles were reversed. If there was one thing she'd learned in the past six months, it was to stop giving advice.

"Well, I'd better let you go. Thanks for listening to me even if I sound crazy."

Gina laughed. "Not crazy, Val. Grieving. Two different things."

"It doesn't feel that different to me."

Gina tsked a sound of pity. "You're under a lot of stress. It's totally understandable, but it's not helping anything to be so wound up. You've gotta give yourself a break. Maybe find a babysitter and go out for a night."

The idea made Val's chest hurt. Even if there was something to do in Owl Creek that would be worth the hassle, who would she go out with? She hadn't stayed in touch with any of her childhood friends since she graduated high school. And she didn't have the energy to foster any relationships now that she was a single mom trying to scrape together a fresh start.

Val hung up the phone and went back to the pile of papers she'd been sorting through. There was no recycling service in Owl Creek—apart from Stan's Market accepting soda cans and plastic bottles for loose change—but she wondered if neighboring Salmon Ridge had options. Otherwise her last hope was the county seat of Pineview, but that was an hour away. It was probably ten times the size of Owl Creek and if there were enough people in Wallace County who cared enough to start a recycling program, they would be in Pineview.

She smiled a little thinking how much she'd changed. Jordan had always said she'd had a city girl brain with a country girl heart. When she'd left Owl Creek as a starry-eyed eighteen-year-old bent on conquering the world, she'd envisioned becoming a sophisticated urbanite. She would have been horrified to see herself over ten years later, back in Owl Creek, a college drop-out living in her parents' house. Her dreams might have crashed and burned. But dang it, she could still recycle.

After piling the papers into a box, she took it out to the corner of the house near the garbage can to get it out of the way. A box of donations came next, then a bag of kitchen trash. But when she opened the lid to the garbage can, she huffed in annoyance. The previous bag had been ripped open, its contents spilling into the can. Flies already swarmed.

"Abby!" Val called, setting down the new bag so she could tend to the one in the can.

When Abby appeared, Val showed her the mess.

"Did you get into the garbage can?"

Abby looked uncertain. She shook her head.

"I know I tied this closed before putting it in. If you need to get something out of the trash, please ask me about it first. Now there's a big mess and I'm going to have to clean the whole thing out. We don't want to attract animals."

"It wasn't me," Abby said, peering into the can and wrinkling her nose. She waved at the flies buzzing around her head.

"Who else could it have been?" Val's voice rose in frustration. "There's only you and me now, and I know it wasn't me." She felt herself working up a full head of steam but wasn't sure how to stop. *It's just trash,* a part of her thought. But still she grabbed Abby's shoulders and crouched down to look her in the eye. "I need you to be honest with me. It's very important that you always tell me the truth."

Abby looked at her and Val could read the fear in her eyes. The desire to tell Val what she wanted to hear.

"Maybe it was a raccoon."

Val exhaled. "A raccoon would have spilled the trash all over the yard. It wouldn't dig through it and then put the lid back. If you can't tell me the truth, then…no movie tonight after dinner."

Abby's narrow shoulders sank with disappointment, and Val burned with shame. What kind of mom would take away the only positive thing in her daughter's life over a little white lie? For that matter, what kind of mom would give her daughter a life where an evening cartoon was the only thing she had to look forward to in her day? And of course, as it always did, fury at Jordan quickly followed, simmering under the surface with a white heat.

She took a deep breath and tried to calm herself.

"It's too hot. Go back inside while I clean this up." The sweet smell of rotting food mixed with the drone of flies made her want to gag, but she pulled out all the trash bags and grabbed the hose.

By the time she was finished—damp from sweat and the spray of the hose—she felt exhausted. Wrung out like the limp rag now drying in the sun. Maybe Gina was right. She was too wound up. She was fixating on cougars and a random jacket found on a dump heap. She'd come to Owl Creek because she needed a safe place to land after the nightmare of the past six months. But she was carrying the nightmare with her, refusing to let it go.

Val slammed the lid on the garbage can. She'd get through this. She'd get the house ready to sell. She'd get a job and move somewhere Abby could make friends and be happy again. And she'd leave Owl Creek for good.

Val yawned and checked the clock on her laptop. 9:56 p.m. That was something. Usually she didn't get sleepy this early. She pulled out her ear buds and saved the transcription document. It was counterproductive to work when she was this tired. She'd just have to go back and check her work in the morning, and some of the clinicians were hard enough to listen to once.

She flipped on her parents' old TV set while she got ready for bed, the low noise helping drown out the sounds of the farmhouse settling around her. Nights were always the worst. Once the chorus of crickets died down, the silence of the country amplified unexpected noises. A distant dog barking. The shriek of bats. Creampuff tipping over a watering can on the back porch. Even the creak of ancient wood sighing as the night cooled.

A breeze tossed the curtains of her open bedroom window, but the air was still stifling. The back of her sinuses burned from the constant smoke as they did most days now.

Val sat on her bed and reached for the remote. She never missed Netflix more than on these lonely nights. Without high speed internet, she was at the whim of whatever the old antenna could pick up, and the local news wasn't enough to distract her for long.

Just before she flipped off the TV, a picture of a man appeared on the screen. Shocked, Val switched it back on, waiting impatiently as the old set warmed up.

She recognized Carter's voice narrating the story of Sam Howser's disappearance from the fire camp in town. Footage of the camp played against his description of Howser with a tip line number on the bottom of the screen. Again, they showed Howser's face, and Val suppressed a shudder.

"Howser has ties to the community," Carter said, "but so far police say they have no idea where he might have gone. There's a concern that he has untreated mental health issues, so they're asking anyone with information about his whereabouts in the past week to contact the Wallace County Sheriff's Office. If you've seen this man or have any information related to his disappearance, please call the number at the bottom of your screen."

The screen switched to a live shot of Carter in front of the fire camp at the elementary school. He always looked so serious when he was reporting, not like the Carter she knew.

Val went to the window and looked out at the dark trees at the edge of the yard. She felt exposed, looking out at the night with the glow of the TV behind her. If Howser was out there watching the house, he would know right where she was.

She shivered and reached for the window, dragging it down and locking it. It was foolish, she knew. But she couldn't shake the feeling that she was being watched.

The news had moved on to a story about a family whose son with special needs had met his favorite athlete. The tip line number was gone and she hadn't written it down. Even if she called the police, what would she say? *I got spooked by your news story, but it probably doesn't mean anything because I get spooked by everything these days.*

Instead, she pulled up Carter's number. She'd run into him shortly after moving in, and he'd invited her to have lunch sometime. She hadn't taken him up on it yet, but was glad she'd saved his number.

Not surprisingly, it went to voicemail.

"Carter, it's Valerie. I'm sorry, I know you're working. I just saw your story on the news—nice haircut, by the way. I wanted to talk to you about…well, just give me a call when you get a minute."

She hung up and didn't know what to do with herself. She did a circuit of the house, checking all the windows and doors. Everything was locked, and the light above the shop cast the front yard in an eerie light. The back yard was lost in shadow.

She got a drink of water and stood at the kitchen sink, looking out at the still night. Imagining what she would do if someone tried to break into the house. How fast could she get Abby to the car? The stairs were by the front door, and her little Prius was parked near the porch. Senses alert, she grabbed her keys just in case.

When her phone buzzed, she started.

The single text from Carter made her smile.

U like my haircut?? Yes!

Another followed shortly after.

It might be a while. How late is too late to call?

I'll be up, she replied. *Thanks.*

She was tempted to stay on her phone to pass the time, but the bright light ruined her night vision. Instead, she sat in the dark imagining fending off an invader with a skillet like the heroine in Abby's favorite movie. Cartoon princesses were always so naive. Rapunzel should have dumped Flynn Rider back out the window before he could open his smarmy mouth.

This reminded Val that she'd seen an old baseball bat in the living room where she was organizing the last of her parents' possessions—all the stuff that her mom hadn't had room for in her new condo. Val carefully moved through the room, using the light from her phone to guide her around the stacks of photo albums, reference books, and novels yellowed with age.

Behind a box filled with electronics she spotted the leather-wrapped handle. She hefted the bat and tried to imagine swinging it at a person. Could she do it? Six months ago she wouldn't have had it in her. That Val—with her gated community and home security system—seemed so much more civilized than this Val living in the hills with only her own strength to protect herself and her daughter.

Val brought the bat back to the kitchen and laid it on the table, wondering if she would have the courage to use it. Praying she wouldn't need to.

It was after midnight when her phone rang. Her relief was immediately tinged with regret. What if Carter thought she was overreacting? They'd been good friends in high school, but that had been years ago.

Steeling herself, she answered. "Hi, Carter." She tried to keep her voice low but it still sounded surprisingly loud in the stillness.

"Val!" The hum of road noise accompanied his voice, and she suspected he was driving. "I'm so glad you called. Are you getting settled in all right? Ready to take a break from all those boxes?"

"Um, no." Val paused, flustered. "That's not…I wanted to talk to you about your news story tonight."

"Oh, yeah? The haircut was that good?" His voice held a smile.

"No," she smiled weakly. "I mean, not *that* good. Maybe if you get rid of that fuzz on your chin."

"It's my signature look! Otherwise I look like I'm about fourteen."

Val chuckled. He wasn't wrong. "You look fine, Carter. Look, this probably sounds really stupid, so I'm sorry to waste your time. But I'm not sure who else to talk to."

The humor stilled. "I'm listening."

"Thanks. For the last few days I've wondered if someone's hanging around the property. When I saw your story, I thought it might be that missing guy."

It sounded ridiculous when she said it out loud, but Carter didn't laugh.

"Hmm. I'd love to hear more about it, but I'm driving and can't take notes. Do you mind if I come by right now? Talk to you in person?"

"No," Val said sharply. "I mean, yes, I mind. It's late and my daughter's asleep. I don't even know if it's worth your time. It could just be my imagination." *And we aren't in high school anymore.*

"Got it. Well, give me the gist." He didn't sound the least bit affronted by her refusal.

Hoping she wasn't rambling, she told him about meeting Paul and discovering the jacket. He murmured encouragingly in all the right places, adding a thoughtful "Huh" after she told him about the jacket disappearing again.

"That alone is weird, right? And now I think someone has been getting into my trash. I'm very careful about keeping the can clean because I can't stand maggots, so I always tie up the bags. Today I found a bag ripped open but still in the can with the lid on it. Tell me, what kind of animal would do that?"

"Interesting," Carter said. "You're right, it does sound suspicious. Have you called the police?"

"No. I worried I was imagining things. But then I saw your news report and thought I should tell someone."

"I'm glad you did. I really think you should call the police."

A loud creak sounded through the house and Val reached for the bat. Just in case. It was a relief for Carter to take her seriously, but the idea that someone really might be sneaking around the property wasn't exactly comforting.

"Do you have the hotline number? I didn't write it down."

"I have something better. I've got Joel's number. You should call him directly and tell him."

Val paused. "Joel? I forgot he was with the police."

"He's a detective now, and he's working this case. I'm sure he'd love to hear from you." Again she heard a smile in his voice.

"Detective so young?"

Carter laughed. "We're not that young anymore, Val. And you know Joel. He distinguished himself pretty early on with that whole Stan's Market thing. When the opening came, he was a shoe-in."

"What happened at Stan's?" Val knew she should probably end the call and go to bed, but it was a relief to have another adult to talk to. Especially one who had more interesting things to talk about than her own problems.

"You really have been out of it! I thought everyone knew about the shootout that happened there a couple years ago."

"I'm sorry. I've been really bad at staying in touch."

"Yeah, well, it was pretty big news here. A robbery gone wrong. A couple of meth heads were looking for cash and didn't think through what would happen when the cops showed up. It was right during the lunch hour too, so the place was full of high school kids. They held eight hostages for almost an hour. Cops were waiting for a team from Medford to help out, but when the junkies started firing, Joel stormed the place and took them down. Saved every one of those kids."

"Wow. I had no idea."

"Yeah, it was all pretty heroic. Made the national news for about two seconds. Joel had departments as far as Colorado trying to recruit him."

"But he stayed?"

"Some of us like it here."

Val winced at the implied criticism, but Carter continued before it had a chance to sink in.

"He didn't have a reason to go. At the time he and Lacey were still married—"

"They split up?"

"Yeah, not long after it happened. I think…well, it

doesn't matter what I think. The point is, Joel's the man in charge and would love to hear from you."

This sudden closure on a juicy story was so unlike the Carter she knew that Val laughed. "All right, send me his number and I'll give him a call."

"Good." She heard the engine die and the slam of a car door. "So, when can I take you to lunch so we can catch up properly? Not that I'm not at my best at almost one in the morning..." He trailed off into a yawn.

"Maybe next week. I'm still trying to get my feet under me."

"Just say the word. And give Joel a call. I don't like the idea of you out there alone with a convicted felon on the loose."

Val straightened. "Wait, what?"

Carter swore under his breath. "Sorry, Val, I'm too tired. I wasn't supposed to say that bit."

"Carter, what are you not telling me?"

"Don't tell Joel I said anything. But Sam Howser was involved in the Ryan Moyer killing."

Now *that* one she'd heard of, although the details were fuzzy. She and Jordan had been living back east, but she'd heard all the major points of the case from Gina and her mom.

"You think a murderer could be hiding in the woods up here?" Val tried to keep her voice calm to hide the panic building in her chest.

"I don't know, Val. But I can come out there if you want. I really don't mind."

Val considered it and looked out again at the black night. She trusted Carter, but it seemed too much to invite him to her home in the middle of the night.

"It's all right. I'll call Joel first thing in the morning."

She almost changed her mind after she hung up. Only one thought stopped her from dialing his number again. Those who had killed Ryan Moyer claimed to have done it in defense of women everywhere. The missing girl's dad had appealed to all fathers, declaring that what he'd done was to protect all the daughters who had been failed by the justice system. If Howser was involved, maybe he felt that way too.

But her skin crawled as she remembered the way he used to look at her.

4

The dirt road winding up the mountain was rutted and in serious need of grading. Joel couldn't remember the last time he'd been to the Rockwell property, but he was sure the road hadn't been that bad back in the years when he'd driven it almost daily. His last clear memory of Val's home was the night of graduation. Everything had changed as their class went their separate ways, the promises written in yearbooks forgotten before the summer ended.

Joel tried not to think about that night as he reached the familiar turnoff. But something about making this drive brought back feelings he hadn't thought about in years. Lacey had gone home from the party early because she'd had a dance competition the next day. As the night had wound down, Carter, Maddie and the others had dwindled away. But Joel had stayed, wanting to hang onto those last moments as long as possible. Feeling they were on the cusp of a seismic shift in their close friend group. Wanting to savor it while it lasted.

And then it had happened. Without warning, while the two of them were alone under the walnut tree, Val had kissed him. He'd been so surprised, he couldn't remember to this day what he'd said or done in the moments following the kiss. But he could still remember the way her skin had looked in the white lights hanging from the branches of the tree. He could still remember —or imagined he did, anyway—the softness of her lips. He definitely remembered feeling shocked and confused, especially when she'd looked at him with light reflecting in her brown eyes and said in a soft murmur, "I just needed to know."

He never asked her what she'd learned from that kiss. He never told her that he had almost broken up with Lacey over it. He never told her that since then, he'd wondered what might have been possible if there had been no Lacey. But whatever she had wanted to know, Val had spent the rest of that summer avoiding him.

And in the fall, she was gone.

They'd seen each other since, of course. Chance meetings at the grocery store when she was visiting for the holidays. More recently at Jim Rockwell's funeral. But those encounters were always disappointing. Friendly, but vaguely distant, as if the closeness between them had died that night. Now, as he approached the farmhouse, he wondered if she even remembered it.

The house had grown shabbier in the years since he'd last been here. The roof of the shop sagged in a way it hadn't before. But the large walnut tree in the front yard and the mature fruit trees lining the eastern fence were unchanged. As he parked his car he felt a great sense of familiarity. Even homecoming.

He wiped his palms on his pants, not wanting Val's first impression of him to be a sweaty handshake. He took his time grabbing his notepad and pen. By the time he got out of the car, the front door was open and a young girl stood on the porch. Blond curls sprang out from her head in a wispy mess. She stared openly at him as he walked up the steps.

"I already saw you coming," she announced.

"Hello. Is your mom here?"

Of course Val was here. He'd just gotten off the phone with her twenty minutes earlier. But he didn't know what else to say to this child with the wide eyes.

The girl nodded and stood aside for him to enter, beckoning with a grand gesture.

Joel stepped inside and paused, unsure how far to go. He knew this house inside and out, had once been considered part of the family. But they were just kids then. He wasn't sure what Val considered him now.

"Sorry, come in!" her voice called from upstairs. "I'll be down in a minute!"

Joel barely had time to register the mess of boxes and books crowding the front room before he heard her footsteps on the stairs.

Seeing her now, his uncertainty melted away. There was a sense of rightness in how she hurried down the stairs, the way she rounded the corner of the landing and skipped the bottom step. He couldn't help but grin.

"Valerie Rockwell. I can't believe you're back!"

"So good to see you!" She greeted him warmly, reaching for a brief hug.

Her hair had darkened to a golden brown, and her features were more defined. More angular than he remembered. If anything, her looks had improved with maturity. Her eyes held a depth of wisdom that spoke of loss and determination. He wondered what she saw when she looked at him.

"Can you believe we've gotten so old?" she asked with a laugh.

"Speak for yourself," he joked to hide a wince. Had she noticed his hair was starting to thin?

As if reading his thoughts, she offered a reassuring, "You look fantastic, Joel. I'm only wondering where the time has gone. I can't believe it's already been, what, eleven years? And look at you! Mr. Detective!"

"And who is this beautiful young lady you have here?" He crouched down to look the girl in the eye.

She shifted closer to Val but her eyes were bright with interest. Eyes that were more green than brown.

"I'm Abby," she said. "Are you a policeman?"

"I am. My name's Joel and I've known your mom since I was almost your age."

Val ran her hand through Abby's curls. "Joel and I need to talk for a few minutes, so I turned on a show on my laptop upstairs."

At this, Abby ran to the stairs without a glance back at Joel.

"Do you mind if we go to the kitchen?" Val asked. "I don't have a good place to sit in the living room. I've been going through the last of my parents' stuff so everything's a disaster right now. Plus, I'd rather Abby didn't hear our conversation."

Joel followed her to the kitchen and accepted a glass

of iced tea. The glass was cool and moist with condensation; he had to stop himself from downing the whole thing in his thirst.

For a moment he wished they could sit and chat like old friends, but Val had called with a specific purpose in mind. He didn't want to give the impression he wasn't taking her seriously. So he sat at the table and opened his notepad.

"What can you tell me about Sam Howser?" he asked.

Val swirled the ice in her glass. "I don't know for sure that it's Hows…sorry, Howser. Hows is what we called him at the mill."

"Wait, you know him?" Joel looked up curiously.

"A little. I met him at the mill the summer after graduation. He was on my dad's crew."

"What were your impressions of him?"

She didn't answer right away, and when he looked at her there was a heightened color in her cheeks.

"It's dumb, but…he gave me the creeps. At first, I felt bad for him. He seemed like the kind of guy who would always be the butt of someone else's jokes, you know? But apparently I was nicer than I intended and gave him the wrong impression." Her blush deepened. "The next thing I knew he was bringing me presents and asking me out. I mean, I was only eighteen. He had to have been at least thirty years older. I had no idea what to do, so I made my dad tell him off. It's so embarrassing. So much for being an adult."

Joel smiled. "Did he leave you alone after that?"

"Yeah. I mean, Dad was his supervisor, and everyone respected him. But I wished I'd had the courage to do it myself. After that, it was just awkward. Like, we actively avoided each other."

I can imagine, Joel thought. "So you recognized him on the news last night. Have you seen him recently?"

Val shook her head. "I don't even know it's him. But I've been noticing strange things that make me think someone might be coming around at night."

"What kind of things?"

Joel took careful notes while Val described finding a jacket near the garage that didn't belong to her, and signs that someone had been into her trash. He kept his face neutral, focused on gathering facts. Conclusions would come later.

She finished with, "It might be nothing. But the idea that he could be out there…well, when I saw the report I thought someone should know."

What was it about a missing person that seemed so malevolent? When Howser was walking the streets of Owl Creek, no one seemed to care. But say he's a missing person and suddenly everyone's suspicious.

"Do you know a man named Paul Sheen?" Val asked abruptly.

Joel paused, wondering where the question had come from. "Doesn't sound familiar. Why?"

"I didn't know him either. I guess he knows my parents, but I've never heard of him. I found him raiding the shop the other day." Val explained her encounter with the stranger and how afterward she learned that her mom had indeed given him permission to be there.

"Could the jacket be his?" Joel asked, hoping he didn't sound condescending.

Val shook her head. "He said it wasn't, and I don't know why he would have lied about it. Plus, the jacket smelled like smoke and he didn't."

Well, then. "What kind of smoke?"

"It's hard to say, it was so brief. I think it was campfire smoke, but I didn't exactly take a big whiff. You say you don't know him?"

Joel shook his head. "If he bothers you again, let me know."

"I told him to check with me before he comes out next time. Honestly, he'll be doing me a favor to empty the garage out so I don't have to do it."

Val's daughter came into the kitchen, her flip-flops smacking against the floor. She placed a piece of paper on the table in front of Joel.

"This is for you. Would you say it's a masterpiece?"

Joel looked at the rough drawing of a stick person with a ridiculously long neck about to get swallowed whole by a blobby, fanged creature. He stifled a laugh.

"I would definitely say that's a masterpiece."

She nodded as if this was expected. "This is me. I thought about drawing my mom and dad, but there were too many risks."

Val stiffened. "What do you mean, Abby?"

"If I drew our family, then I didn't have room to draw the dinosaur. Too many risks."

Val's tension eased. "My late husband was an investment broker. You can imagine the conversations Abby overheard at our house."

Joel smiled, hoping she would say more. But Val didn't volunteer anything else, and Joel knew it would be unprofessional to question her about something so personal.

After clarifying Val's observations, he couldn't think of a reason to linger. He slipped Abby's drawing into his notebook and stood to leave.

"I suspect there's nothing to worry about, but let me know if anything else strikes you as odd. And call 911 immediately if you see a prowler. I'll make sure a deputy patrols out in this area for the next few nights so someone will be close if you need anything."

"Thanks," Val said, but she seemed…disappointed? Annoyed?

Whatever it was, as he replayed their conversation on the drive back to town, Joel couldn't shake the feeling that he'd failed some kind of test.

5

The world was tinged a peachy hue, like sunset in the middle of the day. Wallace Community Bank looked like the set of a nostalgic period film. As Val held the door open for Abby, she frowned at the horizon where a large plume of black smoke rose above the distant hills. The fire wasn't close enough to Owl Creek to be a threat to the town proper, but a dozen homes further upriver had already been lost.

Inside, the bank lobby was blessedly cool and free of the scent of smoke. With no air conditioning at home, Val and Abby were breathing smoke night and day. They were taking allergy medication just to keep the burning eyes and runny noses under control. To breathe clean air felt like a luxury.

Val directed Abby to a leather sofa against the wall and approached the first available teller, a young man in a blue polo shirt with the WCB logo embroidered on the front.

"How can I help you?" he greeted.

"I'm wondering if I could speak with your hiring manager," Val said.

Before the teller could respond, a voice echoed across the lobby. "Valerie Rockwell?"

It took Val a second to recognize the beaming woman as she approached, her heels clicking against the hard floor. Maddie's red hair had been bleached blond and cut in a short pixie. Her makeup was dramatic, tastefully so, but still heavier than Val was used to. Her smile was comfortingly familiar: wide and warm.

Val smiled in return. "Maddie! Hello! I didn't know you worked here."

They hugged and Val thought she picked up the sweet smell of vape. Maddie was a picture of professionalism in her pencil skirt and understated jewelry. When Val told her she was looking for work, Maddie invited her into her office.

It's better this way, Val told herself. *Most jobs come because of who you know.* But still there was a part of her that wished she could talk to a stranger. Someone who would be less interested in her personal life.

"What sort of work are you looking for?" Maddie asked, settling into the chair behind her desk where a nameplate announced her name as Madeline Gottschalk. On the wall behind her hung bland artwork that would fit into any doctor's office waiting room. Val was more interested in the photos on the desk—Maddie with a man she didn't recognize and a sleeping baby. There was also a framed illustration of a comic book character, a curvy woman with red hair and cat eye glasses.

"I'm pretty open at this point, but I have some secretarial experience. Currently I'm working remotely for a mental health clinic, helping them develop an online continuing ed curriculum." That sounded more impressive than simple transcription. "But I'd like something full-time with a little more stability."

"Well, I already know you'll work harder than most of my staff," Maddie said with a laugh. "Do you have a resume?"

Val handed it over and tried not to fidget as Maddie read through her qualifications. She knew all too well it was terribly anemic.

After a long pause, Maddie said, "I don't see a degree on here."

"Yes, I didn't graduate." Val felt her cheeks warming and hoped Maddie wouldn't notice. "My husband's work required a move before I could finish. I always planned to go back, but once Abby came along it got a lot harder."

Abby looked up at the sound of her name and then back down at Val's phone, quickly engrossed in her game.

"She's old enough now that I'm looking into options to finish my degree," Val said, pitching her voice with bright optimism. It wasn't too big of a stretch. There was a community college in Pineview and she'd pulled up their website just that morning. No need to tell Maddie how she'd been so overwhelmed with anxiety that all the words had blurred together, and she couldn't even remember what she'd read.

"What brought you back to Owl Creek?" Maddie asked.

"I'm getting my parents' place ready to sell. But there's a lot of work to do, and with the market what it is, it's going to be a long process."

Maddie laid the resume down and met Val's eyes. "I'll be honest, Val. We can't hire someone who isn't planning on sticking around. I don't work with temps for a reason. We represent the largest financial institution in the county, and having reliable employees is a must."

The words stung, and Val felt a wave of irritation. "I can't promise how long I'll stay, Maddie, but I wouldn't be here if I didn't think it would be worth your time."

Maddie's eyes had lost some of their warmth. "I understand. The truth is, Valerie, I know you're more than capable. But without a degree I could only start you out as a teller. That means minimum wage. Once you finish your degree, we can talk about moving you into a loan officer position. But that all depends on how much you're willing to invest in us, and if we're going to see a return on our investment in you. Is this move to Owl Creek permanent? What's your home situation like? Do you have the support you need to work full-time while finishing school and taking care of your daughter?"

Val was pretty sure Maddie was violating all sorts of laws with these questions, but there was no good way to respond without making it look like she was avoiding them. She and Maddie had too much history. Student body president and vice-president, co-captains of the volleyball team, with countless drama productions, band concerts, and speech and debate contests between them. Not to mention the nights they'd snuck out to the abandoned pump house on Val's property to try whatever Maddie had managed to steal from her dad's liquor cabinet.

She straightened her spine and lifted her chin. "Thank you for understanding the complexity of my situation. At this point, Maddie, I don't have anywhere else to go. I lost Jordan six months ago. It's just Abby and me now. The only reason I can even afford gas and food is because we don't have a mortgage or rental payment while we're living in my parents' house. Is that how I want to live forever? No. But this is where we are now, and until I get back on my feet, I'm not going anywhere. If there comes a time when I can consider better opportunities somewhere else, that'll be a great day. But it's not anywhere on the horizon that I can see."

Val sensed Abby looking at her but she held Maddie's gaze. Maddie, for her part, looked abashed.

"I'm sorry, Val. I didn't know about your husband. Would you like to talk about it?"

"No." Val glanced at Abby.

Understanding flickered in Maddie's eyes, and her tone softened. "Of course I'd like to help, but this is the best I can offer. Fill out an application and think about it. If you think it'll work for you, I can at least promise you an interview."

Val thanked her and tried to take the application with dignity, but she couldn't help feeling like she'd just opened a scabbed-over wound and Maddie was cringing from the stench of pus. She couldn't leave the office quickly enough.

But Abby held back. "Who's that?" she asked, pointing to the illustration of the woman with the red hair and glasses.

Maddie's face softened. "That's Amy Geddon. She's from a webcomic. Have you heard of *Robert Apocalypse*?"

Abby shook her head. "I like her necklace." A large round pendant hung from the woman's neck and she held it with her left hand, her thumb and forefinger brushing the edges.

"That's her Grover-C," Maddie said. "It's like a teleportation device. The story's a lot of fun. You should check it out."

"Thanks, Maddie," Val said, irked by Maddie's sugary-sweet tone. "Let's go, Abby."

When they got out to the car, the heat inside was suffocating even though they hadn't been in the bank for more than thirty minutes. Val rolled down the windows and breathed deeply, waiting for her hands to stop shaking before she started the car.

"Can I see it, Mom? *Robert Apolloclips?*"

Val sighed, trying to ground herself with physical awareness. Perspiration prickling her forehead. The heat of the seat against her back. The dry air tightening her throat with thirst. She started the engine and turned the air conditioning on high.

"We'll see. I'll check it out first. Amy Geddon looked to be nothing more than an indulgence of male fantasy and I don't want our culture's objectification of women to distort your own developing sexuality."

There was silence in the back seat.

"Okay."

Val sighed and rubbed her forehead before shifting

into reverse. The visit with Maddie had been harder than she'd expected. Val wasn't opposed to getting an entry-level job, but she knew that here, of all places, people expected more of her. Maddie's doubt had shaken her weak confidence, and by the time she stopped at the post office to pick up a package—a box for Abby from Jordan's mom—she had a raging headache. Further job inquiries would have to wait for another day.

Joel rang the doorbell and hoped he hadn't made a mistake. He'd driven over an hour to reach this address in the mountains above Salmon Ridge, and the derelict appearance of the house wasn't promising. At the sound of the doorbell, he heard a dog rush to the door and bark excitedly. After a minute, the door opened to reveal a large man in a gray t-shirt and apron holding back an energetic boxer with his leg. The pungent smell of cooking cabbage wafted out the door.

"Can I help you?" the man asked.

"I'm looking for Peter Moyer. I'm Joel Ramirez from the Wallace County Sheriff's Office."

The man looked him over grimly. "I'm Peter. And I know who you are, Detective."

"Do you mind if I ask you a few questions? I'm investigating a missing persons report that might interest you. He's connected to your son's death."

Moyer's eyes darkened. "I don't think there's anything you could say that would interest me."

"Maybe not, sir, and I really am sorry about your

loss. But I'm trying to understand what may have happened to this man."

"Who is it?"

"Samuel Howser."

Moyer grunted. "I'm not sure I can tell you anything that would help, but come on in."

Joel followed him into the house, the boxer sniffing him eagerly. The smell of cabbage was overwhelming.

"Come on, Shiloh. Leave the man alone."

Peter ushered the dog out the door to the back yard as Joel took in the room. Blinds were closed against the sun, and box fans hummed in the kitchen and living room. A window A/C unit offered more noise than relief. The shag carpet was old and threadbare, and the furniture had the unmistakable look of having been gnawed on by the boxer.

But it was neat and tidy, as if Moyer were determined to make the most of his reduced circumstances. Family photos hung on the wall, showing a handsome young man through various stages of childhood, culminating in a brooding senior portrait. His dark hair flopped onto his forehead and his eyes were guarded.

"Thank you for seeing me, Mr. Moyer. I know this can't be an easy thing for you to discuss."

Moyer perched on the edge of a flowery armchair, elbows on his knees. "If you were your predecessor I'd have been tempted to chase you away with a shotgun. But my cousin's kid was one of the ones you saved in that grocery store shootout. So I figure I can give you a few minutes."

"Thank you, sir. I'll keep it brief. Sam Howser disappeared from a fire camp in Owl Creek six nights ago. As far as we know, this is the first time he's been back to town since he was released from prison last winter. What I'm trying to figure out is if there's anyone in the area who may have wanted to hurt him."

Moyer's gray brows drew together. His smile looked more like a grimace. "Do you mean me? I haven't been in Owl Creek in years. But if you're looking for an alibi, I'm afraid Shiloh's all I've got."

"I'm not accusing you of anything, Mr. Moyer. I just wondered if you know of anyone who wanted to do him harm. You mentioned you still have a cousin in Owl Creek?"

Moyer sighed heavily and leaned back in the armchair. "Look," he said slowly, "I don't know what you want from me, but I've got no fight left. We gave up everything trying to clear Ryan's name. Even though he was never charged in that girl's disappearance, everyone was sure he'd killed her. There was no body. No evidence that she's even dead. The girl could've up and run off to Tahiti for all we know."

Joel raised an eyebrow. "You think she's still alive after all this time?"

Moyer shrugged. "Eliza was a fiery one. She jerked Ryan around with her moods so he didn't know what's what. I think they broke up half a dozen times in the four months they were together. I warned him she was trouble. Always toying with him and punishing him if he didn't play to her every whim. It disgusted me, but I figured, they're teenagers. They'll get tired of each other and move on a little smarter for the next time."

"Can you tell me what happened when she disappeared? I've read the police report, but I'd be interested in hearing your side of things."

Moyer rubbed the side of his face, considering. "The details get a little fuzzy, so I'd go with the police report. But here's what I know. Ryan never had anything to do with her after Prom."

"The night they had that big fight?"

"Fight?" Moyer scoffed. "It was just a little argument. Eliza was a drama queen so she played it up for the attention. Screaming at him, walking out of the dance in a huff. He was tempted to leave her there, but knew that wouldn't be very gentlemanly of him. So he found her and took her home because that's the kind of young man he was. But that was the last straw. When he dropped her off that night, he told her they were finished. He never saw her again."

"That was three days before she disappeared, correct?"

"I think so. Your report should tell you that."

"Do you know what they argued about that night?"

"Ryan thought she was carrying on with someone else. She told him it wasn't any of his business, but didn't deny it. I tell you, she was the star of her own soap opera."

Joel thought he was describing half the sixteen-year-olds he'd known in high school, but didn't say so.

"Were you aware she was using drugs?"

"Not until the cops told me. Ryan said he didn't know either. I think he was always a bit blind when it came to Eliza. He just couldn't see her for who she really was."

"And you're sure Ryan had nothing to do with her disappearance?"

"As sure as I am that Shiloh's chewing on the back door jamb as we speak. I mean, he sulked for a few days but he knew he was better off without her. He didn't call her. Didn't text. As far as he was concerned, it was over. Until the cops showed up at our door." His voice cracked with emotion.

Joel put down his notepad and paused. "I'm sorry to ask you to relive this. I know it must be very painful. Would you mind telling me about the events surrounding Ryan's abduction? Anyone in particular, besides you and your wife of course, who was especially affected?"

Moyer wiped his eyes with the hem of his apron. "I don't know that it matters now. It won't bring him back."

Joel waited.

"You have to understand what we went through, Mr. Ramirez. Ryan was never charged with any crime, but that didn't matter to the people in Owl Creek. We'd lived there our whole lives. Knew these people like family. And suddenly we're getting death threats. Our cars were broken into. Kids at school papered Ryan's locker with missing posters of Eliza. They were like mongrel dogs fighting over a bone. There was no letting go once they had a piece of him."

Moyer's eyes darkened with anger. "I used to be a chiropractor, but had to close my practice. We drained our savings hiring a PI to find out what happened to Eliza when it was clear the police didn't know what they were doing. When that didn't work, we moved out here to give him a fresh start. But that didn't help either.

"They were waiting for him after baseball practice one night. Sam Howser said at the trial he thought they were just going to rough him up a little. Scare him into telling them what he did to her. Howser said Ryan was terrified, but of course he couldn't tell them anything because he didn't know anything. Don't you think he would have? When I think of his final moments…that's what I see at night when I can't sleep, my poor boy's frightened eyes."

Moyer took a deep shuddering breath, his lip trembling. "After they killed him, there was nothing left for us to fight. Ryan would have no redemption. People still believed he'd done it, even though the Bellinghams testified that he'd denied it to the end. We thought it would get better once those murderers went to prison. Justice would save us. But justice feels awfully hollow when you still have to face each day knowing your boy isn't coming home. Ruth couldn't take it anymore and just gave up on life. I lost her to the bottle three years ago. Since then, I'm just a living corpse waiting for my turn."

Moyer's depth of sorrow took Joel aback. He didn't know what to say in the face of such grief and felt a wave of guilt for coming into this man's home to dredge up the past. Moyer looked up at Ryan's framed senior picture. In the portrait, Ryan looked moody and defiant, and Joel wondered how much of that was affected for the camera and how much was a defensive hardening due to months of persecution.

"You might think I was angry at Sam Howser,"

Moyer said, "but as far as I'm concerned, he did us a favor. Without his testimony, the Bellinghams might have gotten away with it. I think Howser felt genuinely bad about his role in all of it. But the Bellinghams? They were proud of it, the sick bastards. Proud of killing a defenseless kid. If you should be talking to anyone, it's them. I wouldn't be surprised if they sent someone after Howser. The man was never very bright. He didn't stand a chance."

Joel noted this and asked one final question.

"Can you tell me, what did Ryan think happened to Eliza?"

Moyer grabbed a tissue from a box on a nearby table and blew his nose. "At first he was worried about her. Her car was found abandoned on the side of the road. No keys, phone on the floor. If she'd tried to hitch-hike and got picked up by a stranger, who knows where she could be. But after a while, he wondered if it was staged as a way to get attention. Had a friend pick her up and then run off. He told police about this guy she'd been seeing on the side, someone she called Dr. M, but police never figured out if he existed or if Eliza had made him up to torment Ryan."

"Dr. M?"

"Yeah. I don't know if he was a real doctor or what. I just know that Ryan was sure he was wrapped up in this somehow."

Joel had seen the notes about a doctor in the police files. Several doctors had been questioned, but none had caught the investigators' attention. This was in the day before smart phones, so Eliza's digital blueprint was small and hadn't turned up any leads. In the end, police had dismissed it as a desperate diversionary tactic from Ryan.

Joel left Moyer's house feeling more burdened than when he'd arrived. He didn't know if Howser's disappearance was connected to Ryan's murder, but it was time to pay a visit to the Bellinghams.

6

DRIVING down Main Street on the way out of town took Val past Stan's Market, the small grocery store in a historic building that drew in the high school lunch crowd with fresh sandwiches and rotisserie hot dogs. In recent years, an empty lot across the street had been turned into a tiny park with grass and a pavilion, and Val imagined it must be a popular hangout for teens during the school year.

She thought of what Carter had said about Joel stopping the robbery and saving all those kids. She tried to imagine the courage it would've taken to burst through the old wooden door knowing two gunmen waited for you on the other side. Or maybe he'd gone through the back, sneaking up on them from behind. Either way, Val couldn't have done it, and she was surprised to learn that Joel had. He'd always been the kind of guy who would think his way out of a problem instead of rushing to action.

Seeing him the previous day had been hard. Val was

out of practice with normal conversation. But it had helped that Joel hadn't been that interested in normal conversation. Unlike Carter, Joel hadn't stepped out of his professional role. Even when she'd mentioned Jordan, he let the comment slide without digging deeper. Maybe she should have been offended by his disinterest, but for the first time in months, she felt like someone other than the widow of Jordan Fisher—son of the indomitable Senator Jeanette Fisher.

It was…nice.

She was bothered that Joel hadn't told her about Howser's criminal record, though. She should have asked him, but she hadn't wanted to get Carter in trouble. And she'd really hoped he would tell her himself. If Howser was lurking on her property, didn't she have a right to know about his history? She and Joel had been best friends when they were younger and had told each other everything. Now they were practically strangers.

As she turned onto the county road that led to their house, they passed a rundown property that was so full of debris it looked like a junkyard. Or it would have if it hadn't been for dozens—maybe even hundreds—of mannequins placed in various poses. Most were nude and many were missing heads or limbs, but that didn't stop the owner from positioning them provocatively on discarded furniture, appliances, or cars.

The scenes changed regularly, and today a female figure in black panties was prominently featured in a lewd posture near the road. As usual, Val hoped Abby wouldn't notice.

As usual, she did.

"Mom?"

"Hmm?"

"Why doesn't that mannequin have a shirt on?"

Grateful that's all Abby had noticed, Val searched for an age-appropriate explanation.

"That's a really good question. Maybe the owner ran out of clothes to put on his mannequins."

"Probably." Abby snorted a laugh. "He would need a lot of clothes because he has tons of mannequins. Like, all the stores combined. I don't like them."

"Me neither."

Val's thoughts were scattered as she drove up to the house, so she didn't notice right away the front door was open. They often left it open when they were home to allow air to circulate through the screen door, but she was careful about closing it before they went anywhere.

"Abby, did you go back in the house before we left?" Val asked.

"I don't think so. When can I watch *Robert Apolloclips?*"

Val reached for her phone to call the police and hesitated. Maybe the door hadn't latched all the way, and the wind had blown it open. It wouldn't be the first time. But did she dare risk it?

She thought again of Joel storming into Stan's to save the hostages. She was always looking for someone to save her. It was time she saved herself.

"Wait in the car. I'm going to go check on something."

Val left the engine running so the interior would stay cool, but locked the door and brought her key fob.

With her phone in one hand ready to call 911 and

her key fob in the other ready to run back to the car, she climbed the steps to the porch. This was her house now. It was up to her to make sure it was safe. To keep Abby safe.

At the screen door, she paused. Her voice quavered as she called out, "Hello? Is someone there?"

Slowly, she opened the screen. It creaked loudly, and she strained to hear over the noise. A thump sounded within the house.

"Creampuff? Are you in there?"

The unmistakable squeal of the back door being yanked open made her heart leap out of her chest. Val jumped back, tripping against the screen door. Panicked, she ran across the porch as a figure tore across a corner of the yard. A part of her was vaguely aware she was yelling, but the rest of her was focused on only one thing.

Protect Abby.

Val hurled herself at the car, madly pushing the button on the fob. She threw open the door and slipped in as fast as she could, expecting hands to grab her at any second. Then she jammed it into gear and pressed on the gas.

"What happened? Where are we going?"

Abby's worried questions peppered her as they tore out of the dirt driveway and onto the country road heading down the mountain. Val couldn't even answer, her heart was pounding so furiously. She glanced behind her in the rearview mirror, expecting to see someone in close pursuit, but there was nothing there.

The man was gone.

Val didn't stop until she got to the Parkers' driveway.

She pulled off the road and braked, heaving great gasps of air as if she'd been sprinting.

"I can't...just give me a minute. We're okay. It's okay." She wasn't sure if she was repeating the words for Abby or for herself.

The Parkers' dog, a long-haired collie, came running to meet them, barking insistently. A hand on Val's arm made her turn to see Abby, pale and wide-eyed, straining against her seatbelt to touch her.

"Hey, baby. Go ahead and unbuckle. Come sit with me for a minute." She pulled Abby onto her lap and held her tightly while she called 911. Her voice still held a note of hysteria, but at least she was no longer hyperventilating.

She hadn't gotten a good look at the intruder, but in her mind she pictured Howser's photo from the news story.

Abby rested her head against Val's chest, tucked under Val's chin as she talked to the dispatcher. She smelled of coconut shampoo and perspiration.

When at last Val hung up, Abby asked, "Why was that man at our house?"

"I don't know. He shouldn't have been there. The police are going to come and try to find out. We'll have to go back and meet them there."

"But what if he's still there?"

Val closed her eyes. She couldn't go back. Not alone.

Carter answered on the first ring.

"Hey, Val. I was just getting ready to—"

"He was at my house. I saw him. I came home and he was there." Her hands were tingling with adrenaline.

"Who?" It came out sharp.

"I don't know. But there was a man in my house. I drove away and called 911, but I can't go back there. Not alone. What if it was him? What if it was Hows? "

"I'm coming right now. Where are you?"

Val hiccuped with relief. "I'm sitting in the Parkers' driveway. In my car."

"Where's your daughter?"

"She's with me. We're both safe."

"I'll be there in ten."

Val sighed. "Thank you, Carter."

"Who was that, Mom?" Abby's skin was sticky in spite of the running engine and Val adjusted the A/C vents to blow directly on them both.

"That was a friend of mine. You'll like him. He's coming to make sure we're okay."

"Are we okay?" Abby asked.

"Yes, we're okay." *I hope.*

Joel had just left Salmon Ridge when the call came through that there'd been a home invasion. He immediately recognized the address, and by the time he arrived at the Rockwell place—taking the tight curves way too fast on the mountain road—he could barely remember the drive back. It still wasn't fast enough.

Two county sheriff Yukons sat in the driveway, parked behind Val's blue Prius and Carter's Lexus crossover. Why was Carter there? Joel parked behind Larry's SUV, taking in the group gathered in the shade of the big walnut tree.

Larry was talking to Val and her little girl while Carter hovered protectively. Carter looked up as Joel's door slammed shut, then hurried across the dry grass to intercept him.

"It's about time. What took you so long?" Carter kept his voice low, but it was obvious he was angry.

Joel ignored him. He went straight to Val, interrupting Larry's questioning and scanning quickly for signs of injury on either her or her daughter. Relieved when he saw none.

"Are you both okay?"

Val nodded jerkily. "Yeah, we're all right. Now."

"I was in Salmon Ridge when the call came in or I would have been here sooner. Can you tell me what happened?"

Larry edged away to join Kim, the other deputy circling the yard. It was helpful to get multiple accounts of a single event, and Joel and Larry would compare notes later. No one ever told the same story twice, always choosing different details as the brain tried to process what had happened. But more importantly, Joel wanted to hear for himself that they were okay.

Val scratched absentmindedly at a mosquito bite on her arm. She was dressed in nice slacks and an eyelet blouse and explained that she'd returned from job hunting in town and found the front door wide open.

"You didn't call 911 immediately?"

She dropped her gaze to the dry grass. "I was trying not to overreact. The house is old. There's no deadbolt. Sometimes the front door doesn't quite latch all the way. I didn't want to call out the cavalry for nothing."

"Next time, call the cavalry. I'd rather send a deputy

here for no reason than not send one when you're in danger."

Val's brown eyes met his, sparking with anger. "There'd better not be a next time. You'd better find him Joel. I can't sleep another night knowing he's out there."

"Could you identify him? Do you think it was Howser?"

"I don't know. I want to say 'yes' but as soon as I saw him I ran to the car. He was gone when I looked back. Abby got a better look than I did, but her description isn't exactly helpful. I mean, she's seven. All adults past forty look like her grandpa."

"Do you think she'd be able to identify him from a photo?"

Val shook her head. "I don't know. I'm so tired of this, Joel. I just want it to stop."

"I know." Out of habit, Joel started to reach for her but stopped himself. He didn't think she'd appreciate that friendly gesture now. "It might not seem like it, but this is good. Now we know someone has been here and have a basic idea of what he looks like. And the fact that he ran off tells me that hurting you isn't his intention. It's not much, but it's something."

Carter draped an arm around Val's shoulder. "You've gotta work on your bedside manner, Joel. Nothing about that sounded encouraging."

Joel focused on his notepad to disguise his surprise at seeing Carter's familiarity with Val. For a moment, he wondered if they were a couple, but then she sidled away from him and folded her arms.

Not a couple, then. Just Carter being Carter. Joel couldn't say why he felt gratified by that.

"You and Abby are welcome to stay with me for a few days," Carter offered. "I've got a spare bedroom and lots of video games."

Val looked away, uncomfortable. "No, thank you. I think that'd be too much for Abby."

And for me, Joel thought she was implying.

Carter charged on ahead, undeterred. "Then at least let me stay here. I sleep pretty light and can pitch a tent in the yard. Keep an eye on things."

Val hesitated. "What about work?"

"My producer is great. She'll understand."

"I'll think about it."

"Carter," Joel interrupted. "Can you give us a minute? I have a couple other questions I'd like to ask Val." When they were alone, he turned his back to the house to give them a little privacy. "It's not a bad idea to have someone here, but are you sure you want to ask Carter? He's not trained in protection. I can have a deputy stay if it would make you feel comfortable."

"You said yourself that whoever it is won't hurt me," Val challenged. "Maybe Carter isn't a professional, but at least I trust him."

"That's what concerns me. I'm sure Carter has your best interest at heart; he's about the most genuine guy I know. But he's also genuinely good at his job. Don't forget what he does for a living."

"You think he's just trying to get the scoop for a big story?" Her voice crackled with annoyance.

"He has a hard time staying out of matters that aren't any of his business. I don't want you to get hurt."

"Is that right?" The wind tossed her hair into her face, and she yanked it back. "Then why didn't you tell me Howser was a convicted murderer? If you really cared about keeping me safe you would have been honest with me from the beginning."

Ah. Now it was finally out. "Carter told you?"

"Yes, because he doesn't believe in keeping things from the people who most need to know."

"No, he doesn't believe in keeping anything from anyone. There's a difference. Look, we don't know who you saw today. It could be Sam Howser, but even you aren't sure. Maybe I should've told you, but there's no reason to get you worked up over a lot of sensational gossip that will only make it harder to sleep at night."

"And how much sleep do you think I'll be getting tonight?"

She had a point. "Sorry, Val. I understand why you think I should have said something. But my world operates very differently from Carter's. I focus on facts and evidence and only share what's necessary once I'm certain the benefits outweigh the risks."

"Fine." Val looked toward the house where Carter sat with Abby on the porch. "Do what you need to, Joel. But don't be surprised if I have a hard time trusting you." She stalked away and hurried up the porch steps.

Carter caught Joel's eye and offered a smug smile before following her into the house.

7

Since they'd arrived two weeks earlier, Val had felt like she was suffocating under the thick calm of her childhood home. But now, it had become a circus. Deputies—an older white man whose round youthful face didn't match his graying hair, and a short, black-haired woman whose brown skin was even darker than Joel's—passed in and out through both the front and back doors, examined windows, searched through the garage, and even climbed the hill behind the house.

Unless Val was needed to answer questions, she and Abby stayed out of their way. She tried to identify if something was missing, but it was hard to know whether anything had been taken when the whole house was already in a state of complete upheaval.

It was dusk before the deputies packed up. Joel was the last to leave, but promised to return the next day.

"With your permission, I'd like to bring some photos for Abby to look at," he said.

He'd avoided Val since she'd yelled at him in the

yard, and now his dark eyes were distant. Val felt chagrined at her outburst but had meant every word of it.

"That's fine," she said. "Text me so I know when to expect you."

She followed him to the screen door and watched him drive away.

"Can I help you with some of this stuff?" Carter asked, taking in the haphazard piles in the living room.

Val sighed. "I'm exhausted. I'll work on it more tomorrow."

"I don't mind," he insisted. "I'm used to staying up late. Put me to work."

She almost told him no. But the thought of someone else chipping away at it was appealing.

"You know what? Go for it. Gina and I haven't missed this stuff. We surely won't miss it if we don't know what's here. If you see anything that looks valuable or sentimental enough that we'd have regrets, set it in the dining room. Otherwise, trash goes outside and donation items go on the porch."

"Great! You and Abby go on to bed. I'll be fine here," Carter said with a grin.

Val briefly wondered if she should tell him not to throw out the baseball bat, but she felt foolish admitting that she'd thought of using it as a weapon. She couldn't remember now where she'd left it, but after today she desperately wished she had a better way of protecting herself and Abby.

Val took extra time to read to Abby and tuck her into bed. Abby had been pensive all afternoon, but now that they were alone, her tongue loosened. It was calming to hear her chatter about Creampuff and the healing progress of a scratch on her hand. They talked and snuggled for almost an hour before Abby ran out of words and Val felt like she could leave and get ready for bed herself.

Hearing Carter working downstairs while she brushed her teeth was so comforting that Val went to him a few minutes later with a blanket and a pillow. "Don't bother with the tent. If you can clear enough room off the couch, I'd rather you stayed inside."

He looked surprised. "Oh. Thanks."

"Thank *you*. I hope you won't get in too much trouble at work. But I'm really grateful."

He moved a stack of old VHS tapes from the couch and motioned for her to sit. "Is Abby down for the night? Would you like a drink to unwind?"

Val cringed. "No, thanks. I gave that up when my husband died. I was…it was getting a little scary." Her life was already complicated enough. She didn't need to add alcohol abuse.

"Ah, the responsible mom. I can respect that. Adulthood isn't always as fun as we thought it would be, is it?"

"Not when you have other people counting on you not to wreck your life," Val agreed. "But I've got something almost as good." She went to the kitchen and poured two tall glasses of lemonade before joining Carter on the couch.

He laughed. "The next best thing, eh? Girl, you need to live a little."

"What's more summery than cold lemonade on a hot evening?"

"Can't argue there." Carter tapped his glass against hers before taking a long swig. His fair hair seemed a shade darker in the dim light of the single lamp. His features softer. They sat in companionable silence against the strident call of crickets thrumming in the night. The wind must have shifted because the smell of smoke wasn't as thick in the air, and the breeze through the open windows smelled of dry grass and sun-baked earth.

"I think I was too hard on Joel today," Val confessed. "I didn't mean to get after him like that. Do you think I hurt his feelings?"

Carter shrugged. "Joel's a good guy. And he's good at his job. I'm sure he understands the stress you're under. I wouldn't worry too much about it."

"I feel like I'm barely holding it together these days. I don't like the person I'm becoming, but I can't always stop it. The other day I got so mad at Abby because I thought she was lying to me about getting into the garbage. I couldn't let it go. And then it turns out she was telling the truth!" Val laughed sheepishly. "Any sane person would have been more worried about some drifter going through their trash. But I was just happy Abby wasn't lying to me."

Carter reached out and laid a hand on her knee. "You've been through a lot, Val. I think you're doing a great job. And I'm sure Abby does too."

His hand was warm and freckled and covered in pale hair that caught the light. It felt…real.

She laid her own hand on top of his.

"Did you know Jordan took his own life?"

For a moment, Carter was speechless. Only the chorus of crickets filled the air.

"I didn't know. I'm so sorry, Val."

She didn't look at him. She didn't think she could say the words if she saw the compassion in his eyes. And she really needed to say the words. She needed to get them out before they strangled her.

"Jordan was my world. He came into my life when I wasn't sure there was any point to it. I'd dropped out of Purdue. I'd given up on my future. I was…a mess."

"I don't understand. You were on top of the world our senior year. What happened?"

Val took a sip of lemonade, wondering why she was telling him this now. But it felt right. And she knew instinctively that Carter wouldn't judge her.

"It was so much harder than I expected. I thought I was prepared, but I wasn't. I pushed through that first year, but something went wrong my second year. It hit so hard I didn't see it coming. I couldn't sleep for days at a time, and then other days I couldn't get out of bed. I stopped going to class. I couldn't eat. I dropped fifty pounds and barely had the strength to carry my backpack. I was too ashamed to tell my parents so I avoided their calls, and instead of telling them I was on probation, I took out loans and told them I was staying for summer term. I didn't dare go home."

"Wow. Val, I'm so sorry. I had no idea. But you must have gotten help?"

"When things got really bad, a friend took me to the hospital. They hooked me up with an inpatient program, and slowly, I clawed my way back from disaster. Death, even. A few months later, I met Jordan. He helped me put my life back together, and by the time I'd recovered, we were inseparable. He was almost done with his Master's in Accounting and had a great job offer. He came from a great family—his mom's a senator, for crying out loud—and he had an amazing future and he wanted me to be a part of it. It was a no-brainer."

"Was he good to you?"

"The best. I still had some hard times, especially after Abby was born. But he was kind and supportive. Always getting me the best care. Making sure I had anything I needed. Trying not to burden me with finances or bills or anything like that." Val trailed off, listening to herself as if it were someone else's story. "I know it sounds weird. I mean, I was never the kind of girl who needed a guy to take care of her."

"Yeah, it doesn't sound like you at all."

"I guess it's easy to get stuck in patterns with certain people and then we don't give them room to change. I didn't need to be strong when Jordan was around. He was strong enough for us both, and he hadn't known the girl I was before. After a while, I guess I forgot too."

Carter squeezed her knee. "Well, I know she's still in there somewhere. She's the one getting you through this."

Val cocked her head. "Maybe."

After a moment, Carter asked hesitantly, "So, what happened? Why did Jordan…?"

Val downed the last of her lemonade. "Apparently he'd had his own demons that he didn't share with me. Probably thought I couldn't handle them. The day I found out I didn't really know the man I'd married was the day he drove his car off a cliff into Lake Baruch."

Carter waited for more, but when she didn't offer it, he sighed. "I'm glad you told me. And I'm so glad you came home. If there's anything I can do to help, you know you can count on me, right?" He moved his hand slightly, almost imperceptibly turning his touch into a caress.

Val threw off his hand and stood so fast, she barely knew what had happened. Carter too, looked stunned. His mouth hung open.

"I'm sorry, Val, I thought we were both—"

"Sorry, Carter, I can't—" she began at the same time. "I don't have any room in my life for that right now."

Carter managed a weak smile. "But if you did…"

"I don't," she snapped. Her face flamed hot and she struggled to meet his eyes. "I invited you here as a friend. Nothing more."

For a moment, he looked embarrassed, but then he packed it away and said smoothly, "Sure, I understand. No hard feelings. Sorry if I made you uncomfortable."

"You didn't," she lied. "But it's late, and I'm tired. Thanks for listening. I'll see you in the morning."

As she reached the stairs, she heard him softly call her name.

"Val, I meant what I said. You can count on me for anything. I promise I won't do anything like that again."

She wrapped her arms around her stomach and tried to hold her voice steady as she replied, "Good night, Carter."

8

VAL WOKE to the sound of distant laughter and was immediately disoriented. Thoughts of Jordan flashed through her mind, bringing the longing of another life as if the last six months had been nothing but a nightmare. As she fully woke, she pushed the feeling away.

Not Jordan.

Carter.

She hated these moments when sleep made her forget. It was so much harder to face the day when she had to relive six months of betrayal and grief before she opened her eyes. It had been happening less since coming to Owl Creek, but talking about Jordan to Carter the previous night must have brought it all up again.

The rhythmic creak of the trampoline drew her to the window where she felt a flicker of delight to see a blue sky with no sign of smoke. She breathed in the fresh morning air. It felt new like a beginning.

Below her in the yard, Carter and Abby were

jumping together on the trampoline. Carter was in a t-shirt and basketball shorts, and Abby was dressed in her nightgown. On some command Val couldn't hear, they both collapsed on their backs and then tried to jump back to their feet again. When that failed, they ended up in a rolling heap of giggles.

With a smile, Val went downstairs to make coffee. The kitchen was pleasantly cool, and the breeze coming through the window smelled of lavender from her mother's herb garden. In spite of the excitement, she had slept better last night than she had in months. She wondered how much of it was the security she felt with Carter downstairs.

Maybe she should get a dog.

As she idly Googled "German Shepherds vs. Labradors," the back door opened, and Carter and Abby came tumbling into the kitchen.

"I knew it! I told you Mom was up!" Abby said triumphantly.

"What? You must be a genius," Carter said with a wink at Val. "Or maybe you have x-ray vision. How many fingers am I holding up?" He held his hand behind his back.

"It's not x-ray vision! I smelled the coffee!" Abby laughed in a way that made Val's heart hurt. Abby missed her father deeply, maybe more than Val realized.

Val felt a surge of gratitude toward Carter. But also alarm. She wasn't ready to date again—her reaction to Carter last night had made that clear. But when she was ready, how would she do it without breaking Abby's heart at every turn? She'd had very little experience in relationships even without a child to complicate things.

And her marriage hadn't been what she would call a raving success, considering how it had ended.

But those were thoughts for another day. She poured Carter a cup of coffee and worried for a moment about meeting his eyes. When she did, she saw understanding. Compassion. Safety. What she'd shared with him the previous night hadn't changed what he thought of her.

"Did you sleep okay?" she asked. "That couch doesn't have much support."

"It was fine. I really am a light sleeper, so my first night in a new place is always rough. This wasn't too bad, actually."

Val wondered if the reference to "first" meant he expected there to be others. Time to nip that in the bud.

"Thanks so much for staying. If I ever need an impromptu couch guest, I know who to call."

"I don't mind staying again tonight, if you want. I need to go into work today and finish up a couple of things, but I can—"

"No, it's fine. We'll be all right. Joel said he could send out a deputy if I want him to. Yesterday it was still pretty raw, but I'm feeling a lot better about things now."

Carter shrugged and took a sip of coffee. In the silence that followed, Abby blurted out, "Carter has a tattoo like that Amy Geddon woman. The cartoon in the bank woman's office."

Carter nearly choked on his coffee. "When did you see my tattoo?"

Val looked sharply at Abby.

"When we were jumping on the trampoline. You

tried to do a headstand, remember? And your shirt fell in your face?"

Carter laughed. "You're a very observant little girl. Do you follow *Robert Apocalypse?*"

"My mom won't let me."

"Hold on, I never said that," Val protested. "I said I wanted to check it out first."

"Oh, it's great." Carter's eyes brightened. "I think you'd like it. It's been around for years but it was kind of an underground thing for a long time. Now it's really taken off. There's merchandise and even rumors that they're selling the rights to make a TV series."

"Show Mom your tattoo," Abby commanded.

"It's okay," Val said, heat rising in her face. "You don't have to show me anything."

"It looks like her necklace."

"Where did you see Amy Geddon's necklace if you haven't read the comic?"

"Maddie," Val explained, wondering how much to tell Carter about her pitiful job search. "We were at the bank yesterday and she had a picture in her office."

"Ah, of course. I should have guessed. Bryson and Maddie run a big fan forum. It's gotten huge!"

"Bryson?"

"Bryson Gottschalk? You remember him?"

Val shrugged apologetically, thinking of the picture in Maddie's office and the man she didn't recognize. "Sorry, I'm drawing a blank."

"Salmon Ridge? Star quarterback? The class ahead of us?" Carter shook his head as if it didn't matter. "Joel and I couldn't stand him in high school, but he and Maddie hooked up a few years ago and he's actually pretty cool. He's been a diehard *Robert Apocalypse* fan from the beginning. Runs the Apocalypse Masters page. Last year he and Maddie went to a con in Portland dressed as Robert and Amy and had people lining up to take selfies with them."

Abby climbed onto the counter to reach a box of cereal from the cupboard.

"Let me help you with that," Val said, taking the box and pouring the cereal into a bowl. It was a small reminder of how different she was from her peers who were still single like Carter or just starting their families. She couldn't imagine obsessing over a webcomic and spending weekends going to cons in Portland. Would that be her life now if she hadn't married so young?

Abby dug into her cereal with gusto. "I like Amy Geddon's necklace," she said with her mouth full, a tendril of milk leaking out her lips.

"The Grover-C." Carter nodded, finishing off his coffee. "Amy Geddon invented it and it's the coolest thing. Not only can she use it to teleport, but she can simultaneously manipulate a small bubble of time so it seems like she disappears even when she's in the same spot. Or she can appear to duplicate herself so the bad guys are confused."

"That's convenient," Val said drily.

"It's awesome!"

"It's a weird name," Abby noted. "Why is it named after Super Grover?"

Carter laughed. "That's a good question! Some people think it's an anagram, others think it's named after her dad. Can I tell you a secret that some of the really hard core fans think?"

Abby nodded expectantly.

Carter lowered his voice conspiratorially. "Some people think it's actually named after Grover Cleveland. He was the twenty-second and twenty-fourth president of the United States."

"I know what USA stands for," Abby interjected. "United States of America."

"Um, yeah." Carter paused as if remembering that Abby was not his typical audience and he was unsure how to continue.

Val suppressed a smile.

"So, Grover Cleveland was elected twice but didn't serve consecutive terms," he continued. "At the beginning of his second term, he had a tumor in his mouth that had to be operated on but he wanted to keep it a secret. So he got on a yacht and went offshore to have it removed. He even destroyed the career of a journalist who tried to expose the truth."

"That's terrible," Val said.

"But why name the necklace after him?" Abby asked.

"Well, you see, going offshore put him in no man's land. He was technically not on American soil anymore, so it was sort of like he teleported and left his tumor behind when he returned."

"That seems like a stretch," Val muttered into her mug.

"Bryson makes a great case for it. You'll have to check out his site."

"I still think it's named after Super Grover," Abby declared.

"Well, you've gotta be a fan for your opinion to

count," Carter said good-naturedly. "So, do you want to check it out? So you can be a real fan?"

The rest of the morning the three of them sat together on the couch, huddled over Carter's phone reading *Robert Apocalypse.* Amy Geddon was Abby's favorite character, with her high tech gadgets that conveniently did whatever she needed them to do in any given moment. Except when the plot required failure and disaster. Then nothing worked, and Robert Apocalypse saved the day.

There were some predictable twists, like when Amy's ex-boyfriend who used to develop tech with her was revealed to be the mysterious Doctor Menace who generally caused havoc and tried to destroy the world. But there were also moments that surprised Val, like when Doctor Menace sacrificed himself to save Amy's mom from the bomb that he himself had rigged to blow up the massive Fero City Bridge. Of course, he survived to fight another day. But as the comic unfolded, Amy's complex relationship with the two men drew Val in. Most of it was shallow and campy, but occasionally there would be genuine moments of emotional resonance.

She didn't realize so much time had passed until her phone buzzed with a text from Joel.

"Joel will be here in thirty minutes. Abby, you're still not dressed. Go brush your teeth and get changed." She looked at her own jeans shorts and tried to remember how many days she'd worn them. Maybe it was worth freshening up a little.

"I'd better go into work for a few hours," Carter said, gathering up his messenger bag.

That was fine with Val. She wasn't sure how things were going to go with Abby doing a photo line-up and didn't want an audience.

"Thanks again, Carter. I really appreciate it." She gave him a hug before he left, keeping it short and platonic.

When Carter left, he seemed to take the morning calm with him. Val waited for Joel to arrive, feeling increasingly tense. To distract herself, she reached for the package she'd picked up from the post office the day before.

"Abby, do you want to see what Grandma Fisher sent you?"

It turned out to be a remote-controlled drone with four propellers and a camera.

Abby was over the moon. "Wow! Can we take it out today?"

Val frowned at the recommended age limit of 12+. Oh well. If Jeanette wanted to waste her money on gadgets that were wildly over Abby's coordination level, that was her problem.

Val knew Jordan's death was as hard on his parents as it was on her—maybe harder since the scandal had threatened Jeanette's political career. Under the circumstances, they hadn't tried to convince Val to stay in Illinois. But with the move back to Oregon, Val knew Jeanette and Charles felt like they'd lost them too. If this was how they decided to be a part of their lives, Val could respect the effort.

"Let's do it later when it cools off a little. Detective Ramirez is coming soon to ask you some questions about the man we saw yesterday."

"You mean Joel?"

"Yes, but we don't usually call police officers by their first names."

"You do."

"That's because I knew him long before he was a policeman. We were best friends for years and years. It's hard to remember to call him something different."

Abby cocked her head, the box still in her hands. "You don't act like you're best friends. You seem like you're always mad at him."

Val's neck warmed. "Well, that was a long time ago. We're not best friends now." *I'm not even sure what we are.*

She knew that the weirdness between them was mostly her fault. She and Carter didn't have any baggage between them, so it had been easy to pick up like old times when she saw him again. But Joel was different. Her feelings for him had always been complicated, even when they were young. Just when she'd started to think there might be something more to their friendship, he'd started dating Lacey. Sometimes she'd resented the younger girl, and other times she'd been relieved because it meant her relationship with Joel didn't have to change. They could weather the ups and downs of teenage drama a lot easier as friends.

Until she'd ruined it by kissing him the night of graduation. She didn't know what he'd felt; she was so embarrassed by what she'd done that she never talked to him about it and avoided him the rest of the summer. But she had felt something—promise and loss all at once—and it had haunted her that whole first year they were apart.

Now she was back in Owl Creek, but it certainly

didn't have the feel of second chances. More like desperate irony.

The soft thrum of a car coming up the road brought her back to the present. She did have a second chance to be more civil to him today. And she hoped to use the time to get some answers.

9

Abby leaned her head against her arm, nearly laying it flat against the kitchen table. She sighed, and her breath puffed against the photos, shifting the nearest ones out of place.

"Maybe we should try something else," Joel suggested, keeping his tone light. "Do you think you could draw a picture of the man you saw?"

Abby pulled her hair away from her face. "Maybe. I like drawing. But he was running pretty fast."

Val brought a tin of mismatched markers and a few sheets of copy paper and sat next to Abby.

"You're doing a great job," she murmured, lightly rubbing her back.

Abby selected a green marker and Joel let her draw in silence for a bit, watching the figure take shape.

"What do you remember from yesterday?" He asked.

Abby already seemed more relaxed with a marker in hand.

"He was running by the trampoline and I thought he might trip because I left my book out there and one time I was running down the stairs and I left the Fluffy book on the stairs and I slipped on it and fell all the way down—" she raised her hands and stair-stepped them down for emphasis, "to the bottom. I got a bruise on my leg, like this big."

She made a circle with her fingers.

"So you thought he would trip on your book?" Joel prompted.

"Yeah, but he didn't. He just kept running."

"Did you see where he went?"

Abby bent over her drawing again and shook her head. "Mom got back and we drove away."

"Was he taller or shorter than your mom?"

"Taller. But not as tall as my dad."

"What else did you see? Did he have any tattoos? Or any owies or anything like that?"

Abby looked up, her eyelids lowered in disgust. "You don't have to call it an 'owie.' I'm not a baby."

Val hid a smile.

"Right. Sorry. Did you notice if he had any wounds or scars?"

Abby set aside the green marker and selected a black one. She'd colored his body all green and was now adding black hair.

"He had a beard," she said, moving to cover the face in black. She pressed so hard on the paper that the marker squeaked.

"Did you hear anything strange? Anything you can remember?"

Abby shook her head. When she finished, Joel took her drawing and praised it generously.

"This will help me out a lot. Thank you, Abby."

"Great job," Val said, giving her a squeeze. "You've been working so hard! Why don't you go take a break?" She waited until Abby left before asking, "Is this helpful at all?"

Joel shrugged. "I mean, a clear ID is always nice, but seeing a stranger running away from your house is nothing like staring at a bunch of mug shots."

Val plucked out the picture of Howser from the batch. There were a few other men who had a similar look: thin face, greasy hair. Abby had identified two of these whom she thought might have been the invader. All of them bore a resemblance to Howser, but she hadn't picked out Howser directly. Of course, Howser was clean-shaven in the photo Joel had brought, and Abby said the man she'd seen had a beard.

"I've requested a canine team but Owl Creek doesn't get first pick on county units. They said they might be able to get one here on Friday."

"Two days away?" Val asked incredulously. "Anything could happen by then."

"He also might have run off, you know. Seeing cop cars at your place last night would surely make him think twice about coming back."

"I'd still rather know for certain."

"So would I." Joel stood and stretched, then refilled his glass of water at the sink. "I promise we're doing everything we can. But with the actual crime being a home invasion, not an obvious robbery—"

Val snorted. "Who would even know in this mess?"

"I'm just saying, I can understand why you're concerned, but there's only so much we can do."

Val sighed. Her thick hair was pulled back into a tight ponytail, but little wisps had curled around her face in the heat. She wasn't wearing makeup these days, but Joel found the look refreshing and honest. He liked it.

"Do you have a theory about what he's doing here?" she asked.

Joel gathered up the photos. He suspected he wouldn't get anything more from Abby.

"Maybe he thought the place was empty, and it would be a safe place to hide away from town. He hasn't lived in the area for a long time, but he might have heard your mom had moved while he was in the fire camp."

"Or maybe it was the opposite. I keep wondering if he was looking for my dad," Val said thoughtfully. "I talked to Gina about the Ryan Moyer murder. That was her class, you know, so she was very close to it all. She said it was Dad who persuaded Howser to go to the police in the first place."

"Really?" Joel reached for his notepad.

"Yeah. Apparently Howser confided to him enough that Dad insisted he report it. Dad might have even gone with him when he turned himself in. Gina couldn't remember for sure."

"And if Howser was in prison, he wouldn't have known your dad had passed. It's plausible that if he needed help he might have come here looking for him."

"Look at me, doing your job for you."

"Look at me, taking all the credit."

She grinned.

It was something, just a little softening between them. He would take it. In the silence that followed, Joel took a risk.

"Val, I got a text from Carter this morning. He said you shared some things last night about your husband's death that he wanted me to know. As a friend," he added when Val stiffened.

Carter's text had actually read, *You won't believe this. V's hubby offed himself,* followed by a link to a news article that Joel ignored. He wanted to respect her privacy and give her a chance to tell him herself. Or not. It felt too much like snooping to research the details of the tragedy to satisfy his own curiosity. As a detective, he knew the difference.

Val glanced toward the door to the living room. Concerned about Abby or wanting to escape? Joel wasn't sure.

"I want you to know that I'm really sorry about what happened," Joel said. "You don't have to talk to me about it, but I hope you don't blame yourself."

Val looked at the floor. "Thanks. But I think I got over that a long time ago."

"That's good. His problems were his own, and although you have to live with the consequences, that doesn't make them your fault."

"Thanks," Val repeated. Then she moved to the doorway and called, "Abby, would you like to fly your drone now? Maybe Joel can help us set it up."

"Oh. Sure, I'd be happy to." Joel was certain this was a diversion tactic, but he didn't mind. If it meant building trust with Val and Abby, it would be a good way to spend a few minutes.

Val didn't really need his help, of course. She helped Abby put it together, assembling the fragile propellers and installing an SD card.

"Have you ever flown one of these things?" she asked as she searched in a kitchen drawer for batteries.

"A couple of times. It's fun, actually. Kind of soothing."

"This one has a camera, so it's pretty involved. I mean, look at this remote. How is a seven-year-old supposed to operate it?"

Joel took the remote and oriented the controls. "Nice. This is a good drone, Abby. Just be careful that you don't let it get out of range. It's easy to lose control if you do."

"You wanna give her a demonstration?" Val asked, offering him a crooked smile in invitation. Or was it a taunt?

They went outside and stood under the shade of the walnut tree with the drone in the middle of the yard.

"Try to avoid those trees over there," Joel directed, pointing to the evergreens that bordered the property on the east side. "I'd keep it flying over those fields instead."

He pushed the throttle and the blades started spinning. It always amazed him how delicate these machines were, how responsive to his fingers. The drone lifted into the air and the video feed on the remote lit up. He flew it out over the cars, high enough that it was above the house, then swept around the perimeter of the yard and brought it back to a safe landing.

"That was awesome!" Abby said. "My turn!"

Joel showed her the basics. "Don't worry about these controls here. They're for the camera. You can add that in after you get really good with controlling the drone. Start out small. There you go!"

She raised the drone into the air and then sent it flying toward the driveway. In seconds it was out over the field.

"Whoa, hold on. Just a little bit on the trigger. There you go."

He helped her bring it back and did a loop around the field.

Val watched with a glint in her eye. "Thanks. I would have crashed it by now."

"It's a little tricky at first, but once you get the hang of it, it's not hard."

They watched the drone do another lap.

"Speaking of prying into our personal lives, did you and Lacey have any kids?"

Joel shook his head. "I wanted to wait. I didn't feel ready, especially once I was accepted to the academy."

"Lots of policemen have kids."

"Yeah, but I wanted to make sure Lacey would be okay if anything ever happened to me. I thought after a few years we'd have student loans paid off, build up some savings, and then she'd be in a better place if she found herself raising kids without me."

He realized too late what he was saying and looked away from Val, hoping she didn't think he was commenting on her situation. He remembered how she and her husband had practically oozed wealth when he'd seen them at her dad's funeral. Judging from the nondescript shorts and t-shirt she wore now, and the modest Prius in the driveway, it was easy to see she'd come down in the world.

But she was nonplussed. "That sounds like the cautious Joel I know," was all she said.

"Maybe I was too cautious, I don't know. By the time my career was well underway, something had happened to us. Maybe having a baby would have helped. We still talked about it, but I think we both knew it wasn't going to last."

"That must have been hard."

Joel shrugged. It had been hell. Trying to work it out. Wondering if it would be better to end it. When he'd led the team into Stan's that day to free the hostages, one thing had become clear. He'd thought about Lacey and wondered what she would do if he didn't come home that night. And as much as it hurt to admit, he'd realized that a small part of her would be relieved, maybe even eager to move on with her life.

That's what he'd told Carter later when Carter asked what was going through his mind. Joel was a mess, trying to reconcile the lives he'd saved with the ones he took. Trying to process the look of abject terror on the first boy's face when Joel shot him. Still a teenager, Joel would find out later. What was worse, though, is that the kid wasn't even armed. Witnesses would declare that he'd been trying to talk his agitated friend into surrendering. If Joel had given them a few more minutes, he might have succeeded. Or one of the victims might have been shot, it was impossible to know. He would never know what might have happened, and the uncertainty haunted him.

Something about facing that uncertainty—that fear of what might have been—had given him the courage to let go of Lacey for good. Carter heard it all, but he showed uncommon decency in choosing not to mention any of it later in their on-camera interview.

But Joel couldn't say all that to Val. Instead he said vaguely, "We were holding each other back. It was the right thing to do."

A gasp from Abby drew Joel's attention back to the drone. Too late he saw that she'd flown it too high.

"It's not working!" she complained, thrusting the remote back into his hands.

He jammed the lever but it didn't respond. "It's too high. It's lost reception."

"Not over there! You're flying it toward the trees!"

"It's the wind." Joel winced as the drone was tossed like an errant balloon over the house and toward the forested hillside.

"Oh, no!" Val cried and took off to the back yard. They spotted it just in time to see it drop out of the sky and disappear into the trees.

There was a moment of stunned silence.

"Where is it?" Abby asked. "Did you see where it went?"

Val exhaled noisily. "It's gone, baby. It's lost in the forest now."

Abby looked at them both, and Joel could see the war in her eyes as she tried to hold it together. Then her face crumpled and she ran into the house.

"I'm so sorry, Val," Joel said lamely.

"It's fine," she said, but he could tell she felt the same pain in her heart that he did. It would take a callous monster to look Abby in the eyes and not be moved by her despair.

"Let me try to find it."

"Up on the hill? You'll never find it. It's probably stuck in the top of a tree. And how will you find one tree out of hundreds?"

But Joel would rather face a fruitless search than Abby's tear-filled eyes. "Maybe I'll get lucky. It's worth a look."

Val looked at him quizzically and then back at the house. "Okay, but I'm coming with you. I don't think anyone should be out there alone."

"No, I'm fine. You stay with Abby."

But Val shook her head. "She won't want me until she calms down. I'll check on her and then I'll be right out."

While he waited, Joel called Larry. "I'm at the Rockwell's and going to do a little scouting on the hillside."

"You wanna swing by Lori's bakery and pick up some of those sticky buns on your way back?" Larry replied. "You may need them to sweeten up Caroline Bellingham. She called a little while ago, wanting to know why you were talking to Roger Wright this morning. Apparently he called her after you left."

"Old loyalties run deep, I guess."

"Shane did work for Wright Trucking for over twenty years."

"All right, I'll see what I can do," Joel answered as Val came out wearing a sunhat and sunglasses.

She held out a ball cap with the Cubs logo on it. "Unless you want to work on your tan," she teased.

He took it gratefully.

They went through the back gate to the old logging road that ran up the hillside. Trees lined the road, but the sun beat down mercilessly, burning the back of Joel's neck. Soon he was sweating and his throat was dry. The air was filled with buzzing insects, and Queen Anne's Lace bobbed their white heads as Joel and Val brushed past.

At the first bend in the road, Val stepped off into the dry grass. "I think it was this direction."

Joel followed, searching for conversation to distract him from his thirst. "How long do you think you'll stay in the area?"

"Is that all anyone cares about?" Val asked with annoyance, striding on ahead. "I saw Maddie yesterday, and that's all she could talk about: whether or not I was here to stay."

"I guess because it's nice to have you back. Is that so bad?"

"That's not how it feels," she scoffed. "I get the sense that everyone judged me when I left and feels smug now that I've come back. Do I have to stay in Owl Creek so that people like Maddie feel better about themselves for never leaving in the first place?"

Joel frowned. "That's harsh, Val. I don't think Maddie needs your approval about her life choices—"

"But she thinks she has a right to disapprove of mine?" Val snapped. She stopped short, as if catching herself from saying more. When she continued, her tone was more controlled. "There's a ridge ahead where the trees clear a bit. We may be able to see better from there."

Joel was in good shape, but Val was powered by something which drove her forcefully up the hill. Sure enough, the trees thinned and soon they reached an outcropping of basalt with boulders projecting from the earth like an ancient sacrificial altar. Val leaned against the side of one of the boulders, resting in its shade and breathing heavily from her hike. Joel stood next to her and looked back the way they'd come. They were higher than he'd realized, and the farmhouse was visible below, set against tones of yellow grass and brown earth.

"I can't speak for Maddie," he said after catching his breath. "But I was proud of you when you left to go to Purdue. I was proud of you for having dreams, and I'm proud of you still. Your dreams may have changed, but that doesn't make them less important."

Val's expression was unreadable behind her sunglasses. "You don't think I was betraying my roots by leaving?"

"No more than I've betrayed them by staying."

She picked at the burrs clinging to her sock. "Joel, do you ever wonder how your life might have been different if you hadn't stayed and married Lacey? Not that I'm saying that was a bad choice. I liked Lacey, of course. But do you think you might have followed a different path if it hadn't been for her?"

Joel pulled off the ball cap and wiped his forehead on his sleeve. Now that they'd stopped, he could smell his own sweat and hoped she didn't notice. He wasn't dressed for a hike on the mountain. In the heat. With a smart and attractive woman.

"Let's see, would I have followed a different path?

Of course. That's implicit in the question, right? I think what you're really asking is if I've regretted following the path I took."

Val looked away. "I'm sorry, that's not a fair question. Forget it."

She stepped out from the shade of the boulder and started walking along the rocky ridge, leaving Joel feeling slightly deflated. He wasn't sure how he would have answered the question, but he wished she'd stuck around to hear it.

"I think we gave it our best shot," Val called over her shoulder. "If we go this way, we can take the road back down."

Joel hurried to catch up to her. "My mom always says that every choice you make is actually two choices. Every yes is a no to something else. So even though you may think you're only choosing one thing, you're also choosing *not* to choose something else."

"It's okay, you don't have to—"

A sharp hiss filled the air. Val stopped uncertainly, stepping back toward Joel. The hissing continued and Joel searched the ground, unsure where it was coming from.

Val grabbed his arm. Something was lying in the shade against the rocks above them. A shape like a person, but also wrong somehow. Its clothes were torn away, revealing ripped flesh in dark tones of red and black. Out of a crevice in the rock, barely a hint of gold in the darkness, emerged two pointy ears. A glint of glassy eyes.

And then the cougar screamed, a sound like needles

dragging along Joel's spine. High and shrill, it awakened something primal in him.

Pure, potent fear.

Before he knew what he was doing, he stepped in front of Val, raised his arms and shouted back at the cougar. The scream cut off.

"Back away slowly," he said. "Careful, now. It thinks we're here to steal its food."

"But Joel. Do you see…?" Her words cut off in a choking sound.

"Don't look. Don't think about that, Val. Just move." His voice was unsteady, and his heart raced.

They moved awkwardly back the way they'd come, Joel unable to watch his feet because his eyes were locked on the crevice, imagining the golden shape leaping out into the daylight.

They had just made it to the trees when Joel stumbled in a hole and went down, pulling Val with him. She yelped, and he scrambled to his hands and knees in a panic.

"Run!" he said breathlessly, terror overpowering reason.

Val got to her feet before he did and bounded down the mountain. He ran after her, blackberry vines tearing at his skin and clothes, his chest burning. The slope was treacherous at that pace, with deadfall and roots and hidden foxholes waiting to turn an ankle. But still they ran, slipping and stumbling, chased by visions of the cougar racing after them.

They didn't stop until they reached the logging road. Slowly Joel's brain caught up, reminding him that if the cougar had wanted to kill them, they would be dead already. He slowed to a jog but didn't stop until they'd closed the gate behind them into the yard. He bent over, gasping for air.

Val reached for him and he gathered her into his arms, both leaning on each other for support, trying to catch their breath. For a long moment they couldn't even speak. They held each other up until their breathing slowed.

Joel pulled his work phone out of his pocket, one arm still propping up Val. "Larry, I need you to call Fish and Wildlife ASAP. We've got a situation here and need a team of agents right away to take out a cougar. There's a possible human victim."

He pulled the phone away while Larry let out a stream of curses. "Yes, that's what I said, a human victim. Val's all right. She's here with me. We'll be at the house. Let me know when the agents are on their way."

"That was a person?" Val said weakly. "But…it looked…"

"Let's get inside and get some water. Fish and Wildlife will take care of it. You don't need to worry about it anymore. Everything's going to be okay." But even as Joel said it, he didn't believe it himself.

10

Abby seemed to sense that something was wrong as soon as Val and Joel entered the house. Val was prepared for another volley of tears when she saw that they didn't have her drone. But Abby took one look at their expressions and instead, wrapped her arms around Val's waist and buried her face against her middle. Val held on to her, luxuriating in the warmth of her little body. Stroking Abby's back calmed her trembling hands.

Joel went out to his car and between his cell phone and radio, appeared to be in a steady stream of urgent, sometimes simultaneous conversations. Val stood in the living room and looked at the piles remaining from forty years of life her parents had shared in that house. Suddenly it seemed so unnecessary. Why was she wasting her time combing through forgotten history when there were no guarantees for the future? Why let the past burden today when tomorrow might not even come? Life was tenuous. Today might be all she had.

Making a decision, she started moving all the as-yet-untouched boxes out to the porch. There was a Goodwill donation center in Pineview, just down the road from Walmart. She would fill her trunk every time she went to town, getting rid of it one load at a time. It felt good to clear the space, and by the time the first deputies arrived, she looked around the living room with satisfaction.

It had been different when Jordan died. Getting rid of his things had felt like losing a part of herself. She had desperately held onto that life even when she'd begun to suspect there was more going on beneath the surface than she understood. Jeanette had come to help after the memorial, but she'd been so distraught that Val had sent her away after three days of sobbing every time she touched something that had belonged to him. Val had never seen her mother-in-law so undone.

In the end, friends had come in and done the hard work, sending some of it to his parents and saving a small box of mementos for Val. Even that she'd been tempted to discard when she'd moved back to Owl Creek. She'd felt so betrayed by his death. Keeping anything of his had felt like forgiveness, and she wasn't ready for that.

Inspired by the boxes accumulating on the porch, Val went upstairs and found the last box of Jordan's things she'd stored in the top of her closet. She placed it with the other boxes without opening it. If she opened it, she might lose her resolve. But holding onto a piece of Jordan wouldn't bring him back, and it hadn't helped her forgive him. Maybe it was best to be free of him altogether.

Abby perched on her knees, leaning over the back of the couch to watch the deputies through the living room window. When the Fish and Wildlife agents arrived, she announced excitedly, "That one has a big gun!"

Val watched as the agents talked with Joel. It surprised her how slow and deliberate everyone was being about all of this. It was like they had all the time in the world and hunting a man-eating cougar was part of a normal workday.

When Joel came in to tell her that he was leading them up the hill to find the cougar's den and she and Abby needed to stay in the house, she felt a flicker of fear. How could he endure going back to that scene?

But all she said was, "Are you hungry? I'm going to make tacos."

He blinked. "Uh…No, don't worry about me."

"You sure? Ground beef was on sale last week. I've got plenty."

Again that look like she'd said something totally irrelevant. Inappropriate, even.

"It's okay. We'll bring in some sandwiches or something. If you don't mind letting deputies use your bathroom, we'll stay out of your hair otherwise."

Val shrugged and went to the kitchen to cook the ground beef. But she found that when she loosened the raw meat into the pan, the sight of the blood running out of the packaging made her queasy. She hadn't gotten a good look at the corpse, but it was enough to let her know she didn't want to see more. Red flesh. Blood dried black. Had she imagined the hint of white where bone should have been? With part of a pant leg and boot still intact as if to mock the reality that this had once been a person. She hadn't heard flies over the shrieking of the cougar, but her memory filled them in so that they mixed with the shrill scream.

Val put a lid on the pan and left the meat cooking, no longer hungry. By the time she returned, the bottom of the meat was charred black and smoke seeped out from under the lid. But at least it wasn't red and bloody anymore. She could handle this.

Abby was on her third taco when Val heard the first shot. It was startlingly loud and echoed across the valley, reverberating on the surrounding hillsides.

"Do you think they got it?" Abby's green eyes were wide with concern. She hadn't been happy when Val had explained why the agents with guns were there.

"I don't know."

Another shot rang out.

Val went to the kitchen window and drew in a quick, indignant breath. Carter was in the back yard, gesturing to the hillside, accompanied by a man lugging a large camera.

She stormed out the back door so fast, she scarcely noticed the door sticking when she pulled it open.

"What do you think you're doing?" she demanded, standing on the porch where she hoped she looked commanding.

"Val! This is Milo," Carter said. "I'm showing him around a bit so we can figure out the best place to set up a shot."

"I can tell you the best place to set up," she said, trying to keep calm in spite of the angry pounding of her heart. "You can take your camera and shove it up your butt. Get off my property before I report you for trespassing."

"Whoa!" Carter stopped short. "You all right, Val? I know it's been a stressful day, but—"

"I didn't give you permission to come film on my land, Carter." Val folded her arms, mad enough to want to hit him. That stupid soul patch would make a perfect target.

Carter looked at Milo and muttered something too quiet for Val to hear. But she could imagine it. *Let me deal with her…*

Oh, she dared him to try.

When Milo left, Carter bounded up to the porch. "Val, this is big news. A cougar killed a man practically in your back yard. Don't you think people should know?"

"I don't care what people should or shouldn't know. You're not filming on my property. Not me. Not my house. Not a single fencepost."

Carter nodded. "I totally understand. This whole thing must be really upsetting. How well did you see the cougar? Do you think the body could belong to Samuel Howser?"

Val gaped at his audacity. Then she smiled grimly. "You're not nearly as slick as you think you are, Carter. This is not my first rodeo. Get the details from Joel, since he seems so interested in talking to you. You're not getting anything from me. And I'll remind you there's a minor child in this house. I'm sure your producer wouldn't want to be accused of exploiting her after such a traumatic event."

Carter's eyes narrowed. "You know, we don't need your permission to film from the road."

"Maybe not. But if you film anything besides the mountain, I know a lawyer who will sue your little news agency so fast no one will dare put Carter Millston in front of a camera again."

She hoped Carter wouldn't sense her bluff. Not about the lawyer, that part was true. But Melissa wouldn't waste her time on such a small case. Especially not now that Val was penniless.

Carter hesitated only a fraction of a second, as if waiting to see if Val was joking, before raising his hands in defeat. "All right, you've got my word. We won't get the house or the yard."

"Or mention my name."

"Come on, Val—"

"No names, Carter."

"Fine. No names." He turned away, shaking his head. Then he paused for a parting shot. "You know, Val, not all of us are bad guys. I'd like to think you could trust me, of all people. Even if your previous run-ins with the media were nightmarish, you should know me well enough to know I'm not like them. "

"You have no idea the substance of my nightmares," she spat.

Carter shrugged sadly and walked away, leaving Val shaken. What exactly did he know about Jordan's death? She supposed even people in Owl Creek would have heard about Senator Fisher's son. It was only a matter of time before someone connected the dots, and she should have guessed it would be Carter. It's not like it would be that hard to find out. But somehow she'd still hoped she was safe from all that in Owl Creek.

Just to be sure Carter was true to his word, she watched both the evening and late night news after putting Abby to bed. The cougar attack was the headline story, and Carter's report was exciting with lots of his signature energy and dynamic inflection. He did indeed keep his word, never indicating exactly where he was and not mentioning her name. Joel had consented to an interview, but he, too, left out details of her involvement.

"While performing a routine search for missing person Samuel Howser today, police made a grisly discovery. A human body was found in the hills east of Owl Creek. But what was even more disturbing is that the victim was protected by a vicious mountain lion that did not want to give up its prey without a fight."

Daylight footage of the police cars and wildlife agents moving up and down the mountain accompanied the report, as well as a distant shot of the cougar being carried out on a stretcher, but there was not even a glimpse of the farmhouse. Maybe Carter really was a decent reporter, if such a thing existed.

Val perked up when the view changed to a live shot of Carter interviewing Joel. As promised, they stood on the road away from the house, lights illuminating only the two of them in front of an empty field.

"You actually saw the cougar, is that right?"

"Yes. It was hidden in a crevice and issued an aggressive warning as I approached."

"Could you tell the identity of the body?"

"It was difficult to see any distinguishing features from where I was standing."

"But it was a human body?"

"It appeared so."

"Do you think the body could be that of Samuel Howser?"

"It's too early to say." Joel was so composed and distant as he talked about it. Val would never guess he'd been just as terrified as she was. But she could tell he was holding back. She was sure Carter could see it too.

"But you were searching for him, is that correct?"

"Yes."

"Any particular reason you were searching in this area?"

Val frowned. Carter knew exactly why Joel was there.

"It was a routine search as part of our investigation. We've been looking into every credible lead. This was one of many that we've received over the past week."

Well done, Joel.

"And when do you expect to know the identity of the body?"

"Agents from the Department of Fish and Wildlife killed the cougar earlier this evening. Now that it's safe to approach the area, we're working to gather as much information as we can before bringing the remains off the mountain. It will take some time."

"Can you tell me the condition of the body?"

Do you have to be so macabre? The cougar was feasting on it, what would you expect?

"I'd rather not discuss that, out of respect for the deceased and their family. But a cougar can keep a kill for several days, and agents are pretty confident this was a recent occurrence."

"Do you think the victim was killed by the cougar?"

"It would appear so, yes."

Why did reporters always ask the dumbest questions? *Did you know anything about your husband's illegal activities, Mrs. Fisher? How does it feel to know that your husband stole millions of dollars from senior citizens? What do you want to say to the victims who lost all their retirement savings due to your husband's fraud? Have you heard that at least three of his victims took their own lives because they couldn't deal with the financial ruin? Mrs. Fisher, did you have any idea your husband would kill himself to avoid getting arrested?*

Val switched off the TV and went to the kitchen to make a pot of coffee. Despite the late hour, the police didn't show any signs of leaving, and a generator and floodlights had been brought in to illuminate the hillside where the body was found. Abby was sleeping through the commotion, but Val knew it would be a long night for her. She wouldn't sleep until they were finished.

Underneath all the exhaustion there was a part of her that felt relieved. She hoped the body was that of the intruder she'd found in her house the day before. Whether it was Howser or not, she couldn't say, nor could she say if he deserved a violent end. But the green fabric she'd seen could have matched the jacket she'd found at the garage, and she was glad to know that whoever he was, he wouldn't be bothering them again.

A step on the front porch followed by a light knock brought her to the screen door. Carter waited alone.

"I wanted to let you know we're finished here. Sorry

about before. I didn't mean to make you uncomfortable."

Val nodded stiffly, her arms folded across her chest. "I saw your report. Thank you."

Carter looked out at the news van with the Channel Six logo and hesitated, like he had something important to say but wasn't sure if he should say it.

"Val, I know what Jordan did. I can only imagine what kind of hell that put you through. I guess I should be grateful you don't hate me for what I do for a living."

"I should have guessed you wouldn't have left it alone," she said wearily, but his apology weakened her annoyance.

"Have you told Joel?"

Val shook her head. "I'm not in any rush. Abby still doesn't know. She knows her daddy died, of course, but she doesn't know what he did to all those people."

Carter chewed his lip, considering, then looked her in the eye. "Did *you* know?"

Val felt a surge of anger. How could he even think that of her? But at the same time she thought of the custom home and luxury cars and designer clothes and all the years of wealth she'd enjoyed, naively thinking it was all honestly earned.

I did it for you, his suicide note had said. The shame still bit her after all these months.

And made her mad.

"Get off my porch, Carter."

He looked at her with disappointment, as if she'd confirmed his fears. She slammed shut the heavy door, remembering too late that Abby was upstairs sleeping.

When Joel found her later, she didn't know how

long she'd been sitting on the couch in a stupor, her mind following the same paths it had worn so well these past months. Trying to figure out what had pushed Jordan to prey on the weak and trusting, abandoning any sort of moral compass he once had. Wondering why she hadn't known he was capable of such cruelty. Reliving the wintry morning when the special agents had come to her door with a search warrant. The pity on Agent Giles's face when he brought her the suicide note. The hours of intense fear as she desperately tried to reach Jordan, caring only about him coming home safe. Still unaware of just how much damage he'd done. Still believing he was the same man she'd married, and whatever he'd been mixed up in could be sorted out.

And then they'd tracked his cell phone to the cliffs above the lake in a neighboring county, and she thought it had all been an accident, a tragic combination of icy conditions and distraction from guilt and fear. Until they'd found evidence that he'd intentionally driven over the edge, taking with him any hope that she would find answers. Or peace.

"Sorry to keep you up, Val," Joel said, bringing her back to the present. "You've been great. We all really appreciated the coffee."

Val blinked, trying to get her bearings. Gray daylight rimmed the edges of the windows. Joel's dark eyes were bloodshot, and he was in need of a shave. Val yawned and walked him to the door, wondering if she looked as haggard as he did.

"Why did it take so long?"

"We couldn't risk moving the remains until we finished processing the scene. The body wasn't...let's just say that it didn't come off the mountain in the same condition we found it."

Val shivered at the thought. She was seized with a sudden desire to feel the reassuring warmth of his arms around her again.

"Joel, it's been such a busy night that I haven't thanked you."

He looked up in surprise. "For what?"

For so many things. For not prying into Jordan's death. For not mentioning me in your interview with Carter. For taking care of the intruder. And the cougar.

But what she said was, "When we saw that cougar today…yesterday…you placed yourself in front of me. Like a human shield."

"I did?"

"Yeah, you did. And the fact that you didn't realize it makes me even more grateful. It wasn't an act. You did it without thinking, with no thought for your own safety. You're a good guy, Joel. It's nice to know you have my back."

Joel looked away. "It's no big deal. It's human nature to look out for each other, you know? Anyone else would have done the same thing."

Not necessarily. But Val kept her thoughts to herself, her arms folded tightly instead of reaching for a hug. After an awkward hesitation, he wished her goodnight and walked away into the emerging dawn.

11

JOEL HUNG up the phone and leaned back in his chair. He looked at the clock and sighed. So much for calling it a day. This Howser case didn't want to be put to rest. The past few days he'd been able to focus on other cases, sure that the medical examiner's report would settle things once and for all. A picture had been growing in his mind of Sam Howser, troubled and off his medication, hiding out in the woods near Val's home until the unfortunate cougar attack.

It wasn't a complete narrative and still left questions. Why had Howser left the fire camp in such a rush, leaving his personal effects behind? What had taken him to the hills near the Rockwell home? Was it coincidence or a deliberate choice? But they were questions that became insignificant now that he was dead. It was a grim end to a life plagued by tragedy, but with no crime committed, Joel was prepared to move on.

Apparently not.

He looked over his notes from his phone call with Dustin, the county's ME.

> Victim: Samuel Howser (confirmed dental records)
> Time of death: between 2000-0200 hrs July 20-21 (last known sighting 20 July 1630 hrs, home invasion)
> Cause of death: pending autopsy, evidence of significant head trauma, mountain lion incidental

Incidental. Joel circled the word. Something—or someone—may have killed Howser before the cougar got to him. Howser's remains were on their way to the state's ME office in Clackamas County to find out for sure.

They'd already determined that Howser had been killed in another location and dragged by the cougar to its den. A blood trail had indicated the actual site had been lower on the hillside, within sight of the farmhouse. He'd kept that particular detail from Val; her nerves had been frayed enough as it was. But they'd still assumed it was the cougar who'd killed him.

Joel reached for the case file and pulled out photos of the scene where Howser had died, steeling himself against the site of the mangled corpse. There was nothing to indicate an obvious cause for accidental death. Dustin had been clear that a fall could have only caused that kind of trauma to the skull if it'd been from a great height.

"Car accidents, bike accidents without wearing a helmet, that sort of thing," he'd explained. "This isn't an 'oops I tripped and hit my head on a rock' kind of injury." Which meant either they were wrong about the location, or someone else had been there and removed the instrument from the scene.

Even more puzzling were the designs drawn on some of the more preserved parts of Howser's body. The cougar had gone for the organs first, eviscerating the torso and mangling one half of his face. But part of the left leg and arm had remained untouched. On the forearm and lower leg had been drawn five symbols similar to the symbols Joel had seen in Howser's notebook. They were crudely drawn with a marker, one of them marked out with an X. Maybe it was significant. Maybe it was nothing.

Joel scratched at his neck and flipped to his interview notes. He'd stopped following up on leads once the body had been found, not wanting to divert any more attention to a case that was about to be closed. But now, it was time to consider suspects again.

Joel went back to the top of the list. Aside from Val and Abby, Tom Morrison was the last known person to see Howser alive. It wouldn't hurt to see if he could remember anything else significant about that night.

As it turned out, Tom was between shifts and agreed to come in within the hour. Joel wondered if his mention of air conditioning had sweetened the deal. The interrogation room was little more than a conference room that doubled as a site for gatherings like when Kathy brought in donuts for birthdays or other special occasions. A window looked out on the receptionist area where Kathy bent over her desk, the ends of her black bob swinging against her chin as she moved to staple a packet of receipts to their respective invoices.

When Tom Morrison came in, he eyed the water cooler in the corner of the room.

"Are you thirsty? Help yourself," Joel offered as he closed the door behind him.

Tom shook his head.

Joel reached for his hand. "Thanks for coming in. I appreciate you answering a few more questions about Sam Howser. We're trying to understand why he left the fire camp that night."

"So it's true that he was killed by a cougar?"

"It would seem so, yes." No sense in revealing more than necessary.

Tom swore and ran a hand over his beard. "I ran into a cougar once on a hunting trip. Nearly crapped my pants. Them are some fierce cats."

Joel murmured in agreement, suppressing a shudder at the memory of that primal scream. "Where was that?"

"Up near Moon Lake. Got myself a six-point elk up there that trip."

Joel wasn't a hunter himself, but he smiled appreciatively as if he were. "Are you from there originally?"

"Klamath Falls, actually."

"Nice area."

Joel opened the file and withdrew the small notebook they'd found in Howser's tent.

"Have you ever seen this notebook before?"

Tom's expression lifted in recognition. "Yeah, that's Sam's."

"Did he ever show it to you? Or talk to you about it?"

"No, but he was always writing in it during our down time and late at night. He was pretty protective of it."

"Protective how?"

"I don't know. He got weird about it if anyone asked questions. Like, were we supposed to pretend we didn't notice he was always taking notes about stuff?"

Something about his tone reminded Joel of Bruce's comment about Sam and Tom exchanging words. "Why do you think he didn't take it with him when he left camp that night?"

Tom fidgeted with his keys and looked at his watch as if trying to decide how to answer. "Okay, here's the deal. The night he disappeared he seemed extra…off. It had been kind of a strange evening with reporters there and camera crews. People were getting interviewed about living in the camp and stuff. But Sam was oblivious, just sitting there writing in his little book. Shauna sees him and asks if he wants to be a reporter too with all the notes he was taking. She didn't mean anything by it, but he swears at her and tells her to…you know…to mind her own business. Well, I'd about had it. So when he went to use the john, I snuck into his tent and took the notebook."

Joel raised an eyebrow. "This same notebook?"

Tom picked it up and looked it over. "Yeah, it was this one."

"How did Sam react when he discovered it was missing?"

Tom pushed the notebook back across the table. "I don't know. I left camp before he got back to his tent. Didn't get back until late, so I waited until morning to return it. I went in his tent and that's when I realized he was gone." His eyes flickered to Joel's and away.

"Is there anything else you haven't told me about that night?" Joel asked, trying to keep the annoyance from his voice as he scribbled down this new information.

"That's it. It was a stupid prank, especially now that he's…after what happened. I feel bad, but I don't see how it would have anything to do with him being in them woods."

Joel opened Howser's notebook to a page that held drawings like the ones found on his body. "Do you know what these sketches mean?"

Tom leaned forward and shook his head. "Ain't got no clue. Sorry."

Joel took out a photo of Sam's leg showing one of the drawings of the same symbol. The mottled color of the skin made it hard to see the marker clearly, but if you looked past the pooled blood, it was there. He passed it to Tom.

Tom's eyes narrowed, and he shot a look at Joel. "What is this? Is this from…is this Sam?"

"We found similar drawings on his body. Someone marked him up just like he marked that notebook. So you can see why I need to know everything you can tell me about that night."

Tom swore and look away. "I didn't have nothing

to do with that, Detective. All right, look. We didn't go to McGowan's. We went to that bar around the corner…uh, the Trader. But we didn't have nothing to do with whatever happened to Sam. That's messed up. Looks like some kind of Satan cult stuff or something."

"Why didn't you tell me you'd been to the Trader?" While McGowan's was part family restaurant and as such a popular choice for social gatherings, the Trader attracted a seedier crowd.

"We ain't supposed to drink. I didn't want Bruce to find out where we'd been and I told the other guys I wouldn't tell."

"What else aren't you telling me about that night?"

"Nothing, I swear it." He fidgeted in his chair, clearly rattled.

Joel set the picture aside, but didn't put it back in the folder. He left it where Tom could see it while he got a cup of water from the watercolor. He offered it to Tom, who took it and drank without hesitation.

Joel sat back down and leaned forward with his elbows on the table. "All right, Tom. Let's go over it all again from the beginning. Tell me everything you remember about that day."

"Can we please go to the toy aisle?" Abby asked as Val grabbed a grocery cart from the nearest rack. The asphalt radiated heat as they hurried to the Walmart entrance.

"Let's get our groceries first and then we can stop

there for a few minutes if we have time. But no begging."

The cool interior of Walmart was a welcome relief to the blistering heat outside, and Abby sighed audibly as the sliding doors closed behind them. Val could feel the heat of the day radiating off her skin.

They'd come to Pineview to follow up on some job inquiries, so Val felt a little overdressed in her cropped tweed pants and platform sandals compared to the women in flip-flops and cut-off shorts towing kids in drooping swimsuits who looked like they'd come straight from the river. Val's curled hair hung limp around her sweaty neck, and she wished for a hair elastic so she could pull it up into a quick ponytail.

The effort had been worth it. She'd hit it off with the office manager for a pediatric dentist, and had an interview scheduled for the following week. It wasn't quite enough to make up for the anxiety she felt trying to fill near empty cupboards with a dwindling bank account, but it was something.

She mentally calculated how long it might take before she had a regular paycheck. She knew she shouldn't get her hopes up too soon, but it was hard not to. The office manager had seemed genuinely impressed and the two women working the front desk had been warm and welcoming. It would be nearly an hour commute all the way to Pineview, which meant long days away from Abby. But that was a problem for another day. For now, she had more pressing matters, like whether she could afford the soft toilet paper or would have to settle for the cheaper brand.

She was bent over her shopping list where she'd

notated how much she'd spent so far—doing a quick tally of what she still needed to get—so she didn't notice the couple who entered the aisle until the woman spoke.

"Oh, hi Val!"

Val looked up and quickly tucked the list away, hiding the strain she felt behind a smile.

Maddie edged her cart closer and Val couldn't help noticing the make-up and skin care products littering the bottom of the basket. It had been months since Val had been able to spend that kind of money on beauty products. What had once felt like a fundamental need now seemed a laughable luxury.

Maddie turned to the man behind her by way of introduction. "Have you met my husband? This is Bryson. Bryson, this is my friend, Valerie Rockwell."

Val leaned forward to shake Bryson's hand, looking for a sign of the star quarterback Carter had mentioned. He was dressed like a desk jockey and his hand was pleasantly soft. His grip was firm and his gray eyes behind hipster glasses were bright and interested.

"I've heard a lot about you. Nice to meet you, Valerie."

Val shrank a little, wondering what he'd heard. She kept her smile in place as she pulled her hand away. "Maddie and I have known each other a long time."

Abby tugged Maddie's shirt hem to get her attention. "My mom and I have been reading *Robert Apolloclips*."

Bryson's attention swiveled to Abby. "Who's this?"

"I'm Abby," she announced, brushing her hair out of her eyes. Val was acutely aware of the torn lace on the edge of Abby's skirt and her stained shirt. She was grateful for Abby's complete unawareness of her image, but that same naïveté made Val feel suddenly protective.

Was that an edge of condescension in Maddie's smile?

"Who's your favorite character?" Maddie asked.

"Amy Geddon," Abby said without missing a beat. "But I like Robert too. I don't like Doctor Menace. He's mean and his hair is too pointy."

Bryson laughed. "Robert can be pretty mean to Doctor Menace, though."

"Yeah, but Doctor Menace deserves it. He made all those people sick with the blue poison."

"Give it time. You might feel differently about him later."

"You two should come over some time for dinner," Maddie said brightly. "We could show Abby our cosplay props. Bryson makes a mean Doctor Menace, and he's really good with kids."

"I prefer them to adults most of the time," Bryson said with a laugh.

The way he looked at Abby made Val want to end the conversation. She took Abby by the shoulder and pulled her close.

"We'd better finish our shopping. Good to see you."

"You too, Val. And just so you know, I've sent your application on to my supervisor." Maddie crossed her fingers and gave a hopeful little wave.

And just like that, the power in the conversation shifted, slipping away like earth shifting under Val's feet. Her gaze flitted to Bryson's and sure enough, the pity in his eyes was clear. Maddie had told him everything.

"Great. Thanks, I really appreciate it."

Shame burned her cheeks as she turned away. She was reminded of the first time Jordan took her to a campaign fundraising event for his mom's reelection. Sure that everyone she met would sense she didn't belong, she'd hung to Jordan's arm like the new girl trying to get social cred from the popular crowd. Desperate and pathetic.

This was stupid. She was having an inferiority complex in freaking Walmart.

Val went through the motions to finish her shopping, but she couldn't think straight. The notes on her list didn't make sense anymore and she ended up spending forty dollars over budget. After all her efforts to be so careful.

The whole drive home she puzzled over that forty dollars, chiding herself for not looking at the receipt while she was still in the store. But she'd just wanted to get away from people and go home where she could unpack her meager groceries in peace.

As they passed the house with the mannequins, movement in the rearview mirror caught Val's attention. Abby was shielding her eyes from the scene in the yard, and the sight fired Val's protective instincts. Did the man have family? Grandkids? What did they think about his hobby?

The worst thing about it was that it served as a daily reminder that there were likely other perverts living in the area who weren't so easy to spot.

Val drove up the long drive toward the farmhouse and growled when she saw the red truck parked out front.

"What's wrong, Mom?" Abby asked from the backseat.

"Oh, nothing. Someone's here who shouldn't be, that's all."

"Is it Paul?" Abby leaned forward and looked out the windshield. "I like Paul. He's funny."

Val bit her tongue. Seven-year-olds weren't known for their discretion, and she preferred not to say anything that Abby might repeat.

This was the third time Paul had come to raid the garage, and he still had yet to ask her permission. He came out of the shop when she pulled up, wearing the same faded overalls she'd seen him in each time. Or maybe he had multiple pairs, one for every day of the week.

Paul whistled when she got out of the car.

"Well, aren't you all dolled up? What's the occasion?"

Val didn't comment, but added the catcall to his ever-growing list of offenses. "Mr. Sheen, I believe I clearly asked you to text me before coming over. I even texted you my number to make sure you had it."

He pulled off his gloves and tossed them onto the front seat of the truck. "Please, call me Paul. I was passing by and thought it'd be a good time to pick up a few lengths of pipe. When I saw your car was gone, I figured I'd be in and out right quick. No need to bother you."

"I'm more bothered that you'd come out here without my knowledge. This is my home now. It's up to me to decide if it's a good time for you to come over."

He shrugged as if he couldn't fathom what she was

asking. "Sorry to bother you, ma'am. I'll try to remember to call next time."

He heaved his large body into the cab of the truck and started it. As he pulled away, Abby hung out the car window and waved to him. He beamed at her, waving back.

Val watched him leave, marveling at how for living so far away from town, they seemed to have no shortage of visitors.

While Abby ran inside to use the bathroom, Val started hauling in the groceries. She tossed the bag of popsicles into the freezer—her one cheap splurge for Abby's sake—and went out for another load, thinking of how Abby had chatted up Maddie and Bryson. She didn't want to squelch Abby's friendly nature, but it sure made Val nervous sometimes. After the past six months, she didn't trust anyone with her daughter. How would she find a babysitter next week while she went to her job interview?

She immediately thought of Carter. Val trusted him and he'd been so good with Abby. But Val hadn't spoken with Carter since she'd shut the door in his face the night the cougar was killed. In hindsight, it felt like an immature gesture, but what to do about that now?

Once inside the house, with a dripping popsicle in one hand, she called him, apology at the ready. As it turned out, she didn't even need it.

"Val! Are you finally ready for that lunch date we talked about?"

He sounded so happy to hear from her that she wondered if he even remembered their fight. Maybe in his profession he was used to people slamming doors in his face and didn't take it personally.

"Actually, I have a job interview next week and was wondering how you'd feel about watching Abby for an hour or two."

"Absolutely! What day?"

"Next Wednesday. So, August third?"

"That'll be perfect. I've been wanting to show her the next season of *Robert Apocalypse* anyway. There's some crazy stuff that happens, where Amy Geddon and Dr. Menace have to team up in order to—well, I'd better not give it away."

Val chuckled, and it felt good, loosening some of the tension of the day. "Thanks, Carter. I really appreciate you helping me out."

"Anytime, Val. And I'm serious about that lunch."

"And who would watch Abby then?"

"Hmm. Fair point. Tell you what, how about I come over some night and cook for you both? Then we can watch a movie and share a bottle of wine after she goes to bed."

It wasn't a very good cover for a date, and Val almost refused. She was definitely not ready to date, and Carter wouldn't be her first choice. He was too…safe. Not in the "I only like 'bad boys'" kind of way, but in the "We'll never be more than friends" kind of way.

Which, on second thought, made him perfect.

"All right, I'm in. But no wine. I told you, I don't drink."

"Right, I forgot. I mean, I could bring a little something else…"

"Carter! I don't do that stuff and you shouldn't either."

"I know, I know. I don't do it that often, I swear. Just special occasions. But I'll be good, I promise."

Val shook her head as she hung up. A job interview and a date in one day? She would celebrate with another popsicle.

12

Joel shut down his computer and stuck his head in Larry's office on the way out.

Larry was cracking open the plastic clamshell of a deli salad.

"Meg has you on salad again, eh?"

"This was my idea. It's pretty good. They add all these little things in it to fight high cholesterol."

Joel didn't comment as Larry squeezed a fat package of dressing all over the greens.

"I'm going to see Caroline Bellingham. Can you spend some time going over Howser's notebook and see if you can make sense of it? I didn't get anything useful about it from Tom Morrison."

"Sure. Unless you want me to go with you. I wouldn't want to face Caroline Bellingham by myself. To that whole clan, we're the enemies."

"Thanks, but showing up with extra numbers will just make things worse. If you can take a look at that notebook, that would be a lot more helpful. I don't know when I'm going to get to it."

"Suit yourself," Larry said, then stuffed a heaping forkful of salad into his mouth.

The air outside was smoky, the winds having shifted again. Smoke had poured back into the valley with a vengeance. If only they could get some rain, maybe it would settle things. Instantly, Joel could taste the smoke in the back of his throat, and he hurried to his car to turn on the air.

As he drove, he thought of his painful visit with Peter Moyer and Moyer's warning that the Bellinghams were the ones most likely to want to hurt Howser. He'd talked with a couple of Shane Bellingham's friends—his boss and coworkers from his days hauling logs for Wright Trucking. All had said that although they tried to look out for Caroline, they didn't have any contact with Shane. Prison records had verified it was true. Shane's only visitors were his wife and son.

Caroline Bellingham lived on a little knoll overlooking the high school football field. It offered a pastoral view of the town, though the valley was murky with haze as if a painter had bumped against the wet canvas before the paint had dried.

Joel parked his car and noted the moss collecting on the roof of the brick house. The quaint shutters were in desperate need of fresh paint, their finish cracking from exposure. Shane Bellingham's incarceration clearly hadn't been easy on his family.

A teenage boy in ripped jeans and cowboy boots came out the front door and scarcely glanced toward Joel on his way to an old coupe whose bumper was strapped on with bungee cords. He pulled out of the driveway with the aggressiveness of the inexperienced, and Joel was relieved to see him go. He didn't want an audience when he questioned Caroline.

When Caroline came to the door, she held a cigarette in one hand and a newspaper in the other. She wore a plaid shirt and loose fitting jeans, her hair pulled back in a long ponytail. Her eyes narrowed in recognition.

"You're that detective."

"Joel Ramirez from the Wallace County Sheriff's Office."

"What do you want?"

"I wanted to ask you a few questions about Sam Howser."

She swore and knocked the ashes of her cigarette onto the cement step.

"What makes you think I would want to talk to you about Howser?"

"I'm trying to figure out what might have been going through his mind coming back here to Owl Creek. It seems like a place he would have wanted to stay far away from."

"You got that right. I don't know how he dared show his face. But it sounds like he got what he deserved. That was him the cougar got, right?"

"It was his body that we brought off the mountain, yes. Mrs. Bellingham, would you mind if I come in and ask a few questions? I'm trying to tie up some loose ends to better understand why he was on that mountain in the first place."

She moved the newspaper to the other hand so she could scratch her leg. It seemed hazardous to hold it in the same hand as the cigarette, but she didn't seem to notice. "I don't know why you're wasting time with Sam Howser when my Eliza is still missing. Seems like you police have a special talent for wasting your time."

"Can you tell me how your husband knew Sam?"

"I don't know. I think Ted knew him."

"Your brother-in-law?"

Caroline spat a few choice words. "Ted was always a bad influence on Shane. Shane never would have killed that boy, he just wanted to find out what he did to our Eliza. But Ted never knew when to stop. I told Shane he should have gone to the police as soon as it went too far. But Ted convinced him no one would ever find the body if they were smart about it. And they might have gotten away with it if Ted hadn't been stupid enough to involve Sam Howser. The man didn't even have enough brains to cross the street the right direction. Ran off to the police as soon as he got scared."

"Do you know anyone who might have wanted to threaten him?"

Caroline waved away a mosquito. "I don't know why you'd care now. The man is dead. You already got the cougar that killed him."

"Mrs. Bellingham, there's a chance that Sam Howser was already dead before the cougar found him. I'm trying to figure out if someone took it on themselves to make him pay for his betrayal."

"That's why you were questioning Roger?" She took a deep drag on her cigarette with trembling fingers, and Joel angled his face away from the smoke pouring out her mouth and nose. "You're unbelievable. Looking for more people to lock up with my husband instead of finding my daughter? Shane is a good man. And if someone decided to balance the scales with Howser for getting him thrown in prison, I'd call them a hero."

"Does that include your son, Mrs. Bellingham? Where was he last Wednesday night, if you don't mind my asking? The night of July twentieth?"

Caroline's papery skin went a shade whiter. "Ronnie was at work. The gas station. You can check with his boss."

"All night?"

"He came straight home and went to bed like he always does. Look Detective, you can't imagine what it's like for him, losing his sister and his dad. He was only a kid when my husband went to prison. He's all I have left. He would never do something like that, he's too smart."

Joel sensed she was just shy of throwing him off the property. "How about Ted? Does he have friends or family who might have sought revenge?"

"Maybe. I don't know and I don't care. I'm just focused on trying to give my boy the best chance I can. Revenge won't bring Shane home."

"Can I ask you one more question? Have you ever seen anything like this before?"

He showed her sketches of the designs drawn on Howser's body.

She peered at the paper. "It's from that comic, isn't it? All the kids are into it these days. The one about the scientist and the doctor. Those drawings aren't very good, though."

Doctor? This jogged something in Joel's memory.

"I don't have kids. What comic is that?"

"*Robert Apocalypse.* Eliza was a big fan when it was first starting out. Before anyone else heard of it. She was always cutting edge like that."

"Did you ever hear Eliza talk about a Dr. M? Does that name mean anything to you?"

Caroline's stained smoker teeth showed when she smirked. "You mean Ryan's story about a Dr. M? Yeah, I heard that one. Trying to come up with something to save his skin, but it was just a character from that comic. He wasn't even smart enough to come up with his own villain."

"Dr. M is a character from *Robert Apocalypse?*"

"Doctor Menace. He's the bad guy. The one who's always trying to destroy the world."

"So you don't think Dr. M is a real person?" Joel felt distinctly disappointed.

"No more real than a Kardashian's implants." She chuckled at her own joke.

"What makes you so sure Ryan was responsible for your daughter's disappearance?"

Her eyes darkened, and she took another long drag on her cigarette. "Whoever picked her up that night was someone she trusted. There was no sign of a fight. She went with him willingly. Eliza would have done anything for Ryan, but he was so controlling. Got jealous whenever she spent time with her other friends. I didn't see it at the time, but now I realize how afraid she was. Worried about making him mad. Always trying to please him."

"Did he ever hit or threaten her?"

Caroline shrugged. "Not that she said. But she wouldn't have told us if he did because then we would have made her break up with him. When she did break up with him after Prom, he was so mad he couldn't get over her. I think he sabotaged her car that night so she would break down on that road. But the police didn't believe me." She raised an eyebrow as if daring him to disagree with her.

"You say that she broke up with him? Ryan's father said it was the other way around."

"Oh, he would say that. It makes me sick the way he makes his son out to be the victim. Poor helpless Ryan, stealing Eliza from us and not even having the decency to tell us where she is so we could have a proper burial." Her voice cracked and her eyes watered. She crushed the cigarette butt under her heel with a vengeance.

Joel felt a surge of sympathy for the woman, in spite of her crude hostility. Considering what she'd been through, who could blame her?

"So you don't believe Eliza is alive?"

Caroline looked at a point in the air above his head and blinked away tears. "That's the worst of it. If she's alive, then where's she been these last seven years? Why hasn't she come home? Did she get sold to some pimp? I've heard of girls that's happened to. As much as I hate it, I'd rather believe she's dead and her suffering was quick. Because if she's still alive, and I'm not out there looking for her…I just couldn't live with that."

"I understand. Thanks for your time, Mrs. Bellingham." Joel handed her his card. "That's my direct number. If you think of anything that could help, please let me know."

She looked at his card as if not seeing it, then met his eyes with a fierce expression. "Ryan Moyer deserved to die for what he did to my baby girl. My husband doesn't deserve to be in prison for bringing him to justice. If you police had done your job, this never would have happened. I've said all I ever care to say to you, Detective."

Rough-hewn logs served as posts for the new Donovan Lumber Company sign, which was painted in a brisk white and trimmed in green. Val did a double-take as she drove into the parking lot, taking in the DLC logo with the stylized tree, trying to remember what the old logo had looked like. Her dad had worked here for thirty years, weathering intermittent layoffs and the Spotted Owl controversy in the early nineties. She'd passed the old sign countless times, including all summer after graduation when she'd worked swing shift as a skoog operator. But now, she couldn't remember what it had looked like.

She parked in the shade of a flowering plum tree near the squat office building and checked her reflection one last time in the mirror.

"You ready?" she asked Abby, catching her eye in the mirror. "This won't take long, I promise."

"You said that last time," Abby complained as she unbuckled her seatbelt.

"Last time was different, and it's a good thing too because they might want to give me a job. But this won't have a place to play like the dentist office did, so I'll make sure to keep it quick."

"No TV either?"

"Sorry."

Abby made a show of heaving herself dutifully out of the car. Her ruffled skirt was matted in the back where she'd been sitting, and her sandals scuffed despondently on the gravel.

As they crossed the lot, the heady, citrusy scent of fresh douglas fir flooded Val with memories of plugging knots in plywood with sweat beading under her hard hat. She could almost feel the weight of the steel-toed boots on her feet.

The cedar shake siding of the small office building had faded to gray long before Val's time and the wooden steps creaked under her feet. She pulled open the glass door and ushered Abby inside, pausing to remove her sunglasses.

The office was exactly how she remembered it, except for the woman sitting behind the desk. She was Val's age, or maybe younger, and Val wondered if she should remember her from school.

"Good afternoon!" the receptionist greeted from behind the tall counter. "What can I do for you?"

Her long black hair was pulled into a bun, which emphasized her dramatic widow's peak and large eyes. She wore skinny jeans and a simple plaid shirt over a tank top, but wore them like she belonged in an ad for casual wear. In spite of her striking appearance, Val sensed an undertone of uncertainty about her, like she was trying too hard.

Val understood that all too well.

"Hi. Is Randy in today, by chance?" Val asked, steering Abby away from the candy machine whose gumballs were probably original to the building.

The young woman's brow wrinkled slightly.

"Mr. Donovan?" Val tried again.

"You mean Kevin?"

"Oh. Sure, I suppose I could talk to Kevin."

"Hold on a minute." The receptionist's frown deepened as she turned to the Cisco phone on the desk and gingerly picked up the handle. She paused, considering the buttons, stabbed one, and then sounded relieved when someone answered. "Kevin? You have a visitor. A…"

Here she looked pointedly at Val.

"Valerie Rockwell."

"Valerie Rockwell. Can I send her back?" She paused as Kevin responded, and Val thought she could hear the faint murmur of a man's voice from down the hall. When she hung up, the receptionist turned to Val with a bright grin. "Go on ahead, Mrs. Rockwell. Last door on the left."

There were only two doors on the left, and the first had belonged to Val's dad when he'd been a foreman. A nameplate for a George Hutchings sat there now. On the last door, Kevin Donovan's name sat in place of his dad's.

She knocked hesitantly and opened the door. Kevin stood when she entered, reaching out a hand in greeting. Val took it, noting that aside from his thinning hair and red goatee, he looked much as she remembered him. The room looked exactly like it had when his dad had run things too, from the dark wood paneling to the antlers mounted on the wall.

These were exactly the sort of people Jordan would have sneered at and here she was, asking for a job.

"Hello, Valerie," Kevin said. "You're the last person I expected to see today. How's it going?"

"This is a surprise for me too. I didn't realize you were running the place."

"My dad retired last year." He glanced at Abby, who was bumping against Val's leg in boredom.

"This is my daughter, Abby. We won't take up too much of your time, but I wanted to see if you had any openings in the office. We just moved into my parents' place and I'm looking for work with reliable shifts and daytime hours."

His eyes shot to Abby again and Val realized she was digging her finger up her nose. Val pulled Abby's finger away and hunted in her purse for hand sanitizer, all without breaking eye contact with Kevin.

"I wish I could say I had something, but we just hired Hannah last week and we don't have any other openings."

"Ah, of course," Val said, thinking of the uncertain receptionist out front. She must have only missed the job opening by a few weeks. Hoping it wouldn't come to this, she asked, "Are you still hiring through the temp agency for laborers? As I remember you guys always have openings there."

Kevin frowned. "I guess you aren't reading the papers."

Val shook her head, feeling color rising in her cheeks as Abby's thumping against her leg grew more insistent.

"We're not hiring. In fact, we're trying to negotiate a pay cut with the union. It's either that or we've gotta do some massive layoffs."

Now it was Val's turn to be surprised. "Oh, that's too bad." She wanted to ask where the money for the fancy rebrand had come from, but resisted.

"Yeah, no one wants that. I'm doing everything I can to keep the jobs we already have. But there's no room for hiring."

Val smiled like it didn't matter to her either way. *Every rejection gets you that much closer to an acceptance.* It had become her new mantra.

"I completely understand. Thank you, Kevin, for letting me drop in today. I really appreciate it and I hope things work out for you and your employees."

She kept her smile plastered to her face all the way down the hall, so that she wouldn't accidentally shoot a resentful glare at Hannah on her way out.

13

"You have a date with Carter?" Gina's voice crackled with incredulity over the phone.

Val grimaced. "It's not serious. He's just a friend. I thought you'd be happy to hear I'm trying to get out more." She didn't mention she wasn't actually leaving the house.

"No, that's good. I'm glad. Just surprised. He's not really your type, is he?"

"Do I even have a type anymore? I don't exactly have a great track record."

"Sorry, I don't mean to criticize. Carter's great. Had a couple of rough years after high school, from what I remember."

"Didn't we all?" Val said grimly.

"Fair. But he's doing good now, isn't he? He's like a reporter now or something?"

"Yeah, for Channel Six. He's good at it too."

"Cool. He's a good guy, don't get me wrong. Always helped out with the church youth group and stuff. Just kind of weird to think of the two of you going on a date."

It was strange that Gina knew more about what Val's high school friends had done after graduation than she did. Gina had started high school while Val was in college, so she would have had a front row seat to any town drama that unfolded.

Val dug her fingernail into a crack in the kitchen table where crumbs had collected. "Well, like I said, he's just a friend. I figured I should start somewhere. I don't think he expects anything." *I hope.*

"No, probably not. Good for you. It sounds like a good first step." Gina's tone was cheerful enough, but Val could feel the condescension. When had their roles reversed? The younger sister becoming the one who knew everything? Or at least thought she did.

"How are you doing after all the craziness this week?" Gina asked.

"Fine. I mean, it was awful, but it's such a relief to know it's over. I'm just glad it was that drifter. Ugh, that sounds bad. I'm not glad that man was killed, but I'm so relieved the cougar didn't get Abby. I know it's selfish, but I can't help it."

"No, that makes sense. Do they know if it was Howser?"

"Not that I've heard. Joel said the autopsy could take a while."

"What a mess." Gina tsked on the other end of the line. "I'm glad Dad isn't here to see it. He was always so protective of Howser. Felt like he'd been taken advantage of by the Bellinghams. Dad always thought he deserved another chance. He'd be crushed to know his second chance didn't turn out any better."

"If Dad were still alive, Howser would have had someone to go to and wouldn't have ended up living in the woods where a cougar could attack him."

"Hmm. True."

It was a ghastly thought, and they were both silent for a moment.

Val's thoughts wandered the direction they frequently traveled these days. "After all these years, do they still not know what happened to Eliza Bellingham?"

Abby had been born around the time of Eliza's disappearance, and even though she'd been clear across the country, Val distinctly remembered holding her newborn and fighting a sense of panic at the thought that she would ever grow old enough to leave the house where Val couldn't protect her.

"No, isn't it weird? Her car was found abandoned on Highway 12 with no sign of a struggle or anything. She'd vanished without a trace. The Bellinghams screwed up when they killed Ryan. He was the only person who could have told them where she was, and now he's gone."

"So you think he did it?"

Gina sighed. "I don't know. I liked Ryan. We had a few classes together. None of us thought he could do something like that. But do we really know what people are capable of?"

"No," Val agreed, thinking of Jordan.

"Police never arrested him, but that doesn't mean anything. And even if he was guilty, I'm not saying he deserved to be beaten to death. Without knowing for sure what happened to Eliza, we can't say what he deserved. And now, we'll probably never know."

"That's so wrong. If Abby disappeared like that, I'd go crazy. And then to never know what happened to her?" Val shook her head and instinctively looked out the window to where Abby was swinging. Just to be sure.

In the distance, she spotted a black car making its way up the road.

"Looks like I've got company, Gina. I'll have to call you back."

"Do. I want to get all the details of your date."

"We don't even have it scheduled yet."

"Okay, but don't put it off too long. You've gotta get through the practice date before you can move on to someone real!"

Val ended the call, wondering if she was taking advantage of Carter by using him as dating practice. Should she be clear about her expectations? She didn't want to lead him on, but she also didn't want to leap to conclusions. Maybe he was only in it for friendship like she was.

Val recognized the black Charger as it pulled into the driveway, and something very strange flickered in her chest. Something she hadn't felt in a long time. Something like anticipation.

Why was she so happy to see Joel? They were just friends too, right? But she realized she would never dare go on a date with Joel. Even the thought of him asking her out made her feel a little panicked. Joel was definitely *not* safe.

She came out onto the porch as Joel got out of his car, looking smart and trim in his business dress shirt and sunglasses. And what was it about the badge at his hip that just looked so hot?

Careful…

Abby left the swing and ran to meet him.

"Detective Joel! Do you want to hear a joke?" Her voice surged with excitement. "What do you call a yeti who goes to school?"

"Uh…a student yeti?" Joel replied, catching Val's eye and suppressing a smile as he came toward the porch.

"A yeti school!" Abby announced gleefully. She burst into giggles, and Joel paused, clearly taken aback at the nonsensical punchline. "It's a trick riddle joke because it's about the school, not the yeti. You think you're talking about the yeti, but really it's the school."

Val grinned at Joel's confusion. "Seven," she mouthed with a shrug.

"That's a great joke," he said, and Abby beamed.

"You have my number, right?" Val leaned against the porch railing. "You don't have to drive all this way just to check on us."

Joel's smile faltered, and Val realized how rude she'd sounded, like she didn't want him there.

"I mean, I don't mind, but it seems like a lot of effort," she backpedaled awkwardly.

"I actually have something I needed to talk to you about and didn't want to do it over the phone."

"Oh." Of course. It wasn't about seeing her. It was about work. "Do you mind if we sit here on the porch? There's room for two whole chairs now."

"I noticed." He eyed the remaining stack of boxes as he sat in one of the plastic lawn chairs. "You're making progress. Soon you might even be able to get to the swing."

"I just have to stop myself from opening these boxes. It's best if I don't know what's in there. Every time I go to Pineview I take another load. It's taking forever, but we'll clear it out eventually."

"Mom, can I have a popsicle?" Abby asked, leaning on Val's chair and threatening to make it collapse.

"Yes, but eat it in the yard, please. Joel and I need to talk."

Abby turned to Joel. "Do you want a popsicle?"

"Um…" He glanced at Val and back at Abby, who watched him hopefully. "I don't know. I don't usually eat popsicles on the job." But he cocked one dark eyebrow suggestively.

"I won't tell your boss," Abby said in a loud stage whisper.

"Then in that case, I'll take it."

Abby passed the popsicles around and issued clear instructions to Joel that he was not to leave the stick on the ground, but should put it back in its wrapper and throw them both away when he was finished. He nodded soberly and, finally, she tripped down the steps and back out into the yard.

Val's shirt stuck to her back and wildfire smoke tinted everything in brown, but with a cold popsicle dripping in her hand, it felt about as idyllic a summer afternoon as she could wish for.

"All right, Joel," Val said, when the rhythmic squeaking of the old swing set announced that Abby was at a safe distance. "What brings you here? Not the popsicles, I gather."

Joel's expression grew serious, and he removed his sunglasses to look her in the eyes. "We identified the body. It was Sam Howser."

Val nodded. She'd expected that and looked for something to say. "What a horrible way to die."

"That's the thing. I wish I didn't have to tell you this, Val, but it looks like the cougar didn't kill Howser."

Val sat up straighter. "What do you mean?"

"Something else killed him before the cougar got to him."

"Something or someone?"

"At this point, we're not sure. We'll need to revisit the scene to see if there's anything we missed. A potential murder weapon, trace evidence left by a second party, that sort of thing."

"You think he was murdered?" An ugly dread crept into Val's stomach.

"I don't know. He was most likely killed by a blow to the head. Not something a cougar could have caused."

"A blow to the head? Not just falling on a rock?"

"No. That's one of the reasons I need to go back to the scene."

"Can't they tell from fibers or whatever?"

Joel grunted. "It's not like on TV. We don't even have a forensic pathologist in the county, so his remains have been sent up north. It'll be a while before we get their report, so in the meantime it's just good old-fashioned police work."

Val leaned back, letting the words sink in. "So someone else was on the mountain."

Joel pressed his lips together, and she sensed his inner conflict. Wanting to tell her no, but also not wanting to lie.

"It does seem the most likely scenario at this point, but we're open to other possibilities. I've been doing this job long enough to know that it's best not to jump to conclusions. So I don't want you to worry too much about it. If he was murdered, I'm pretty sure it was a targeted killing, possibly in revenge for Ryan Moyer's death. Or for turning in the Bellinghams. I don't have any reason to think it's someone who would be a threat to you and Abby."

Val let out a shaky breath. "Just when I was starting to think everything was going to be okay."

"I'm sorry, Val. You can see why I didn't want to talk about this over the phone."

She managed a strained smile. "I'm going to get PTSD every time I see your car drive up the road."

He smiled weakly in return.

Val felt a cold drip on her fingers and hurried to lick it up. She'd neglected her popsicle in the wake of Joel's disturbing news. Checking to make sure Abby was still on the swing, she asked the question that had been on her mind since talking to Gina.

"Do the police really not know what happened to Eliza Bellingham?"

"That was before my time, but from what I understand, she just vanished." He grimaced at her expression. "I know, it sounds hokey. It's not realistic to disappear without leaving any evidence whatsoever. But in this instance, without any witnesses, it's true."

"Gina said they found her car abandoned on

Highway 12. No clue where she'd gone or if anyone had been with her."

"Well, that's partly true. She was a teenage driver, half the high school's prints were in her car. Dogs couldn't pick up a scent in the woods, though they did find some marijuana and traces of harder stuff in her backpack."

"So she left her stuff behind?"

"Backpack, phone. Her purse and keys were missing, which shows she probably went willingly. Probably trusted whoever stopped to help her."

"Weird that she left her phone."

"That part was probably not intentional. It had slipped down between the seat and the door. And remember, this was in the days before smartphones. It's not like now when losing your phone sends you into a panic. She probably didn't even notice she'd left it."

"Or she had another one."

"What do you mean?" Joel looked at her with interest.

Val felt herself blushing. "Remember that time your phone stopped working? You couldn't get it to turn on so you threw it away in Calc."

"Vaguely."

"Well…" She laughed nervously. "I took it home with me. I took it all apart and saw that there was a wire disconnected. When I put it back together, it worked again."

There was a moment's pause, and then Joel burst out a laugh. "You're kidding me! You fixed it?"

"Yeah, but I couldn't tell you because then I'd have to tell you that I stole it from the trash can." Val pushed the words out as fast as she could. "By then, you'd gotten another phone and I felt weird about having kept it a secret. Like I was hiding something. It seemed better to not say anything. I factory-reset it—I promise I wasn't spying on you." Her face flamed hotter.

He laughed. "I threw it away, I wouldn't have cared. I would have been impressed that you'd fixed it. So what did you do with it?"

"Tinkered with it a bit until it died for good. It didn't last long." Val was relieved that he wasn't angry. She *had* factory-reset it. But only after she'd skimmed through his texts with Lacey. Until she'd felt like a bad person and stopped. It filled her with shame just thinking about it.

"So you think Eliza Bellingham might have had a second phone? Her parents only reported the one."

"It wouldn't be the first time a teenage girl had an extra phone she kept secret from her parents."

"I had no idea teenage girls could be so devious," Joel said with a glint in his eye.

"Really? No wonder you married Lacey." Val had meant to be clever, but the stricken look in his eyes made her want to swallow the words. "I'm sorry, Joel. I didn't mean it that way. It was just a stupid joke."

His smile looked more like a grimace. "A trick joke riddle?"

"Yeah. Maybe I should get out more. My humor has suffered with only a seven-year-old for company."

"Your humor was never that good to begin with," he said drily.

She smiled. In his teasing she felt forgiveness.

He sighed and rubbed the back of his neck. "You're

not wrong about Lacey. I was more naive than I realized. We didn't even know ourselves yet, let alone each other. What did we think we were doing? Playing house?"

"Lots of people marry their high school sweethearts," Val said, surprised to hear herself playing devil's advocate. "There's nothing wrong with that."

"I don't know. I wish I'd broken things off with her when I left for school instead of trying to keep up a long-distance relationship. Given us both a chance to see other people and figure out what we wanted. I didn't think so at the time, but I look back now, and I think I was scared. Lacey was…safe. I liked having a safety net. But I think all relationships have an expiration date, and we stupidly assumed the shelf life was longer than it was."

It was a grim sentiment.

"Not all relationships," Val said quietly. "Some marriages last. Parent-child relationships. Brothers. Sisters."

"Friends," Joel added, and he looked at her in a way that made her cheeks warm again.

"Yeah. Friends too."

Joel was silent for a moment then said, "I guess I shouldn't complain to you about marriage. Sorry, that's not very sensitive of me."

The warmth drained away. Val knew she should tell him the truth about Jordan. But she thought of Carter asking her that excruciating question, *Did you know?* She couldn't bear to hear that question from Joel. To see the suspicion in his eyes.

"It's all right," she said. "I don't mind."

Their popsicles finished, the sticks carefully tucked into the plastic wrappers, Joel stood to leave. "Do you mind if I spend a little time looking around now? I want to check things out to determine if there's anything we missed the first time around."

"Sure, no problem," Val said, but his words reminded her that unless he could find a plausible excuse for accidental death, there had been not one but two murderers in those woods in the past week. The feeling of serenity that had been growing the past few days was gone.

14

Joel pulled his car onto the gravel shoulder next to a tall cedar fence. It was new, and the tones of the stained wood were fresh and warm. He remembered this property when there had only been a chainlink fence. As he approached the gate, he thought back to the little dog which had always greeted him on his paper route when he was a kid. Carl Lewis, he and the other paper kids had called him. He was fast, and boy, could he jump. As soon as he heard Joel coming, he'd barrel to the gate, snapping his jaws and barking loud enough to be heard on the next block. Then he'd stand at the gate, leaping on his back legs so his teeth were uncomfortably close to the newspaper box as Joel hurriedly shoved in the paper.

Over and over, night after night, he leaped with a fierce determination that belied his size.

Night after night, Joel gritted his teeth, hoping Carl wouldn't show up.

Night after night, he did.

When he finally bit Joel one night as he was doing his monthly collection rounds, he wasn't sure who had been more startled, Carl or Joel. Joel had yelped, swatted him on the nose with a newspaper, and shot out of the yard. Once safe, he inspected his pants for holes, but they were fine. The skin beneath was tender and bruised, but not broken. From that night on, Carl's jumping took on a smug quality, as if he were laughing at Joel.

Former detective Shannon O'Dell lived here now and had improved the place with a new cedar fence and brick walkway. Thick shrubbery softened the lines of the clapboard house, giving it a secluded cottage appeal. Rusted iron lawn ornaments fluttered in the breeze—a windmill, a spinning orb, and something beaded that caught the light as it dangled from a tree branch.

Shannon came from the side yard, holding a bundle of sticks in one hand and large garden shears in the other.

"Hey, Joel. Let me put this on the burn pile and I'll be right there."

Joel waited while the oscillating sprinkler waved its gentle curtain onto the walkway in front of him, then pulled away so he could pass.

Shannon returned a moment later, pulling off thick garden gloves to shake Joel's hand.

"It's been a while. Good to see you."

"You too, Shannon. Retirement agrees with you. You've got quite the oasis here."

Shannon looked over her yard with pleasure, her brow damp with sweat. "Thank you. It's good for my soul, I tell you what. That and golf. I play three times a week."

"Good for you."

"Do you?"

"Do I…"

"Golf?"

"Occasionally. I'm not that good at it."

"You should come with me sometime. It's a great chance to be both in your head and out of it at the same time. Apply all that focus and concentration to something concrete. I've solved a lot of cases out on the green."

A familiar feeling of inadequacy rose within Joel, and he tried to suppress it. He didn't think Shannon meant to be condescending, but it still reminded Joel that some within the sheriff's office thought he had been unfairly promoted because of the Stan's Market incident. Some of them never missed an opportunity to put him in his place.

"How's Cooper treating you?" Shannon asked, as she led Joel to a shady patch of yard under an arbor. She settled heavily onto a wooden bench, and Joel picked a matching chair for himself.

"Cooper's great." Joel hesitated to say too much. If he shared that the lieutenant was hands off with most of Joel's investigative work, would Shannon caution him about getting in over his head? If he said Cooper was a great resource, would Shannon remind Joel that he needed to show more initiative?

So he said nothing.

But Shannon didn't seem to notice. "So. You have some questions about the Bellingham case."

"Bellingham and Moyer, but I understand you didn't work the Moyer case."

"No, that was back when Salmon Ridge had their own department. But we collaborated a lot. Howser turned himself in at our office, and I did some of the searches down here."

"Can you tell me why Howser turned himself in?"

"He had a conscience. I know, hard to believe, but he did. He was tormented by what they'd done. Said they'd killed an innocent kid."

"He believed Moyer was innocent, then? Why?"

"You've seen his confession, haven't you?"

"Yeah, I've seen the official record. But I want to get your impressions."

Shannon took a handkerchief out of her shirt front pocket and wiped her forehead. Damp gray hair clung to her scalp.

"Honestly, I didn't worry too much about why Howser decided to turn himself in. I was just glad he did. Made our jobs a lot easier. Impounded Howser's car. Searched the Bellingham residences. It was all there. The duct tape. Plastic garbage bags with sunflower seeds at the bottom that matched the ones found in Ryan's pocket when Howser led us to the body. I wish all murder cases were solved that easily."

"From what I remember the trial wasn't that simple, though. I followed it while I was at the U. Everyone was talking about it. Biggest trial of the year."

"Oh, yeah. It was ugly. People picketing the courthouse and saying the Bellinghams should be exonerated since the police had failed to find Eliza and bring her murderer to justice. I remember one crackpot went on the news and called Shane the 'destroying angel.' He was ridding the world of a child killer."

"Never mind Moyer was a child himself?"

Shannon shrugged. "People get crazy when mob mentality sets in. You'll learn."

Joel ignored that and pulled out the sketch of the designs found on Howser's body.

"What do you make of these?" he asked.

Shannon peered at the sheet of paper, experimenting with distance. "My reading glasses are in the house. What is it?"

"They're marks found on Howser's body."

"Tattoos?"

"No, just crude drawings. Permanent marker."

Shannon shook her head. "I've never seen anything like that before."

"They're from a popular webcomic. I wondered if you might have seen these symbols in relation to Ryan's death. Or Eliza's disappearance."

Shannon frowned. "No, I don't think so. They would be listed with the evidence if I had. What's the W for?"

"Or M. If Howser drew these himself, it's likely to be an M."

"Moyer," Shannon suggested. "He was still haunted by his part in Ryan's murder."

"Maybe. Didn't Ryan Moyer say that Eliza had been involved with a Dr. M?"

"He did. But no one could corroborate his story."

Joel folded up the sketch and returned it to his notebook.

"There's a character in this webcomic named Doctor Menace."

Shannon pursed her lips. "You think there's a connection?"

"The comic came out the year before Eliza disappeared. It was nothing, a project by a few college kids. Didn't get any traction for a couple of years. But Eliza was an early fan. It seems like too much of a coincidence."

"I don't believe in coincidences."

"Then how about this one? We recovered a notebook in Howser's possession filled with sketches and quotes also taken from the comic. Over and over again, like he was obsessed."

Shannon narrowed her eyes, emphasizing the lines near the corners. "What are you saying, Joel?"

Joel leaned forward. "What if Howser thought this Dr. M really existed? It sounds like Moyer believed it. If Howser felt guilty enough about Moyer's death, could he have gotten obsessed with the comic, thinking it might hold a clue to Eliza's disappearance?"

"Maybe. But I don't know how he would make that connection. I don't think he was the sharpest tool in the shed, if you know what I mean. Besides, what relevance does it have now?"

"Not sure." Joel wasn't ready to share his thoughts, but he suspected that understanding Howser's frame of mind could explain why he had left the fire camp in the first place. Which might in turn lead them to find who or what it was he was running from.

"So you think all of this about Howser is related to

Eliza's disappearance? You'd be Sheriff Larson's darling for sure if you could solve that case."

Joel ignored her skepticism. "Eliza's phone was recovered at the scene of her abduction, right?"

"Yeah."

"What if that wasn't her only phone? What if she had another phone, one her parents didn't know about?"

"Hmm..." Shannon considered this in silence, the only sound the pattering of the sprinkler as it dribbled on the waxy leaves of a large rhododendron bordering the lawn. "It always bothered me that we couldn't pinpoint her disappearance any better than we did. One reason was because she didn't ask for help when her car broke down. Isn't that strange? She'd been at a friend's house watching a movie and working on homework. At least, that's what her parents thought."

"You mean 'homework' was code for smoking marijuana?" Joel knew all this from the reports, but listened carefully as Shannon's story unfolded.

"Right. What always got me is that she didn't text or call anyone for help. She's stranded on the road in the middle of the night, she's got a phone right there, but she doesn't use it."

"She's worried about getting in trouble?" Joel guessed.

"I don't know," Shannon said. "We thought maybe she was too high to realize what was going on. Maybe she decided to sleep it off in the car. She left the friend's house at around 10:30 pm, but no one reported the abandoned car until almost 4:00 a.m."

"That's a big window to pinpoint an abduction."

"Right. How long did she sit there before someone found her? Was she alone in the car? If she'd sent even one text telling someone she'd broken down, we could have had one more piece to figure out what happened that night. But she didn't. Why?"

"Unless she had another phone." It was pure conjecture, but it would explain a lot. Especially if the secret phone was in some way tied to the mysterious Dr. M.

15

"WHEN ARE we going to star gaze?" Abby asked Val as they were picking blackberries along the road near the house.

"We've gotta hope these skies clear before we can do that. But don't worry. The Perseids are the best time to see shooting stars and that won't be until August."

"I thought August starts tomorrow."

"Yes, but the Perseids aren't for another couple of weeks. If the skies clear by then, we can lay out on the trampoline and watch the stars all night. You won't believe how many stars you can see from here. Way more than we could see at home."

The sun felt scalding and a hot breeze gusted waves of irrepressible heat over Val's skin. The blackberries were dusty from being so close to the dirt road. It wasn't long before Abby gave up and sat on the road throwing rocks into the ditch.

"Why am I the only one picking?" Val asked with

mock indignation. "Does that mean I'm the only one who gets to eat the cobbler?"

"It's so hot!" Abby complained. "And the blackberry bushes are too tall. I can't reach."

"All right, let's go in the house and get you cooled off."

She took Abby's bucket—stained with purple juice even though the bottom wasn't even covered—and dumped the handful of berries into her own. It was a meager showing, but would be enough for the two of them.

Until they got inside and poured the berries into a sink of clean water and Abby announced, "We should invite Carter to come eat the cobbler with us."

"Maybe," Val said noncommittally.

"I think he'd like it."

"We didn't get enough berries to share. We'd have to pick some more."

Abby considered this, her hands running through the sink, berries passing between her fingers. Val knew how hypnotic that sensation was. The cold water, the soft berries bumping against her skin. It was as familiar a part of her childhood as her own name.

"Maybe we could buy some blackberries at the store," Abby suggested.

Val laughed. "Spend a fortune on blackberries when they're growing for free all around us? Oh, you city girl."

Abby inspected the red welts on her hands. "But at least they wouldn't scratch me."

"Your Grandpa Rockwell always said the ones that hurt the most tasted the best. He took us out for hours on Saturdays every summer, early in the morning before it got so hot. There's an old pump house across the field where the blackberries were always the thickest and juiciest."

"Ugh. I'm glad Dad never made *me* pick blackberries."

Val's smile faded. She never knew how to respond to Abby when she brought up Jordan.

"Do you miss your dad?" she asked. *What a stupid question.*

Abby nodded.

"I miss him too." It was true. But it also made her angry. Jordan didn't deserve to be missed, but Abby didn't understand that. "Maybe you should try writing a letter to him. Tell him everything you would say if he were here."

Abby looked up, tossing her unruly hair out of her face. "But where would I send it?"

"I don't know. Maybe we just keep it somewhere safe. Even if we can't send it, writing the letter might be nice."

It was too hot to run the oven for the cobbler, so Val strained the berries and set the colander on a plate for later. Abby was disappointed, until she realized she had free access to the blackberries while they sat and drained.

While Val looked for paper, Abby ran to get an old coffee tin full of markers. Trying to find one that worked was quite a production, and soon she was making piles of those that worked, those that were dried up, and the ones that fell somewhere in between. The "almost goods," as she called them. By the time

Abby was ready to begin, Val had gotten lost on her phone.

"Are you reading *Robert Apolloclips* without me?" Abby accused.

"I wouldn't dare." But some of the plots had taken a darker turn and Val wanted to preview them to skip any chapters Abby shouldn't see. Doctor Menace had kidnapped Amy Geddon and stolen the Grover-C, intent on copying it for his own nefarious purposes. Amy had refused to help, and tried to convince Doctor Menace that the power to manipulate time and space came with its own cost. But Doctor Menace had persisted, calling his own creation the O.Blivion.

"Cute," Val muttered. While she skimmed, she answered Abby's spelling questions.

"How do you spell 'Dear?'"

"What does it sound like? D-d-d-dear."

"D?"

Then a few minutes later, "How do you spell 'Grandma?'"

Her sweat cooling on her skin, Val felt a sense of near contentment settling over her as she listened to Abby's humming. When her phone buzzed, her heart gave a little jump of excitement. It was the pediatric dentist's office.

"This is Valerie," she answered, holding up a hand to delay Abby's next question.

"Hi Valerie, this is Michelle from Dr. Waverly's office."

"Hello, Michelle!" She tried to give her voice that perfect mix of professional and personal. A tone that said, *I'd be amazing to work with.* "How can I help you?"

"Well, it's just that I have some bad news. I so appreciate your willingness to come in for an interview, but it turns out that the position we were going to hire for isn't open after all. The gal had planned to stay home with her new baby but now she's decided to come back, and it's easier to keep her on than train someone new. I'm sure you understand."

"Oh, of course." Val wasn't sure what to say as hope for a future with steady income slipped away. "Thanks for letting me know."

"I do wish you luck in finding something soon. And again, I'm sorry it's not going to work out."

Not as sorry as I am.

Deflated, Val put her phone down and eyed the colander of blackberries. Half the berries were gone, and Abby's teeth were stained purple. Val took a deep breath to release her frustration without letting it color her words to Abby.

"Hmm. This isn't enough for a cobbler. What should we do?"

"Maybe you could go pick some more?" Abby squinted up at Val hopefully.

Val chuckled and tweaked Abby's wrinkled nose. "Maybe I could. But it's been years since I've been down to the pump house, and I'm not sure I want you to come until I know it's safe. Why don't you stay here and watch a show while I go check it out."

"Whew!" Abby said. "I thought you were going to say I had to go with you."

"And eat all the blackberries as fast as I can pick them? No way."

While Abby ran to pick out a movie, Val glanced

over the letter she'd written in her childish scrawl. The words she'd asked for help on were spelled correctly, but others she'd confidently spelled phonetically. It was like deciphering another language. Except for her own name, Abby couldn't get her lower case B's and D's straight, so to Val it sounded like she had a cold.

Dear Dab,

I miss you a lot. Mom and I ar at Granbma's house now. Its nice, dut kinb of weerb without Granbma here. I mabe a new frend. His name is Poll and he givs me Tootsie Rolls. I miss my olb frenz. We hab a cugar on the hill. Some pepl came and shot it. I think the cugar bib sumthin dab. It was sab.

Love,
Abby

Val folded the letter and tucked it into her pocket, feeling uneasy at the mention of Paul Sheen. She didn't know Abby had been interacting with him when he came to the house. Val would have to be more careful about keeping an eye on her when he visited. Not that she thought Paul meant any harm, necessarily. But Abby was so trusting that just knowing his name was enough to make him a friend. She didn't understand he was still a stranger to them both.

With the movie started, Val reapplied sunscreen and grabbed her wide-brimmed hat. Dressed in long jeans and a thick denim shirt to provide protection against the wicked barbs, Val cursed the great irony of picking blackberries on the hottest day of the year when she'd rather be in shorts and a tank top.

Promising Abby she wouldn't be gone long, Val went out the back door into the heat. The buzz of insects greeted her and thickened the oppressive feeling in the air. *At least there's no humidity,* she reminded herself. She'd intentionally moved early in the summer to avoid spending another season suffocating in the sauna that was summer in Chicago.

Taking small comfort in the bone dry heat, Val trudged to the overgrown road, grateful it was late enough in the afternoon that she could get a little shade.

She couldn't say what drew her to take the same path she and Joel had followed the previous week when they'd discovered the cougar, but she bypassed the turnoff to the old pump house. Instead, she continued up the hill to the rocky outcropping. Her uncle had once taught her the difference between basalt and greywacke, but she couldn't remember which one described the giant stretch of black rock emerging from the earth.

This is where she'd seen Howser—or what was left of him. There was the cleft in the rock where she'd seen the outline of the cougar. Heard its terrifying scream. Now, the tall summer grass was trampled from police combing through the area, and a brown stain indicated where Howser had lain. Flies buzzed, and Val felt slightly sick.

She'd hunted with her dad as a teenager, so she was familiar with the mess that came from field dressing a deer. But this was something different. Knowing the kill was human made it so much worse. She knew that when the rain returned in the fall, it wouldn't take long before time and weather would eliminate all trace of the ghastly scene. But she'd have to make sure Abby didn't come up here in the meantime.

For the first time, Val wondered if there was similar violent evidence at the scene where Howser had died. She should have asked Joel where that was so she could keep Abby away from there too.

Stepping gingerly around the site, she followed the trail of matted grass. Sweat trickled down her neck and made her scalp itch. She remembered the basics of tracking a wounded deer, and this was easier since Howser's body had been dragged by the cougar. She knew the place when she found it, a spot that overlooked the empty field to the west of the house.

Despite the heat, Val shivered. A man had died here. The dried blood was human. Had someone done the unthinkable, brutally murdering him and watching the life drain from his eyes? Or had it been a freakish accident?

She hadn't heard from Joel lately about how his investigation was proceeding, and standing here in this place, she fought the urge to look over her shoulder. If Howser had been murdered, how had the murderer found him? How could she know for sure that she and Abby were safe?

All thought of blackberries forgotten, Val trudged through the undergrowth and back to the road. The terrain was rough, and she had to watch her step carefully. Eyes focused on the ground, a flash of purple under a trailing fern caught her attention. She stopped and lifted the leaves. It was a purple Sharpie that matched a set in the coffee tin that Abby had sorted through that very afternoon. There was no sign of fading or weather exposure.

This marker hadn't been outside for long.

Val snapped a picture of it and texted it to Joel.

Just found this on the hill near where Howser was killed. Could it be important?

Joel responded immediately.

Don't touch it. Yes, it could be important. I'll be there in thirty.

Val took her hat and hung it on the nearest tree so she could find the spot again. As she continued her trek down the hill, she thought back to when she'd surprised Howser in the house. Had he stolen the marker then? Why?

The memory brought back an intense stab of fear, and she quickened her pace. Abby probably hadn't even noticed how long she'd been gone, but Val suddenly wished she hadn't left her alone.

She crossed the yard and pushed through the back door, using extra force against the sticking frame. The cartoon was still running; she heard it as soon as she stepped into the hallway.

"Hey, sweetie, I'm back. I didn't get any blackberries, though. Maybe I'll—"

Val stopped as she entered the living room. The TV was on, but Abby wasn't there.

"Abby, where'd you go?" She poked her head back into the hallway. The bathroom door was open. The room was empty.

Val went to the stairs and called, "Abby! Are you upstairs?"

She waited. No response.

Don't jump to conclusions. She doesn't always answer, even when she hears you.

Val ran up the stairs calling Abby's name. "If you can hear me, I need you to respond." In her voice she heard an edge that she knew was fear but Abby would hear as anger. She tried to calm herself. "I'm not mad, but I am getting worried. If you can hear me, tell me where you are."

She searched Abby's room: under her bed, in the closet, behind the door. She searched her own room, the extra bedroom filled with boxes, and even considered for a moment going into the attic. But Abby would have needed a ladder to access the hatch.

Heart pounding, she went outside and through the yard, calling for Abby, her voice sounding anemic across the open fields. She looked in the garage, checking behind a large cabinet and opening the sliding doors. She looked behind the last of the boxes on the porch to see if Abby was hiding on the old wooden swing, checked the car, and even peered through the lattice covering the space under the porch. If Abby were there, she would have responded by now.

She knew, with horrible certainty, that Abby was gone.

Grabbing her phone, she dialed 911. She felt detached as she heard herself talk to the operator, voice quavering.

Hold it together, Val.

"I can't find my little girl. I've looked everywhere for her but she's not here."

"Can I get your address, ma'am?" The operator sounded completely disinterested.

Val rattled it off.

"Is this your daughter who's missing?"

"Yes. Her name is Abigail Fisher. She's seven years old. Has green eyes and shoulder length blond hair. Curly."

"Do you know her height and weight?"

"Uh…not off the top of my head, but I'm sure I could look it up. She had her well child exam three months ago." *She's the height of my waist. She's the weight of a snuggle under a blanket when we read together at bedtime.*

"Are there other people in the house, ma'am?"

"No, it's just me. But I wasn't in the house. I was outside, up on the hill."

"Your daughter was left alone?"

"Yes, but I didn't leave her for long. We live all alone up here. I would know if someone came to the house." *Wouldn't I?*

At that moment, she saw Joel's car pulling up the road.

"Never mind. Detective Ramirez is coming. I see his car."

"Ma'am, if you could just—"

But Val hung up before the operator finished. She ran toward Joel's car, talking before he'd even opened the door.

"Abby is missing. I've looked everywhere. I left her in the house while I went up on the hill, but when I came back she was gone."

Joel frowned. "You checked the shop?"

"Yes, of course." Val listed everywhere she'd looked as she followed Joel back through the house.

"She's probably still here somewhere," he said reassuringly. "My parents once called the police because we couldn't find my sister, and it turned out she'd fallen asleep under an end table."

It was reassuring to have someone else there looking with her. Joel was even more thorough in his search, checking moving boxes, closets, kitchen cabinets, and behind the washer and dryer in the laundry room. The longer they looked, the more obscure the hiding places became. The more desperate Val felt.

"If she were here, she should have shown up by now."

Two uniformed deputies showed up in response to the 911 call and joined in the search. She recognized one of them, a genial man named Larry. Should she be worried that she was learning the deputies' names?

Val pulled Joel aside. "What if he got her? Whoever killed Howser?"

The dark look in his eye confirmed he'd thought of that too. But he shook his head. "We've been all up and down that hillside. He's long since been scared off."

"It's already been over an hour. If someone took her, they could be all the way to Pineview by now."

"Don't assume the worst yet. Does she ever go down to the Parkers?"

"Never. But—" Hope flickered in her chest. "She might have gone to the pump house. I told her that's where I was going to pick blackberries."

"Let's go."

Val jogged as fast as she could down the overgrown road that skirted the field to the pump house. She called Abby's name the further they got from the house, but couldn't hear anything over her own breathing and the pounding of her heart. What if Abby had fallen into the old well? Were they too late to save her? How much time would she have?

The pump house hadn't been used since before Val was born, when her dad had dug a new well closer to the house. But as kids, she, Maddie, Joel, and Carter had played there, imagining it as a secret hideout. Later, they'd snuck there to try the whiskey Maddie had stolen from her dad.

The pump house was more derelict than she remembered. No wonder her parents had forbidden them from playing in it. Part of the roof sagged and a massive wall of blackberry brambles overwhelmed one side. It looked like the kind of place that would house a child-stealing witch.

The padlock was missing from the door. Val pushed the door open.

"Abby?"

The shack was small, just large enough to house the old pump's plumbing and the opening of the well. Abby wasn't there, and the old particle board covering the mouth of the well—though swollen with water damage—was still intact.

Joel circled around outside, calling Abby's name. Val joined him, peering into the blackberry canes for any sign that they'd been disturbed. They grew thick and lush here from the high water table, forming an impenetrable wall.

There was no sign of Abby.

"She's not here," Joel said in frustration.

Val turned to him, feeling almost strangled by desperation. "I was hoping…But she didn't even know where it was. I've never brought her here. She could have wandered off anywhere looking for me." *Why did I leave her alone?*

"Do you have any friends who she might have gone with?"

Val remembered Abby's letter and pulled it out of her pocket. "She wrote this letter to her dad this afternoon."

"Who's this 'Poll'?"

"Paul," Val corrected. "He's the man I asked you about, remember? Paul Sheen? He comes over every so often to get supplies and odds and ends from the garage. I've told him a hundred times to text me first. He didn't say he was coming today. But Abby likes him, and he clearly doesn't respect boundaries." She knew she was getting her hopes up again, but she had to keep hoping. If she gave up, the only thing waiting for her was despair.

Joel turned on his heel and headed back to the house, grabbing his phone as he walked. He gave instructions to Larry, asking Val for clarification.

"Sheen?"

"Yes, Paul Sheen."

"Any idea where he lives?"

Val shook her head.

"It's okay, we can find him."

As Joel talked to Larry, Val remembered the original reason for his visit. When he got off the phone, she asked, "What about the marker?"

"Oh, right." He glanced up at the hillside. "Larry's going out to track down Paul Sheen and see if he knows anything. I'll send Brian after the marker if you remember where it is."

Val described where she'd been, gesturing as they approached the house. It seemed so insignificant now. Who cared about a stupid Sharpie left on the hillside when she may have lost Abby forever?

She was relieved Joel sent the other deputy instead of going himself. She didn't want to be left alone.

"Anyone else you can think of we should check out?" Joel asked.

Val racked her memory. "She likes Carter, but I seriously doubt he'd come pick her up without talking to me first."

"Why don't you give him a call just to make sure?"

Val obeyed, frustrated when the call went to voicemail. She sent him a quick text.

Can't find Abby. Call ASAP.

"Who else has she met since you moved here?"

"She met Maddie and her husband, but that was just in passing. Except..."

"What?"

"She's really into that comic and so are they. But I'm sure Maddie wouldn't come out here unannounced."

"Do you want to call or should I?" Joel asked.

"If you wouldn't mind..." Thinking of Maddie still

stung. Val didn't want to call her as a high strung mom who'd lost her kid. At least Joel would sound official.

As they reached the house, Carter called her back.

"Have you found her?" he asked urgently as soon as Val answered.

"No." She didn't realize how much she'd hoped that Carter had Abby until that moment as her stomach sank. She would have been furious at him, but at least Abby would have been okay.

"What can I do? Do you want me to come out and help look for her?"

"No, the police are here. Thanks, though. I was really hoping maybe you'd come by and taken her out."

"I wish I had. Sorry, Val. Keep me posted, okay? I'm headed to work, but I won't be able to focus on anything until I know she's okay."

Val felt so sick it was like her whole insides were stewing in toxic waste. But the adrenaline wouldn't let her stop looking for something to do. She vaguely realized she needed a shower, but she didn't want to leave the front yard. What if she saw something important? What if she heard something? What if suddenly Abby came running across the field, her golden hair shining like the dry grass?

In the midst of all her racing thoughts, she even found a reason to blame Jordan. If Jordan hadn't been a criminal, if Jordan were still alive, she and Abby wouldn't be there. They'd be back in their suburban home with a security system and video cameras and no way for a child to vanish without a trace.

That phrase reminded her of Eliza Bellingham. Val felt a sudden rush of sympathy for the Bellingham family. And a surge of panic. What if Abby were never found? What if she became another lost child in this backwater town? How long had Eliza's mother tried to convince herself that there was a logical explanation for her daughter's disappearance That the worst hadn't happened and Eliza would come home? When had she given up hope, and how did she live with it?

Val thought she might throw up. She went to the kitchen for a drink of water and drank it slowly, her hands trembling. Joel followed a few minutes later.

"How are you doing?" he asked.

She grabbed the counter and breathed deeply. "I can't lose her, Joel. It would destroy me. I just…can't." *I'd never forgive myself for leaving her alone.*

To his credit, Joel didn't offer any hollow platitudes. He placed his hand over hers and joined her in looking out at the empty trampoline sitting desolate in the brown landscape. The silence grew long between them. Full of fear and uncertainty. With every passing minute, the chances of Abby being in danger increased.

When Brian appeared in their view, walking across the back yard and carrying Val's sunhat, Joel stirred.

"I'll be back in a minute," he murmured, squeezing her hand before he left.

Alone, Val leaned against the counter. Her stomach roiled, and she yearned to heave its contents into the sink. But she knew the relief it gave would be temporary. She had to keep it together. She couldn't fall apart when Abby needed her.

Tears pricked her eyes, and she bent over, leaning her forehead against the cool edge of the counter. She tried to ground herself in the feeling of the smooth laminate against her skin, the purple stain beneath her fingers where a blackberry had left its mark.

Steps sounded quick and heavy as someone jogged down the hall. Val straightened as Joel came into the room, his eyes alight.

"She's okay. Larry found her."

Val blinked, her brain sluggish.

"Are you sure? He found Abby?"

"Yes, she's okay. He's bringing her home now."

The immediate relief that washed over Val made her almost collapse. She sagged against the counter, and Joel reached for her, enveloping her in his arms. She breathed in the clean smell of him, letting him hold her weight for a moment. Knowing she should probably be embarrassed at falling apart like this, but not even caring.

"She's really okay?"

"It sounds like it. They'll be here soon. She was at Paul Sheen's."

Anger flared so hot and sudden that Val backed away and threw off his touch.

"Paul took her?"

"I don't know any more than that. Another deputy is bringing him in for questioning."

"If he so much as touched her—" Val broke off, the rage too intense. She suddenly understood how Eliza's father might have been driven to murder. If Paul Sheen had walked up her path right then, Val would have been sorely tempted to do the same. She downed the rest of her water and slammed the glass on the counter, disappointed when it didn't shatter.

It was no more than twelve minutes after Val began

her vigil on the porch that she saw a county sheriff SUV drive up the road. But they were the longest twelve minutes of her life. Longer than the afternoon watching federal agents systematically dismantle her life and pack it into a large truck—furniture, artwork, appliances, jewelry. Longer than the hours spent watching the snow pile up while waiting for Jordan to come home. Longer than the days waiting for the recovery team to tell her they couldn't continue to search for his body in the icy lake water without putting themselves at undue risk. Within that twelve minutes, Val lived a hundred lifetimes of worry for Abby and what may or may not have happened while she was gone.

Nothing was more beautiful than the sight of the little blond head bobbing in the backseat of the Yukon as Larry pulled up in front of the house. Val didn't remember crossing the yard. One moment she was on the porch, and the next, she was standing in the driveway hugging her long-limbed little girl, saying, "I was so worried. Are you okay? I didn't know where you'd gone." Meaningless words that didn't even begin to express the horror she'd felt.

"Paul said he had kitties, and I asked if I could see them. I tried to ask you but I didn't know where you were."

Where to even begin?

"I was outside, remember?" *And he shouldn't have come over without my permission. And you shouldn't have gone out to visit him without me. And you should never invite yourself to a stranger's house. And he never should have taken you. And…and…*

Val pulled Abby away from her body and looked

her sternly in the eye. "You are never to talk to Paul again, do you understand? What he did today was very, very wrong."

Abby looked confused and abashed, as if she were the one getting in trouble.

"Mr. Sheen is cooperating," Larry explained. "He took me right to the barn where she was looking at the kittens with his granddaughter. And Abby and I had a good chat on the way home. I think she's just fine."

"I don't want him on my property again. Can I request a restraining order or something?"

Joel exchanged a look with Larry. "Let's talk about that later. You've already been through a lot today."

Her heart feeling lighter, Val wanted nothing more than to be left alone with Abby. To reassure herself that the nightmare was over.

As if sensing her thoughts, Joel said, "If everything's okay, we'll get out of your hair. Let me know if you need anything else."

She felt a rush of appreciation and gave him a grateful hug. "Thank you so much. I don't know what I would have done without you. You stopped me from going completely crazy."

Joel smiled, and for a moment Val regretted that she was still in her work clothes smelling of sweat, her nails stained black from berries. He really did have a nice smile.

"I was pretty impressed, actually," he said. "You held it together really well."

"Well, it helped having you here." Val felt like an awkward teenager again, not knowing how to compliment a boy. "Thank you," she said simply.

"You know how to reach me," he said in parting, tousling Abby's hair as he turned to leave. "Glad you're okay, kiddo. I'll check in with you tomorrow. But please don't have any emergencies before then."

Val laughed, the sound a little too bright, full of relief. "If I do, you're in my Favorites." She hugged Larry for good measure.

"Am I in your Favorites?" he teased.

"You keep this up, and you will be," she said, then scooped up Abby and squeezed her until she squealed.

16

THREE DAYS after the scare with Abby, Joel drove past the elementary school parking lot and noticed that the fire camp had doubled overnight. High winds and the relentless heat wave had continued to make conditions impossible for firefighters, and the two fires nearest Owl Creek had merged into one major complex. It was only ten percent contained, and all of the town was on Level 1 alert in case things shifted quickly and an evacuation order was issued. Some of the surrounding areas higher in the hills were at Level 2, meaning that they needed to have a bag packed in case things escalated to Level 3 and they were forced to evacuate immediately. Some residents had preemptively packed up and left.

The sun appeared as a perfect red sphere in the sky behind a thick brown haze. It looked like something out of a sci-fi movie. Gravel crunched beneath Joel's tires as he approached the station through the narrow alley that ran between City Hall and a car repair shop. Carter's silver Lexus was parked in front of the building.

Joel paused to text Val before getting out of the car.

Do you have a place to go if you need to evacuate?

Carter offered, she responded quickly.

Of course he did. Joel didn't mean to be peevish, but he was tired of Carter being a step ahead of him.

Pineview would be safer. They've got a few nice hotels if you need suggestions.

There was a long pause before she replied.

Thanks. We'll be fine.

What did that even mean? Was she trying to tell him it wasn't his business? Had he offended her with his suggestion to get a hotel? He didn't mean to imply that she couldn't handle herself. He just wanted to let her know he cared.

But not let her know he cared too much. He didn't want to be Carter.

Let me know if you need anything, he texted to finish the exchange.

It sounded lame, but he didn't know what else to say.

Carter was sitting in the chair by the reception desk, one knee bouncing impatiently, his gray messenger bag on the floor next to his chair. He popped up before the door closed behind Joel.

Joel glanced at the clock. He'd had a late night looking through the *Robert Apocalypse* comic, but it hadn't stopped him from getting an early start. Yet there Carter was, shaved—except for that silly soul patch—gelled, and with eyes sharp like an eagle on the hunt.

"Morning, Carter," he greeted, shifting his coffee to his left hand to shake Carter's with his right.

"How's Val doing? Is Abby okay?"

"They're fine," Joel said, wondering at Carter's urgency. Surely he'd talked to Val himself and didn't need Joel's affirmation. "What brings you here so early?"

"I need to talk to you about something." Carter kept his voice low as they passed the reception desk.

Joel nodded good morning to Kathy, who was already on the phone fielding a call from someone complaining about neighbors weed-eating their ditch. The angry voice drifted toward him from the receiver.

"If my place burns down because they start a fire in that tinderbox…"

Carter followed Joel into his office and closed the door behind him. "I know you probably can't talk much about your investigation, but I have to know. Is Abby really okay? Did Sheen…are you sure he didn't hurt her?"

Joel put his coffee on his desk and sat down. "Take a seat, Carter. What's going on? You didn't come all this way to ask me about Abby. You could have called. Did Val say anything to make you worry?"

"No, she says they're doing fine. But Joel, I've been

doing a little digging on Paul Sheen. I assume you know about his criminal history in California?"

Joel nodded. He didn't mind that Carter did his own investigating. It was part of his job and he shared things with Joel from time to time. There was only so much research Joel could do on any one case, and Carter's access to news outlets meant he had different resources to tap into. The downside was, their accounts were often incomplete, misleading, or downright inflammatory.

"I've been over his police record," Joel said mildly. "Are you talking about the alleged incident with the wrestler?"

"'Alleged incident?' I'm here as a friend, not a reporter. So you can cut out that crap. The kid claimed that Sheen was abusing others on the team."

"That's not what I found. It was a single accusation that was later retracted. Police found no evidence of wrongdoing, and no charges were filed."

Carter pressed his lips together in annoyance. "That's because this was twenty years ago. The fact that this kid even had the nerve to come forward was a miracle. Are you surprised that he bowed to pressure and changed his story?"

"I can't say anything about that. I only know what the police report said."

"So you're not taking it seriously?"

Now Joel was annoyed. "I'm taking it as seriously as it warrants. We questioned Paul Sheen thoroughly. There's no reason to think that he meant any harm."

"So you're not going to charge him with anything?" Carter's voice cracked with incredulity.

"That's none of your business. At best, this is a nice old man who doesn't understand that we live in a different world than he grew up in. If that's the case, he deserves to be educated, not raked over the coals. At worst, he intended Abby harm, which can be nearly impossible to prove. We're doing our best to get to the bottom of it. But it's an ongoing investigation and I can't comment on what may or may not come of it."

Carter leaned forward in his chair, enunciating his words forcefully. "He. Took. Her. From. Her. Home. Without the knowledge or permission of her mother."

"Yes, I know."

"But that's not enough for an arrest?"

"Under the circumstances, it's enough to spark an investigation. I really can't say more than that."

Carter blew out a frustrated breath, the plastic chair creaking as he shifted. "I can't believe you, Joel. After all they've been through, I would think you'd be a little more serious about trying to help."

"Of course I'm trying to help."

"Are you? Do you even know for sure whether or not Howser was murdered? Have you offered police protection to Val in case there's still a murderer hiding out on her property?"

"Is this about Paul Sheen or about Val?"

"Of course it's about Val! She came here for safety, and instead look what she gets!" He ticked them off on his fingers. "A home invasion, a convicted murderer on her property, a wild cougar on the prowl, and now a sex offender targeting her daughter."

"He's not a convicted sex offender," Joel snapped.

"Listen to yourself. It's no wonder the man left California for a fresh start."

"Or he was running from his past. It wouldn't be the first time. Did you read those articles I sent you about Val's husband?"

"No," Joel said, surprised at the change of topic. "It's none of my business. I don't Google my friends for the latest gossip."

Pink spots appeared in Carter's cheeks. "Well, maybe you should, so you know what you're dealing with. Otherwise, you're always two steps behind."

Joel felt a flush of anger, especially since he'd just been thinking the same thing. He sipped his coffee to calm himself. This was Carter, after all. He was a reasonable man, if too quick to jump to conclusions.

"I understand your frustration. I want to help them too, I really do. But I have to operate within the law and not use it for my own agenda. You know what this community would do to Sheen if people took things the wrong way."

"Is there any right way to take it?"

"The facts are that he wasn't charged with anything in California, and no other accusers came forward."

"I found at least three—"

"I don't mean to the press. I mean to the police. I have a hard time taking seriously any accounts that gave the accusers five minutes of fame but weren't serious enough to take to the authorities."

"And if Coach Scott had ever done anything inappropriate, and it was your word against his, would you have gone to the police?"

Joel hesitated.

"That's what I thought." Carter looked triumphant. "It takes so much courage to come forward. Can you blame them for going to the one place that will listen?"

"I don't know, Carter. We have a justice system for a reason. Otherwise, people crucify each other based on hearsay. I've been looking into Ryan Moyer's murder and it's horrifying the way the public responded. Makes me wonder what happened to the decent people in this community."

Carter's expression darkened, and his voice grew calmer. "Okay, that's true. I'm not suggesting we do the same thing with Paul Sheen."

"I would hope not. And I hope you'll use your professional influence appropriately."

"Don't worry. I got a front row seat with that Moyer mess, interning at *The Pineview Daily*. That one got ugly. I'm more careful than that."

"I know you are. But you can't come in here levying accusations against a man and expect me to rush out with handcuffs. I have to be careful too."

Carter nodded. "That's fair." He leaned back and held Joel's gaze steadily. "So, do you think whoever killed Howser did it in retribution for Ryan's death? Or to make him pay for sending the Bellinghams to prison?"

"That's the crux of it, isn't it? Somehow, Howser ended up on the wrong end of both sides. Or maybe it's just a coincidence and whoever killed him was completely unconnected to the Moyers or the Bellinghams."

"True. He could have made some enemies in prison."

"One thing I haven't been able to figure out is why Howser was so certain Ryan was innocent. If you were working at *The Daily* at the time, do you have any idea?"

Carter shook his head. "They didn't really dig into Howser's story. It was more about the girl's disappearance and speculation about her death. Giving context to why Ryan was murdered and reminding the public that Eliza was still missing."

"Did you know either one of them at all? I know you used to help out with the church group."

"Yeah, that was fun. Good kids. I knew Ryan a little, but I worked more with the younger group. I didn't know Eliza. She might have come with him once or twice, but she wasn't a regular."

"Were you surprised when Ryan was accused of her disappearance?"

"Yeah, of course. We all were. He was a nice kid. But I was away at college when it happened, so I heard about it the same way you did. By the time I came home for the summer, he'd dropped off the map. I can't even remember the last time I saw him. Maybe Christmas, the year before Eliza disappeared?"

A knock on the door was followed by Kathy poking her head into the room. "Ronnie Bellingham is asking to see you."

"Which one is that?" Joel asked. He'd talked to cousins, brothers, and nephews of Shane Bellingham. He couldn't keep them all straight.

"The son. Eliza's brother."

Ah. "Give me a minute," he said to Carter, following Kathy out to the waiting room.

When Ronnie Bellingham stood up, Joel was

reminded of a lanky sock monkey, the kind from his childhood that had seen a resurgence in recent years, with their disturbingly red lips. He was long-limbed, with a fleshy jaw and protruding mouth, and he moved as if he didn't yet have full control over his joints. If Joel had to guess, he would put him at sixteen or seventeen, having recently hit a growth spurt but not yet comfortable with it.

"You're Ronnie Bellingham?" Joel offered his hand.

Ronnie's hand was warm and slightly sticky. "Yeah, Shane and Caroline are my parents. Eliza was my sister." He mumbled a little when he spoke, and Joel thought he detected a slight lisp.

"Let's step in here," Joel said, gesturing to the interview room. "That'll give us a little more privacy."

Ronnie sat cautiously, folding himself awkwardly in a chair. Joel chose a chair nearby, hoping to make him feel more comfortable.

"How can I help you?" he asked, keeping his tone friendly.

"I heard you've been talking to all my uncles and cousins and stuff. And I wanted to say that if you think they did anything to that man—Sam Howser—you're wrong."

Joel waited to see if he would say anything more. Ronnie picked at a hole in his jeans, nervously tearing at the threads.

"Thank you, Ronnie. Can you tell me more? Why are you so sure no one in your family had anything to do with Sam Howser's death?"

"I just know that they wouldn't have done that. We

didn't even know he was here until it was all over the news about him disappearing."

"And how did you and your family feel about it when you learned that he'd come back to Owl Creek?"

Ronnie narrowed his eyes. "What do you expect me to say? That we wanted to kill him? We were just as confused as you, Officer. Some of us might've been mad, sure. But not enough to hunt him down, not like that."

"Do you see your father much, Ronnie?"

Ronnie lowered his gaze and picked at the fraying hole again. "We visit him when we can."

"What did your father say when he found out Sam Howser was dead?"

A flush crept into Ronnie's cheeks. "Well, he wasn't sorry to hear it."

"Did he seem surprised?"

Ronnie's head snapped up again. "I don't think I should be talking to you about my dad. I only came here to tell you to leave my family alone. They didn't have anything to do with that man's death. And if you don't leave us alone, we're gonna file a harassment suit."

Joel leaned back and gave space for the words to settle in the air before he spoke again. To give Ronnie his moment of power.

"Thank you for coming to see me today, Ronnie. I can only imagine how hard these past few years have been for you and your family. I appreciate you coming in and showing your willingness to work with the authorities."

Ronnie's brow creased suspiciously. "I didn't say I was working with you."

"No, but you've shown great maturity in coming here today. You've shown that you respect the law, and I'm proud of you. I'm sure your dad is proud of you too."

Ronnie stood uneasily. "I just want you to leave us alone. That's all."

"I'm sure you want the truth just as much as I do. If you ever want to chat about things, you're welcome to come by any time."

But Ronnie was already to the door. Joel watched him slouch his way past Kathy's desk, left hand reaching for his phone, head bent over like it was too heavy to hold upright.

Kathy looked up as he stalked out.

"What was that about?"

Joel smiled a little, but felt no humor in it. "He came to threaten me. But he hasn't figured out how to do it right. Give him a few years and he'll learn."

"Poor kid." Kathy shook her head. "It's not his fault his family's fallen apart."

"No, but he would be better off staying out of it. I'm not sure he's smart enough to realize that."

When he went back to his office, Carter looked up. "What's this?" he asked, holding a wrinkled sheet of paper. Joel immediately recognized it as the sketch of the drawings found on Howser's body.

"It was laying on the floor," Carter said when he saw Joel's expression. "I wasn't snooping. You think I want you to throw me out?"

"It's from a webcomic called *Robert Apocalypse*."

Carter brightened. "You are so much cooler than I thought."

"You know it?"

"Yeah, but I didn't know you were into it."

"I'm not. Just heard of it yesterday."

"Okay, a little less cool then," Carter amended.

"Do you know what these symbols mean?" Joel had spent hours the previous night going through the series as fast as he could, but he'd only made it to season three before falling asleep with his tablet.

Carter pointed to one of the drawings. "This one is the Grover-C. It's a time manipulation and teleportation device. This other one is a weaponized version."

"They look the same."

"Mmm…sort of, if you don't know what you're looking for. Doctor Menace modeled the O.Blivion off Amy Geddon's Grover-C, but you can see subtle differences. This shape is actually a B set inside an O."

Joel peered at the sketch. "I just thought it was imperfectly replicated."

"No, it's intentional. The comic's pretty cool. I've been introducing it to Abby. She's ready to go to Comic Con as Amy Geddon."

"So you know it pretty well then?" An idea was forming in Joel's mind.

"Oh yeah. Why?"

"Can I show you something if you promise to keep it in strict confidence?"

Carter perked up. "Confidence is my middle name."

"Riiiight. Hold on. And don't touch anything," Joel called over his shoulder as he went to Larry's office to get the notebook they'd found in Howser's belongings. Larry had been combing through the comic more slowly, looking for possible explanations about the drawings in Howser's book. But he hadn't hit on anything yet.

Joel could almost feel the curiosity pulsing off Carter as he handed him the notebook. "Do you have any idea what these drawings could mean?"

Carter flipped through the notebook, then sat down again to go through it more slowly. "Interesting. Not a great copy, but these are definitely taken from *Robert Apocalypse*. This is the scene where Amy Geddon learns Doctor Menace's true identity." He thumbed through a few more pages. "And this is where Robert finally tells her that he loves her. End of season five, I think."

Joel noted down the scenes as Carter described them. This would save Larry lots of time if he could zero in on where the drawings came from.

"Whoa," Carter said, turning to another page.

"What's that?"

Carter didn't answer. He read intently, turning pages while Joel waited. Finally he looked up. "These last ones aren't from the comic."

"You're sure?"

"Yeah. I mean, Doctor Menace kidnaps Amy Geddon a few times. But he never kills Robert Apocalypse. This never happens."

"No kidding." Joel looked over his shoulder at the rough sketch of the villain standing over the hero's body with a sharp-pointed cudgel. The next page showed Amy Geddon weeping over his body, followed by Doctor Menace stealing her away. "What do you think that means?"

Carter didn't answer right away, flipping through the rest of the notebook's blank pages to see if there were any more drawings. "I don't know. Maybe this guy hates Robert Apocalypse. Lots of people are into the love triangle. Clearly he's rooting for Dr. Menace."

"Hmm." Joel considered this. It could be that simple, that Howser was a fan. But the connection with Eliza Bellingham seemed too coincidental to ignore. He decided to take a chance.

"Do you have any idea why Howser would have drawn these symbols on himself before he died?"

Carter paused, his expression grim. "These were on Howser's body?"

"Drawn with a marker. We think he drew them himself."

"Maybe because he didn't have his notebook?" Carter guessed. "But why?"

"I don't know. That's why I wondered if you knew Ryan or Eliza. I can't help but think it's all connected to Eliza's disappearance."

"In what way?"

"Not sure. Ryan said Eliza was secretly seeing a Dr. M and thought he might have had something to do with her disappearance. At the time, police thought he meant a real doctor."

"But you think he meant Doctor Menace?" Carter's eyes got that sharp look again.

"That's what I'm trying to figure out. No one at the time knew anything about the comic, so they couldn't ask the right questions. Not even Ryan."

"Yeah, it would have been pretty new. I discovered it in college, but it was already a couple of years old by then."

"Any ideas how I could find other fans in the area?

Those who might have known about it when Eliza did?"

Carter rubbed at the fuzz on his chin thoughtfully. "You'll wanna talk to Bryson Gottschalk. He started one of the first fan forums back in the early days and it's huge now. Does stuff on Reddit and Tumblr too. He might know who else around here is into it."

Joel wrote down Bryson's name. "You don't happen to have his number, do you?"

Carter scrolled through his phone. "No, but I have Maddie's."

"That's all right, I'll find it. Thanks for coming in, Carter. You've given me some things to think about. Too bad you didn't consider law enforcement. You would have made a fair detective."

Carter smirked. "I prefer the camera, thanks. But I'm glad I could help. And think about what I said about Paul Sheen. You've gotta find out what he's hiding before anyone else gets hurt."

"You think about what I said too," Joel replied firmly. "The last thing we need in this town is another witch hunt. A little less emotion and a little more reason would go a long way."

The door opened again and Kathy's face appeared. "I'm so sorry to disturb you again—"

"It's okay, I was just leaving," Carter said, standing. "Thanks for your time, Joel."

But Joel only had eyes for Kathy. Her penciled eyebrows were drawn together in a worried frown.

"It's your car," she explained apologetically. "Larry noticed on his way in."

His car? He followed Kathy out to the gravel parking lot, Carter close on his heels.

When he saw the Charger, he swore under his breath. Shallow scratches in the driver's side door spelled out a predictable curse word.

Poor Ronnie, indeed.

"I'm so sorry, Joel," Kathy murmured sympathetically. "I'll get you the CCTV footage."

"What were you saying about emotion and reason?" Carter asked drily.

Joel shook his head. He did feel bad for the kid, but he couldn't help but reflect on the way he'd spoken of his sister. Caroline had talked like Eliza could still be alive. But Ronnie had consistently referred to Eliza in the past tense. Was he embracing the most likely truth? Or did he know something his mother didn't?

17

If it hadn't been pushing one hundred degrees, Val could have almost convinced herself it was late fall and that was thick fog forming in the fields and blanketing the town. But it was August, and it wasn't fog. Her sinuses were in state of constant irritation, and she was fighting a perpetual headache. She and Abby had slept the past two nights with the windows closed against the night's breeze, using damp towels instead of blankets like primitive air conditioning. Still the smoke seeped into everything and ash fell from the sky like shy snowflakes preceding a winter storm.

It was worse in town where the surrounding hills trapped the heavy smoke in the valley. Drivers kept their lights on as a general precaution, and the headlights shone a sickly orange. It reminded Val of the series in *Robert Apocalypse* when Robert and Amy were trapped in the future after a nuclear holocaust. The illustrator had used an overall wash of murky brown to convey a sense of desperation. Val had liked those chapters in particular, because Robert had finally acknowledged that Amy's skill set was far more useful than his. What was the point of being able to shoot or smash your enemy when your enemy was death and destruction? As usual, Amy's logic and inventiveness had saved them, and with a lot less cleavage than in the earlier strips. Clearly some new voices had been added to the team after the early years.

Val parked in front of the elementary school, and her windshield immediately started collecting white and black ash fall. The fire camp now covered the baseball diamond, outfield, asphalt playground, and the old track down at the bottom of the hill. Rough-looking men passed her car, glancing at her curiously, and Val waited until they were gone before getting out. She felt very out of place in her clean clothes and styled hair and didn't want to attract more attention.

Abby unbuckled her seatbelt in a complicated sequence of movements that still allowed her to tear fibers of string cheese from her cheese stick at the same time.

"I think I'm starting to like cheese sticks," she said as her tongue wrapped around a long strand and pulled it into her mouth. "When I was younger, like six, I didn't like them. But now that I'm older, they're so good!" She wrinkled her nose as she got out of the car. "Ugh. This smoke is so stinky. I wish they would bring in some fans to blow it all away."

"I don't think they make fans big enough for all this smoke," Val said, taking Abby's small hand in hers.

"Yeah, they do. Like those big white ones we saw when we were moving out here."

"Ah. Windmills. Those are very big fans, aren't they? But I think even those wouldn't be big enough to make all this smoke go away."

They reached the door of the old school, and Val was hit with a strong sense of nostalgia. Unlike high school, which held a bittersweet mix of memories, her years in this building had left an overwhelming sense of belonging in its wake, with bright traces of joy like the glitter used to decorate the oversized murals for the annual Christmas Concert. It felt more like coming home than anywhere else she'd been in this town.

Val opened the door and paused, disoriented. Instead of the wide open hallway she remembered, a large wall blocked the entry and funneled her toward the office, which stood in a different location than it had when Val was a child.

Val ushered Abby through the door and was welcomed with a cheery, "Good afternoon!"

The woman behind the counter paused and removed her glasses, letting them hang from a jeweled lanyard around her neck. Her false eyelashes exaggerated her look of surprise.

"Valerie Rockwell, hello! And who is this beautiful child with you?"

Abby hung back, looking nervously up at the stacks of boxes crowding the room.

"Hi, Sue! This is my daughter, Abigail. She'll be attending school this fall so we need to get her enrolled."

"Well, come give me a hug," Sue said, leaning over the counter. "I didn't know you were back. What a surprise!"

"Yeah, it's a surprise to us too," Val answered, leaning to meet the older woman in an awkward hug. Sue was soft and smelled of coffee, as a school secretary should. *Might as well get it out from the start.* "My husband passed away earlier this year, so we've had a lot of unexpected changes."

Sue's face fell. "I'm so sorry to hear that. Was he sick or…?"

"Car accident," Val said briefly, her stomach tightening, prepared to field the next set of questions.

Sue's eyes shone with sympathy as she looked at Abby. "I'm so sorry. But I promise we'll take good care of you. What grade will you be in this year, Abigail?"

"Second," Abby answered, but she kept an eye on the boxes towering nearby.

"Don't mind those. We've been doing a little moving ourselves. It'll all be cleaned up before school starts, I promise!"

"And what about the mess outside?" Val asked.

"Ah, yes. Those brave men and women. We're hoping the fires will be out before school starts, of course. But if we need to delay starting, we'll let the parents know."

"This is different," Val said, gesturing to the new entrance.

"Yes, we made some changes after Sandy Hook," Sue said matter-of-factly.

Val's nostalgia was brought up short with the mention of the tragic school shooting a few years earlier. A jarring reminder that the world was not as safe as it had once been.

"Now, what shall I call you?" Sue said to Abby. "Do you like to go by Abigail? Or do you have a nickname?"

Abby shook her head.

"Really? You seem like you would have a nice nickname. Can I call you Abby? Or how about Gail? I've always liked the name Gail."

Abby looked at Val in horror.

"She goes by Abby," Val explained.

"Abby's a wonderful name."

"No. Abigail." Abby insisted.

Val raised an eyebrow. "Are you sure? You want to go by Abigail?"

"Here, at this school, yes. I was 'Abby' at my other school."

Val exchanged a glance with Sue.

"Abigail it is," Sue said with a twinkle in her eye. "I'm going to get some forms for your mom to fill out. Would you like to read something while you wait? The library's open, and we have lots of wonderful books."

Val took the paperwork and went down the hall to the library. She smiled involuntarily as she entered. It seemed so tiny now. She remembered the shelves towering almost to the ceiling, but now she realized they couldn't be more than six feet tall. If she'd had to guess she would have said there had been dozens of aisles, but now she saw there were only a handful. It still had the same welcoming feeling, with its wide bank of windows letting in copious amounts of light, though now the light was filtered through dirty smoke. She could barely see her car parked out front and the thin layer of ash dusting it.

Val settled herself at a table meant for children,

turning sideways since her legs wouldn't fit under the top. As she filled out the forms, Abby wandered the aisles and eventually found the picture book section. She picked one and sat by Val, turning the pages quietly.

Val had just finished the medical and insurance form when her phone buzzed. It was a local number she didn't recognize.

Feeling a little rebellious considering she was in a library, Val answered.

It was Maddie asking her to come for an interview at the bank the next day.

"Tomorrow?" Val repeated, surprised they were giving her such short notice. Should she ask for more time to arrange child care? Or was Maddie testing her to see how badly she wanted the job? An entry level job where she would start out at minimum wage and still struggle to make ends meet.

But it was more conveniently located than the other jobs she'd applied for—with daytime hours, too—and so far, she hadn't had any other interviews.

"I'd love to, thank you!" she answered enthusiastically. "What time?"

As they arranged the details, she felt increasingly sick. The feelings of shame weren't as intense as before, but they were still there, telling her she should be better than this. Telling her that if she hadn't dropped out of college, she would be able to get a job that would actually support her family. That she should have already had her own career and not depended so much on Jordan. She might have been able to move wherever she wanted after he died and taken care of Abby on her own without crawling home in disgrace. Instead, she'd screwed up and missed her opportunity to really do something with her life and how would she ever afford to go back to school now with an income that would barely meet basic expenses and a daughter who was counting on her and would be increasingly resentful the older she got as she realized how pitiful her mother was.

Val's breath came quick and shallow as she hung up the phone, her heart pounding. She held her head in her hands and breathed deeply, trying to ride it out.

"Mom, are you okay?"

Val looked at Abby and tried to force a smile. "Yes, I'm fine. I've got a job interview tomorrow, isn't that great? I'm just feeling a little worried about some things."

"Like this new school?" Abby said, looking around.

"Are you worried about going here?"

"It seems really old."

Val tried to see the room through Abby's eyes. It was old, but clean and well cared for. Abby would see it differently, though. Her former school had been brand new, and a recent grant had supplied them with all the latest tech.

"It is old. Very old. But it's got some of the best people working here. You'll know all the kids in your whole grade, not just your class. They have more recesses than your old school, and the teachers are very kind."

"But I don't know anyone."

"Not yet. It won't take long before you'll have some good friends, and soon everyone will know you. I remember whenever we'd get a new student, we were all so excited to get to know them that it was a competition to see who would be their friend first."

Abby smiled a little at that.

Val felt Abby's hesitant smile as a weight in her chest, dragging her down into the depths of a churning river. How could she help her daughter feel secure in her new life when she herself was fighting a losing battle to reach the shore?

One step at a time. One day at a time.

And today was a big one. She had registered Abby for school, and her first post-Jordan date was happening that evening with Carter.

The thought cheered her slightly. As much as she wanted to go home and stew in her worries, she knew it would be better to do something social with someone who could help get her mind off her troubles.

As they left the library, someone called her name. Val turned, surprised to see Joel jogging toward her down the long hallway. She waited for him, feeling a tingling of anticipation like she used to feel when she was a teenager. She tried to push it down. They weren't teenagers anymore.

"I saw your car out front as I was driving past," he said. "How are you holding up?"

"You mean aside from never wanting Abby out of my sight? I'd say pretty good."

"That's understandable. But she's doing okay? Carter came to see me yesterday and I wondered if anything had come up to make him worry."

Is that the only reason Joel was here? Because Carter had told him to check up on her? The thought was disappointing.

But she was used to disappointment.

"We're fine. Getting back to normal, whatever that means. We're getting Abby enrolled in school right now," she said brightly, tucking a curl behind Abby's ear. "Though she's decided she wants to go by Abigail now."

"Oh," Joel said. "Well, Abigail is a very mature name. Just right for a third grader."

"Second."

"Right, second. Do you want me to call you Abigail too?" he asked her solemnly.

"No, you can call me Abby. But only when my mom's around. When other people are around, call me Abigail."

Val glanced at her. Where was this coming from? Would she expect Val to call her Abigail in front of strangers? She needed to talk to her about it to make sure she knew the new rules.

Val leaned against the cinder block wall. It was cool to the touch, smoothed over with years of layered paint. She wanted to ask Joel about his investigation into Howser's death, but didn't want to talk about it in front of Abby. She wondered if that's what Joel was thinking of when the conversation stalled awkwardly, neither of them able to say what was on their minds.

"I've been meaning to ask you—" Joel began at the same time Val said, "I have a job interview tomorrow."

Joel stopped. "You have a job interview? That's great news."

Val colored. "Sorry, what were you trying to say?"

"Just that I've been wondering if you need help preparing defensible space around your property. I know a guy who could bring in a tractor if you need it."

"Ugh, one more thing I'm neglecting. Thanks for the reminder."

"But you have a job interview? Tell me about it."

"It's nothing. Just for a teller position at the bank." Val's cheeks warmed further.

"That's great. Get your foot in the door and who knows what will come from it."

"Yeah, but they didn't give me much time to prepare. I've gotta find child care, and I don't know what to do about that. You might be surprised to hear I'm feeling pretty protective of Abby these days."

Joel smiled wrily. "I'd think there was something wrong if you weren't. What if you bring her to the station and she can hang out with me there?"

Val stared. "I can't ask you to babysit while you're working!"

"It's no big deal. When Larry's kids were little he used to bring them in for take-your-child-to-work day, and Kathy brings her granddaughter sometimes. Abby might be a little bored, but no one will mind."

Val wanted to say no, but instead she found herself smiling in relief. "That…that would be amazing. Would you mind? I can't think of a safer place for her to be. But if it's too much—"

"Nah, it'll be fine."

"What do you think, Abby? Do you want to hang out tomorrow with Joel while I go to my job interview? You could see what a real police station looks like."

"In real life?" Abby asked, her eyes squinting suspiciously. "Can I see the jail?

"I don't work at the jail, but I could show you where we ask people questions."

"Oh, yeah! I totally want to do that!"

"Seriously, Joel," Val said, laying a hand on his arm. "You don't even know how helpful this is. It takes a huge load off my mind."

Joel beamed, his dark eyes alight. "It's my pleasure." He laid his hand on hers, and it was warm and comforting.

Val's heart skipped a beat.

"I have a date with Carter tonight," she blurted before she realized what she was doing. Horrified, she pulled her hand away.

Joel's smile dimmed. "Okay."

"It's not anything serious. We're just friends. I'm sorry, I don't know why I told you that."

"It's fine. We're friends too, right? Friends can share their lives with each other."

"Yeah, I just—I'm sorry." She was glad for the shadowy hallway because she knew she must be blushing furiously. "I don't know why I thought you'd care."

What is wrong with me?

Joel blinked, uncertain what to say.

Shut up before you say another word! But Val couldn't seem to stop filling the silence.

"I'm sorry! I don't mean it like that. It's just that, I don't know how to date anymore. This is really weird for me. I thought Carter would be safe. But I clearly have no idea how to even act around men." *Just kill me now,* she thought, mentally slapping her forehead with her palm.

A curtain fell behind Joel's eyes. "Don't apologize. I'm sure you'll have a good time. Just think about what you want from the evening, and make sure he respects you."

It was like a pep talk from a brother to a little sister who'd never held hands with a boy.

"Thanks. I really think it'll be fine. We're just friends."

"Yeah. Well, I'd better head back to work. I was passing on my lunch break and thought I'd try to catch you."

"Okay." Val couldn't look him in the eyes, she was so mortified. "Thanks for checking in. I really appreciate it. I guess I'll see you tomorrow?"

"Sure. You can tell me all about your date," Joel teased as they walked back to the office, but his humor sounded forced.

Val busied herself turning in the forms so she and Joel wouldn't leave together.

"Did I hear right that you have a job interview?" Sue asked as Val moved toward the door.

Val blushed hotter. Had Sue heard their whole conversation?

"Yeah, I do." She pushed the door fiercely, eager to escape.

"Have you ever thought of working here? We have several positions open and are always looking for people who are good with kids."

"Really?" Val stopped, the door resting against her hip. "I didn't finish my degree."

"Neither did I, dear. But you wouldn't need a degree to start out as an aide or part of our support team. There's some certification involved, but you could work on that after you got the job."

"And then I'd have the same days off as Abby," Val realized.

"Abigail," Abby corrected.

"The pay isn't great. It's education, after all. But we've got good benefits, and free summers. Think about it."

Val nodded. "Thank you, Sue." It didn't change the fact that she'd just humiliated herself in front of Joel with Sue listening. But if it meant she had a another job option, it was almost worth it.

A gust of oppressive heat met them as they walked out of the building, and Val's headache throbbed insistently. Joel was pulling out of the lot, and she wanted to look away, to busy herself with her keys, but something on his car door caught her eye. Someone had scratched an obscenity into the paint.

Her phone buzzed.

Joel looked her way, and Val hurriedly looked at her phone, embarrassed to be caught staring. What was wrong with her? She was a grown woman, but she didn't have any more social skills than a twelve-year-old.

She didn't recognize the number, so she silenced her phone. Considering her recent track record, it was probably best she didn't talk to anyone right now.

18

JOEL SWITCHED from the county property records website back to the criminal records database, trying to push away the buzz of irritation in his head. He couldn't pinpoint exactly when Paul Sheen had moved to Owl Creek, but he'd bought his property in 2007—a property that was accessed via Highway 12.

Whether he'd bought it before or after he moved, Joel couldn't say, but his vehicle license registration had also been issued in late 2007, so it was pretty safe to assume he'd been living in the area by then.

Why did Val think she needed to tell him about her date with Carter? Was she trying to warn him that she wasn't interested?

Had he given her any reason to think he was?

Joel sorted through the results of his search for missing persons, but it was tedious and his mind wandered. He kept going over how he'd acted with Val and if there was anything he'd done to show he was interested in more than friendship. The last thing he wanted to do was make her feel uncomfortable, knowing she was still grieving her late husband and probably needed time. But apparently he was wrong. And once again, Carter had been two steps ahead of him.

Joel narrowed the parameters of his search, limiting it to females age thirteen to thirty.

He didn't want to date Val. At least, not right now. He could sense she wasn't in a good place emotionally for a healthy relationship. He remembered what his first couple of relationships had been like after the divorce. Looking back, he couldn't even recognize himself—the manic way he'd pursued some women, or the cold way he'd distanced others. It had taken a good year before he'd recovered enough to settle down. If Val and Carter hooked up this quick, it was bound to be a disaster.

He didn't want to date her.

And yet, he couldn't stop thinking about her.

When he was with her, he felt both comfortable and an exciting new tension that hadn't been there when they were teenagers. Something that made him want to see where a friendship could lead. Something that made him think way too much about that kiss over ten years ago and how much he wished he'd kissed her back.

This was stupid. He wasn't getting anything done. Joel stood and stretched, taking a little walk out to the front desk. Kathy looked up at him and smiled.

"I had an idea for the little girl you're bringing in tomorrow. What did you say her name is?"

"You'd better call her Abigail or I'll get in trouble."

"I've got my kids' Legos packed up in the garage. Do you think she'd like it if I brought those in? My kids used to play with them for hours, but I don't know if kids are still into that these days."

Joel shrugged. "I have no idea, but I can find out."

"I'll warn you, it's pretty noisy when they dig through the box. It's like someone's running spoons through a blender. But it's just for the afternoon. I think we'll live."

"I'll check right now," Joel said, sending a quick text to Val. It was ridiculous how happy it made him to see her respond so quickly.

Abby would love that! I haven't unpacked our Legos so it'll be like Christmas for her. You're a genius!

Kathy's the genius. But I'll cheerfully take the credit.

Was that too flirty? He almost erased it and started again, but stopped himself. They were friends, right? Friends tease each other.

And friends are also there for each other to help pick up the pieces when rebound relationships fail spectacularly.

Feeling slightly better, Joel returned to his desk to resume his search. That's when he saw it. A fifteen-year-old girl had disappeared while walking home after a football game in the same California town where Paul Sheen had lived two years before he moved to Owl Creek. There weren't any witnesses or signs of violence. She'd last been seen separating from friends after the game, but never made it home. Her body, just like Eliza's, had never been found. There was no way to know how well Sheen had known the victim, but her brother was a wrestler, and Sheen was the head coach. It was likely he'd known the family. Enough for the sister to trust him and get in his truck if he offered her a ride?

There were other disappearances in nearby communities as well. A thirteen-year-old had gone missing on her way to the gas station to pump up her bike tire. A nineteen-year-old who worked the late shift at the local grocery store disappeared one night from the parking lot. None of the disappearances were obviously connected to Sheen, but it was worth digging deeper.

Was it only a coincidence that two years after Paul Sheen moved to Owl Creek, a seventeen-year-old girl disappeared under similar circumstances?

Joel went back to the report on Eliza's disappearance. She'd worked in the local hardware store, which meant she was probably well-known to most of the handymen in the area. Joel jotted down the names of her coworkers. Hopefully after seven years they would still remember whether or not she had known Sheen. Before he talked to Sheen directly, he wanted corroboration from others.

The investigators hadn't looked at Sheen as a person of interest when Eliza disappeared. There had been no reason to. If it hadn't been for the scare with Abby, Joel wouldn't be looking at him now. Even still, Joel had to admit, these were pretty tenuous connections. Circumstantial at best.

But something else drove Joel forward. Sheen was familiar with the Rockwell property, and had been on site in the days following Sam Howser's disappearance. Assuming Sheen had a reason to kill Howser, he would have had ample opportunity. It was no smoking gun by any means, but taken all together it suggested a new theory that was worth investigating. And in a frustrating case like this, a new lead could keep things stirring enough that something worthwhile floated to the top.

19

VAL CLEANED the house as best she could in preparation for her date with Carter. She didn't want to work too hard at it, but also wanted to show that she respected Carter enough to put in a little effort. The problem was, the old farmhouse had been neglected so long that even a good cleaning didn't make much difference. The carpet in the living room was stained and worn. The wallpaper in the downstairs bathroom was peeling behind the toilet, and the mounted vanity was coming loose from the wall. Walls looked barren without the family pictures that had hung there for decades. It didn't look very inviting.

Maybe she should hang a few pictures to make it feel more cozy. But what would she hang? Should she display a picture of their family when Jordan was alive? Would she be able to stomach it? But it wasn't just about her. Jordan was Abby's father. It wasn't fair to erase him completely from their lives.

Val decided to test herself by visiting the spare

bedroom and pulling out a box of framed photos. Immediately, she knew it was a mistake. Seeing Jordan's face hit her so hard she rocked back on her heels. His neatly trimmed sandy hair and single dimple that flashed when he grinned. That smile that always seemed a little bit self-conscious. It provided just the right counterpoint to the privilege he wore as naturally as breathing, making him seem more down-to-earth than he should have as the only son of high profile parents whose wealth and status opened doors Val could only dream of.

There were days in those early years when Val couldn't believe he'd chosen her. They'd met in the library on campus when she'd mistaken him for her TA who was supposed to be holding a midterm review session for her Economics class. When the TA didn't show, Jordan offered to review the material with her himself, having taken the same course a few years earlier. When she called to tell him how well she'd done, he'd asked her out.

Looking back, Val realized how that first meeting characterized their whole relationship. Val in distress. Jordan to the rescue. Val always feeling like she owed him. Not in a resentful way, but in a way that made her want to become whatever he needed and then feel honored for the chance.

But now, looking at photos of their life together gave her a vague feeling of disgust. What had once been favorite memories now brought only pain. How many poor retirees living on a fixed income had paid for that trip to Thailand? Or their anniversary in Paris? One photo made her feel physically sick, as she noticed a lovely set of diamond earrings he'd given her for her birthday a year earlier. They'd been taken by the feds with everything else.

She'd just decided she couldn't do it when Abby walked into the room.

"What are you doing, Mom? Are you hanging pictures?" she asked excitedly.

"I don't know. I was just looking."

"Can we hang some on the walls? Please?"

"I don't want to hang a bunch of pictures now if we're going to have to pack them again when the house sells."

But looking at Abby's hopeful face, Val realized that Abby needed to see the pictures on display for the same reason that Val wanted to hide them. Because her world had crumbled around her, and she was trying to figure out where the pieces fit. Where *she* fit.

"Maybe we can hang a couple in the living room. Which ones would you pick?"

Abby picked out a photo of her as a sleeping baby, with Val and Jordan looking on in rapture. She also chose one of her on the first day of kindergarten and the last family portrait they had taken when Jordan was alive. Val liked that one the least because she was looking up at Jordan with an expression of perfect contentment and love.

Trust.

Naiveté.

But Abby was so excited that Val decided she could make this small concession. Someday, she would have to tell her what her daddy had really been like. But now, for Abby's sake, she would honor the man they thought he had been.

Val changed into a clean pair of white cropped pants and a loose, flowing shirt made of soft rayon, then debated whether or not to wear makeup. She settled on a little mascara, deciding that it showed some effort without a major investment. Exactly how she felt about this date.

While she waited for Carter, she checked the evacuation alert map as she did several times a day now. She had a bag packed and ready to go in case she and Abby had to leave. There wasn't much they'd leave behind that they couldn't live without. But if she lost the old Victorian farmhouse…that would be unthinkable. It had tethered her in a way that she hadn't expected since returning to Owl Creek, giving her one constant she could rely on. Even if that constant included sticking doors and no air conditioning.

She refreshed her screen again, just to reassure herself the map hadn't changed. Then she checked her voicemail. The unknown caller from before had left a message, and Val almost deleted it, figuring it was probably a wrong number or a pharmaceutical scam. She was surprised when the woman who left the message addressed her by name.

"Mrs. Fisher, this is Deputy US Marshal Wendy Bines. It's urgent that I speak with you regarding your late husband, Jordan Fisher. Please call me at this number as soon as possible."

Val's stomach sank. Would the nightmare never end? What had the investigators discovered now? They had nothing left to take from her, and she had already told them everything she could. If Jordan had been guilty of even worse crimes, she didn't want to know. She'd call back tomorrow. Maybe.

When Carter arrived, he was dressed in slim-fitting jeans and a shirt cut in a modern, trim style. He smelled of cologne and carried a bouquet of brightly colored daylilies and dahlias. Val was immediately glad she'd put on the mascara and wondered if she should have added lipstick. While she put the flowers in water, Abby pulled Carter into the living room to show him the pictures they'd hung.

What he thought of seeing Jordan's face on their wall, she couldn't guess. But from the kitchen she heard his enthusiastic replies to Abby about how happy she looked. Val's hands trembled as she arranged the flowers, and she paused to take a few deep, calming breaths.

It was one evening with a friend. No more commitment than that.

Over the course of the next hour, she wondered why she'd been so nervous. Carter was his typical friendly self, always knowing just what to say when the conversation lagged so she never felt like she had to work at it. Their conversation moved easily from Abby's early childhood to high school memories to *Robert Apocalypse*.

"You haven't made it to season four yet?" Carter said in dismay, hand paused over the cheese grater where he was pulverizing a lump of fresh ginger.

"Each season is like hundreds of strips each!" Val protested. She was slicing a fresh pineapple, trimming off the outer skin without taking too much of the sweet goodness inside. "Believe it or not, I have other things to do with my time."

"Yeah, but you haven't even gotten to the really crazy stuff. Like who Amy Geddon's mother is and why Robert Apocalypse can't use the Grover-C."

"I thought it had to do with a bio print or something."

"Uh, no. There's so much more to it than that."

Val shook her head. "I'll take your word for it. It seems like the writers change their minds every couple of months and conveniently reverse engineer whatever direction they were going to fit a new plot twist."

"Shh…I won't listen to your negativity. It's amazing. Just wait until Doctor Menace goes back to the Berlin games in '36."

"Okay, and Doctor Menace is one I can't quite figure out. Is he a good guy or a bad guy?"

"I know, isn't it great? He's so complicated!"

"As soon as I start to like him, he does something despicable to remind me he's a horrible person."

"I think he's a great foil for Amy Geddon," Carter said, slipping a slice of pineapple from the bowl and handing it to Abby. "If she hadn't had Robert Apocalypse to give her purpose for her gifts, she might have ended up just like Doctor Menace."

"Seriously?" Val stopped, one hand on a cocked hip and the other waving the knife to punctuate her point. "That's giving Robert Apocalypse way too much credit. And letting Doctor Menace off the hook as if he didn't choose his own path. I think Amy Geddon needs to get away from both of those men!"

"Just wait. Tell me what you think when you get to season eight."

Their banter was interrupted by Val's phone ringing. It was an out-of-state number again, and she suspected it was the federal marshal.

"You can get that if you want," Carter offered.

"No, it's no one I want to talk to."

Dinner was handmade potstickers and stir fry, and soon a haze from the cooking oil hung heavily in the kitchen, even with a box fan blowing in the window. Carter was clearly comfortable in the kitchen. The only time he fumbled was shaking up the soy sauce with the cap not completely sealed, showering his shirt in dark spots.

Val laughed in sympathy at the stains. "Better wash it out before it sets."

"This is a new shirt, too," Carter moaned. But Val couldn't help but wonder if he wasn't a little too eager to take it off so that he could rinse it in the sink. He wore a tank top underneath, and the muscles of his bare arms were more defined than she remembered from high school.

She idly wondered if being single gave him more time to work out. She couldn't remember the last time she'd had a regular exercise regimen. Certainly not since Jordan's death.

"Nice tattoo," she said with a smile, noticing the Grover-C symbol on his left shoulder as he bent over the sink. "Please tell me you don't have posters of Amy Geddon in your bedroom.

He grinned at her over his shoulder. "Amy Geddon is a bad a—" He stopped himself, glancing at Abby.

"Amy Geddon is awesome. But it's not the Grover-C. Can you tell the difference?"

Val looked more closely, feeling a little peculiar at being so close to a man's skin who wasn't Jordan. "Ah, you're right. It's the O.Blivion. You don't have posters of Doctor Menace in your bedroom, do you?" she intoned suggestively.

Carter laughed. "No, but you have to admit, he's pretty cool."

"Cool enough for a tattoo?"

"Well…" He colored slightly, wringing out the wet shirt with gusto. "That's what happens when you drink too much with a roommate and his friend the aspiring tattoo artist."

"Ah, college sins," Val said knowingly. She took the shirt from him and hung it over the box fan to dry. It didn't take long in the August heat, and by the time they sat down to dinner, Carter was dressed again, though slightly more rumpled for the ordeal.

The meal was delicious, and Carter beamed at Val's compliments. Even Abby asked for seconds, though she picked out the vegetables.

"Abby and I wanted to make a blackberry cobbler," Val said as she began clearing the table, "but it didn't seem worth going out into the smoke. So we'll have to make do with Umpqua ice cream instead."

"Good choice!" Carter said, jumping up to help.

When he started running water in the sink, Val objected. "You don't have to wash all these dishes."

"I dirtied them, didn't I? Besides, what kind of a gentleman would I be if I invited myself over and then made you clean up after me?"

Val refused to let him work alone. While he washed, Abby rinsed and Val dried and put the clean ones away. She was secretly glad there were so many pots and pans to wash. The longer they dragged out this part of the evening, the longer she put off the awkward part when Abby would go upstairs to bed and she and Carter would be alone.

But it came soon enough. As the sun dropped toward the horizon, she sent Abby to change into her nightgown and brush her teeth. At Abby's insistence, Carter read her three stories and then tucked her into bed. Val appreciated his thoughtfulness, but hoped Abby was only thinking of Carter as a nice friend and not as a replacement for her dad. She didn't want to get Abby's hopes up. Carter was great, really he was, but she couldn't see herself ever feeling that way for him.

Still, it was nice having someone else who could share the parenting load for an evening. She hadn't realized how much she'd missed that.

Carter hadn't returned downstairs yet when her phone rang again. Seeing the same number again, Val answered it. Might as well get it over with so the marshal would stop bothering her.

"Hello?"

"Valerie Fisher?" The woman's voice held a faint drawl. "This is Wendy Bines from the US Marshals Service."

"Yes, Ms. Bines. I got your message from earlier, but I'm afraid I can't help you. Whatever else you've learned about my husband has nothing to do with me. I'm trying to put that behind me. I feel bad for all the people he hurt, but I can't do anything to help them now. I'd really appreciate being left alone."

There was a slight pause.

"I understand, ma'am. And I wouldn't be calling you now if this didn't concern you, but you deserve to know."

"Okay," Val sighed, steeling herself for more bad news.

"Your husband, Jordan Fisher, is alive."

20

VAL FELT TIME SHIFT, the way it had when she'd seen the cougar. What must have been mere seconds seemed to drag out in agonizing slowness, almost as if she could feel the neurons in her brain misfiring, restarting, trying again. Trying to comprehend the words.

"What do you mean, he's alive?" Her voice cracked on the words. She felt separated from her own body, like a casual observer noticing that she was leaning against the counter. Now sliding down the cabinet to sit on the floor. Vaguely grateful they'd already swept.

"It seems that your husband staged his own death to avoid arrest. We think he's spent the past six months in Guam, Tonga and possibly Indonesia. But he recently returned to the United States, entering through the port of Seattle."

"That's impossible. Why would you say that?"

"I'm sorry. I know this must be a shock. We understand that you've recently moved to Oregon, is that correct?"

"Yes." Val heard Carter's footsteps as he came down the stairs. He stopped in the doorway, his brow furrowing with concern. She could only imagine what he saw on her face.

"And your husband hasn't contacted you at all?"

"Stop calling him that!"

Another pause. "I'm sorry, ma'am. Can I assume then that you're willing to help us apprehend him?"

"I don't want to have anything to do with him," Val said fiercely. "I just want this to be over."

Carter cautiously sat next to her on the floor, not touching her.

"I understand. We're doing everything we can to find him. If Jordan Fisher contacts you, call this number or your local law enforcement. Don't tell him we've been in contact. Don't help or assist him in any way. We'll try to keep you out of it if at all possible. But if there's a chance he's planning to come to you for help, you need to be warned."

"Thank you," Val said, then wondered what she was thanking the marshal for.

When she hung up, she sat in silence, watching the ceiling turn pink from the reflected light of sunset.

"Can I help?" Carter asked softly.

Val had forgotten he was there. She looked at him and was suddenly grateful she had already told him about Jordan. There was less to explain. And considering that she didn't understand it herself, she wouldn't have known where to start.

"That was a federal marshal telling me Jordan isn't dead after all."

Carter gaped. "You mean he faked his own death?"

"Apparently."

"He abandoned you and Abby to clean up his mess?"

His anger made Val feel good. Validated. She thought she might be angry too, but she couldn't feel it yet. Couldn't feel anything except shock.

"They wanted to warn me in case he tries to contact me. I doubt he will. He's not that stupid, and he's got to know I won't help him after what he put me through."

"Val, I'm so sorry," Carter said. He moved to put an arm around her shoulders, but she pulled away.

"No. I'm sorry, Carter, but I think it's best if you go."

His face fell, but with a nod he stood and began gathering his things.

Val felt a flash of guilt as she watched him load up the box full of ingredients. "I'm sorry, I shouldn't have answered the call. Thank you for everything. I really had a wonderful time."

"So did I. I just wish I could do something to help."

He turned to her with such warmth in his eyes that she looked away and grabbed a bottle of soy sauce to give her something to do.

"No one can fix this."

Carter hefted the box, and she walked him to the door. She gave him a short hug in farewell, awkward with the box between them.

"Maybe," Carter offered, "when you're up for it, we can do this again."

I'm still a married woman, Val realized. Not that she

owed Jordan any loyalty after what he'd done. But the thought made her feel sick. Burdened.

"I don't think so," she said sadly. "But thank you for understanding."

As soon as the door closed behind Carter, Val went to the living room and collapsed onto the couch, feeling so nauseated she wanted to vomit. Despite the evening warmth, she hugged a throw around herself, trying to stave off the trembling.

Jordan was alive. He'd lied to them all. He'd written a suicide note, knowing she would mourn him. Leaving her to contend with the authorities. He'd abandoned her. He'd abandoned Abby.

She called Gina and timed her tirade—six minutes—just to give her something else to fixate on.

"I told you he was a narcissist," Gina spat. "Maybe even a sociopath. You've got to get out of there, Val. Go somewhere he can't find you."

"Why would he be looking for me? He's the one who abandoned us, remember?"

"Who knows? The man's a fugitive. He's probably running out of options. Where else would he go?"

"His parents for starters…"

"I'm just saying, you have no idea what he's capable of."

"He's not dangerous. He committed fraud, not violent crimes." Val pictured chasing off an invader, only this time it was Jordan who was hanging around the house, stealing food. It was disturbing how easy it was to imagine.

Gina interrupted her thoughts. "I'm telling you, the

man's desperate. He's already proven that he'll do whatever it takes to get what he wants, and he doesn't care if you get hurt in the process. Who knows what he's been doing the past six months? A little violent crime might be part of his repertoire by now."

"You're not doing anything to help my stress, Gina." Val's throat tightened.

"Blame Jordan, not me. I don't want to see you get hurt. Get out of there. Come to Arizona. If you insist on staying, at least get yourself a gun."

By the time Val got off the phone, it was dark outside, except for the orange glow of wildfire in the distance. Jordan was too smart to come looking for her. Surely he knew she would never help him.

But then another thought flickered in her mind. What if he wasn't coming for her?

What if he came for Abby?

Val's chest seized with fear. She thought of Howser hiding in the woods, breaking in when she was gone. What if...just what if...Jordan had already come looking for Abby, but had found someone hiding in the woods instead?

She sat up straight and dialed. He answered on the second ring.

"Joel? I think I may know who killed Howser."

Joel closed his car door quietly. It was late, and a cacophony of crickets and frogs thrummed in the night air. The sweet scent of dry grass blew in from across the sun-baked fields. Val had insisted on meeting him in person. She wouldn't divulge anything over the phone, but had promised she would explain it all when he got to her house. He'd just gotten off the treadmill when she called—the constant smoke forced him to exercise indoors—and had taken the fastest shower of his life, grabbing a pair of jeans and a t-shirt before he fully toweled off. He hadn't even bothered with socks as he raced for his keys.

Val met him on the porch, slipping carefully out the screen door and closing it slowly so it didn't slam. She held a steaming cup of coffee.

"Do you mind if we talk out here? It's cooler than inside, and I don't want to wake Abby."

The porch light emphasized shadows under her eyes. She was dressed in white pants and a silky top, but her hair was pulled up in a messy bun as if she'd gotten distracted with her appearance at the last minute. Joel found the combination unexpectedly alluring. He stopped himself from asking about her date. That's not why he was here. And he wasn't sure he wanted to know.

They sat together on the porch swing, looking out over the yard lit a sickly orange from the shop light above the garage. All the donation boxes had been cleared away, allowing them to reclaim the porch's purpose as a gathering place. The old wooden swing had always been a coveted spot.

"I don't know how to tell you this," Val began. "I probably should have told you earlier, but I didn't want you to think poorly of me. You have to understand that I didn't choose this. There are some things that I realize in hindsight should have been warning signs. But he was my husband. Why wouldn't I trust him?"

Joel frowned. This wasn't the direction he'd expected her to go.

"You know that Jordan killed himself. But what I didn't tell you is that he was guilty of massive affinity fraud, taking millions of dollars from senior citizens through various real estate investment scams. I don't understand how it all worked. I didn't have a clue until the day the feds showed up on my doorstep. That was the day he drove his car off a cliff. Or…" Val paused, crossing her legs and tugging at her sandal strap. "At least, that's what I thought. Until tonight when a federal marshal called to tell me he's alive and has been living overseas the past six months."

Joel's quick intake of breath made her turn toward him, but then she stopped herself and looked away. Her shoulders were hunched as if in pain, as if she were barely holding herself together. Connections came together in his mind. Carter's insistence that he look up details of Jordan Fisher's death. Val's apparent descent from affluence to near poverty. The shell she'd worn about her to keep people at a distance. Her obsessive worry over Abby. This was more than typical grief. This was betrayal on such a large scale that Joel couldn't wrap his mind around it.

No wonder she had trust issues.

"I had no idea," he said, trying to find words adequate to express what he felt at her disclosure. "I'm so sorry you've been dealing with this. But I don't know how it could make me think poorly of you. I know you, Val, and I know you never would have been a part of something like that. You're as much a victim as anyone else."

She risked a quick glance. "Thank you. I feel like my whole life has been a lie. Even now. People feel sorry for me, but I'm not the grieving widow they all think I am. I hate him. A part of me misses him sometimes, but mostly I'm just so angry for what he put me through. Trying to explain to Abby why everything she loved was being packed into a trailer and taken away. The reporters camping outside my house and following me around town. Do you know what it feels like to see your face on the news and hear people talking about you? And you can't do anything to stop them?"

Joel did, but he didn't say so. All the attention he'd gotten after the Stan's Market shooting had been invasive and made him feel like a hypocrite. Shooting a couple of kids didn't deserve hero status, but the public had disagreed.

But he didn't want to disrupt Val's story, so he kept silent.

She continued, "Am I as bad as he is that I let people think what they will? I know they feel sorry for me, but I'd rather that than they learn the truth and think something far worse."

"It's not any of their business," Joel said firmly. "You're entitled to your privacy, and to grieve however you need to." After a paused, he asked, "Does Abby know the truth?"

"No. That's why I called you. Abby meant everything to Jordan. In his note, he said he couldn't bear for her to see her daddy go to prison. He'd rather die—or make us believe he had—than have her learn the truth.

But I think he's changed his mind. The marshal said he was in Seattle a couple of weeks ago. He's come back to the States, and there's only one person he loves enough to risk coming back for."

"You think he's coming for Abby?"

"I think..." Val paused. "I think he may have already come, but things didn't go how he planned."

Joel leaned back, the swing rocking gently as he shifted. "You think that Jordan met Sam Howser in the woods up on the hill and...what?"

"I don't know. Fought with him over food? Thought he was protecting us? I don't even know who he is anymore. The man faked his own death and fled the country to avoid prosecution. I can't say what he'd do if he felt threatened, especially after risking so much. If he came back to get his daughter, what would he do to someone who tried to stop him?"

Joel looked out past the line of light to the shadows fringing the yard. Orange hot spots from the wildfire striated the distant hills. "Did you tell the marshal this?"

Val shook her head. "I could barely process what she was saying. It was only later when talking to Gina that I realized the timeline fit. Am I making things up? Just being paranoid?" Her gaze was searching. Looking for reassurance.

"I think you need to tell the marshal what you told me. If Jordan did come back for Abby, he could be a very dangerous man."

Val nodded and brought out her phone, placing the call immediately. Her voice trembled as she asked for the marshal, and Joel reached for her hand instinctively.

She gripped his in return and didn't let it go until the call ended.

"They're sending marshals from Portland right away. I don't know how I'll sleep again until they find him. He's had months to plan. He'll have thought of everything. I don't want to suffocate her, but how can I know he won't be waiting the second I'm not watching? At recess or waiting to get on the bus after school. She would go with him willingly."

"You're going to have to tell her he's alive, and warn her to stay away from him."

"It will break her heart." Val yanked her hair elastic and shook out the bun angrily. "She won't understand. How can I do that to her?"

"You have to, for her own safety. He's evaded capture so far, which means he knows what he's doing. Install a burglar alarm. Motion sensors around the house. What happened with Howser might have scared him away for a while, but if you're right he'll be back once things calm down."

Val sighed heavily and scooted closer. She laid her head on his shoulder, as natural as if they were eighteen again. He was grateful he'd taken time to shower before coming over as he reached his arm around her. This was what friends would do, right?

"I just want the marshals to find him. And then I want to be far away when they put him on trial."

"If anyone can find him, they will. But he's probably been scared off. Since we found Howser's body, I've been on that hill a dozen times and didn't see signs of anyone besides him living there. If Jordan killed Howser, he's probably long gone. You'll be safe while the marshals are here, at least. No way he'll hang around with feds combing the area."

Val grew quiet, fiddling with her hair elastic.

Long minutes passed with only the night sounds and the faint squeak of the swing as it swung from the joists. Joel's back started to ache, but he didn't want to move and disturb Val. The weight of her against him was the most comforting feeling he'd had with a woman in a long time. He didn't want to ruin the moment, even if it didn't mean the same for her as it did for him.

Almost without thinking, he reached up and touched her hair. She leaned into his hand, letting him stroke her tangled waves. They sat like that for a few moments, the intimacy of touch without speech. Then she turned her face to his, and her breath was on his cheek.

Her lips brushed his. Hesitantly. She looked up and there was a spark of hope in her eyes. He could barely breathe with her so close. His heart thumped so loud he was sure she could hear it.

This was definitely not what friends would do.

But looking in her eyes, he saw she wanted it too.

He kissed her back. Kissed her like he wished he'd kissed her that summer night under the walnut tree. Gently, then more firmly, with one hand still in her hair and the other tracing her jawline and sliding behind her neck.

Her breath quickened with his, and she shifted, coming up on her knees to reach her arms around his neck, pulling him closer. Her lips were warm and moist, and he felt as if he could lose himself forever. It was…

right. Like they'd been headed toward this moment since the first day they'd met.

And then it wasn't.

Val's hands slid down his chest and slipped under his shirt. Her fingers were soft and ignited a sudden yearning, an inevitability as powerful as the tide. It triggered a warning, and he pulled back abruptly. Scrambling away from her, he stood, trying to clear his head.

"What's wrong?" Val sounded hurt.

"We can't...we don't want to do this," he said, though everything in his body was telling him otherwise. He gripped the porch railing and looked out over the yard, taking a deep breath to calm his racing heart before turning back. "You've had a shock, and I don't want you to do anything you'll regret."

"Who says I'll regret it?" she challenged, her eyes bright.

"I'll regret it. You're not thinking straight. You just barely found out your husband is alive."

"Screw Jordan," she spat angrily. "I'm tired of not being able to live the life I want because of him." But she sat back and drew her knees up to her chest, wrapping her arms around them.

The mood was over.

Disappointment washed over Joel, but it left behind a certainty that he'd done the right thing. He sat down again by her side.

"I care about you, Val. I really do. I don't want to throw away a chance with you on an impulsive night that you might regret. Trust me, I know. I did a lot of stupid things after Lacey left."

She squinted at him suspiciously. "What if I don't regret it? What if this is exactly what I want? I think a part of me has always wanted you, Joel Ramirez. I've spent my whole life waiting for you to notice."

Hope flared in Joel's chest. Not only desire or passion: a hope for something real. He wanted to reach for her and take her in his arms, but that hope held him back.

"Then let's not screw this up. Let's take it slow. We have all the time in the world to do it right."

Val's shoulders straightened, and she blew out a long sigh. "Okay. I like that. I can do slow. It would be best for Abby anyway. Besides," she laughed bitterly. "I guess I've got to figure out how to divorce my dead husband. Sorry, I don't know what I was thinking."

A part of Joel wished he hadn't been thinking as much, but he knew it was for the best. When the sun rose in the morning, he wanted to be able to look her squarely in the eyes without shame, knowing they still respected each other.

Val grabbed a couple of light blankets from the house, and they sat together on the swing without touching. At first he couldn't think about anything else besides the warmth of her lips and her arms around his neck. But even that passed as she talked about her life over the past six months. How she'd gone from one desperate prayer to another. *Please let it all be a mistake. Please let him come home. Please let them find his body. Please make them leave us alone. Please make it stop.*

She told him how she'd refused to hold a memorial service for Jordan, so his parents had done it themselves, and she had only attended for Abby's sake. How they'd had to keep it a secret from the press. She talked about the times she dreamed of Jordan and hoped it was all a nightmare, only to have the crushing weight that the nightmare was real descend on her again when she woke.

For the next few hours, Joel listened and Val talked until there was nothing more to say. When she was finished, the first of the US Marshals had arrived in a black SUV.

Marshal Bines took great interest in Joel once she learned he was the lead detective on the Howser murder. By the time she'd finished questioning him, the sky was beginning to lighten in the east. From the porch, Joel saw Val inside, curled up asleep on the couch. She stirred as the screen door squeaked open.

"Are you leaving?" she asked.

"Yeah. They're bringing in a team to search the area. If Jordan is here, they'll find him. They're very good at what they do."

Val walked him to his car. Her eyes were bleary with sleep, but she was still beautiful. It was nice to be able to admit it to himself. Maybe someday he could admit it to her.

When he opened his car door, a piece of paper fell to the ground, and she reached for it. It was a copy of the designs found on Howser's body that he'd shown Shannon.

"What's this?" she asked.

"This is what Howser was doing with the marker he took from your house."

She looked at him in surprise. "What?"

"These designs were drawn on his body. We think he did it himself."

"Why?"

Joel shook his head. He was so tired, it was difficult to think straight. "I don't know. He'd been keeping a notebook with sketches of *Robert Apocalypse* scenes, but I haven't figured out if it's relevant or not. Everyone says Howser wasn't very bright, and prison didn't help. I'm not sure what it means, but it seems he was fixated on these symbols before he died. Did they have something to do with whoever he was running away from? Did he know something about Eliza Bellingham's disappearance? More and more, I think this is connected to her, but I still can't see how. Ryan Moyer said she had a secret boyfriend, a Dr. M."

"M as in Menace?"

"You've seen the webcomic too?"

"A bit. You should ask Carter about it. He knows way more than I do."

"I did. He had some good suggestions. I still need to interview all of Eliza's friends and see which of them knew about the webcomic and if they think there might have been a connection. Only one supported Ryan's story that Eliza had mentioned a Dr. M, but she doesn't live here anymore. So either Eliza was really good at keeping secrets or Ryan made it all up." Joel yawned. He didn't want to tell Val about his investigation into Paul Sheen. With the news about Jordan, it seemed pointless to make her worry, especially if it didn't amount to anything.

"Well," Val said with a smile, slipping an arm around his waist, "maybe now that the feds are here, I won't be so high maintenance. You'll actually be able to focus on someone else for a while."

"Now that would be a real shame." Joel wrapped his arms around her and pulled her close. Her hair smelled faintly of fried oil, and he was reminded again of how she'd spent her evening. This time, though, when he thought of her date with Carter, he didn't feel even a trace of jealousy.

21

When Val dropped Abby off at the police station, she couldn't help feeling giddy at the thought of seeing Joel. It had only been a few hours since he'd left her, and they'd texted frequently since, mostly about the marshals' search. But there was an easiness to their texts, now. Less self-consciousness. She felt like the same words now carried an important subtext: *I care.*

A woman with a short black bob sat at the reception counter. She looked up as they came in.

"Hello there! You must be Valerie! My name is Kathy. And are you Abigail?"

Abby nodded, but her eyes were on a Spider-Man bobblehead sitting on the edge of the counter.

"Go ahead. Touch it," Kathy said.

Abby did, and as it wobbled ridiculously, a small smile twitched her lips. Abby hadn't been thrilled to wake up and find marshals prowling around the property. She'd been in a foul mood ever since.

"Thank you so much for helping out today," Val said to Kathy. "It's been a rough morning."

"We have strangers at the house," Abby said. "I just want Detective Joel, not any other police."

"Speak of the devil," Kathy murmured as Joel came into the room.

"I thought I knew those voices," he said, smiling.

Val's heart fluttered like she was ten years younger. She hoped Kathy wouldn't notice her blushing.

Abby offered him a high five, then tried to teach him a special handshake she'd done with her friends at her old school.

"I hope she won't be any trouble," Val said to Kathy. "I don't know how long this will take, but I expect no longer than an hour."

"Don't worry about it. I brought some Legos from home and laid them out in the interrogation room. It's not—" she amended, seeing the look on Val's face. "It's just an empty office. Lunchroom, conference room. Whatever we need it to be. She'll be fine."

"Good luck," Joel said as Val gave Abby a quick hug and kiss. She would have liked to hug Joel too, but didn't dare in front of Kathy. So she just smiled and thanked them both.

Her phone rang as she reached her car. Seeing Carter's name gave her a stab of guilt. She hadn't even thought about Carter since she sent him home the night before.

She answered brightly to compensate. "Hi there!"

"Val?"

"Yeah, it's me."

"Oh. I thought…I was just calling to check on you.

I've been worried about you since last night."

Too cheery. She brought her voice down to a moderate pitch.

"I'm all right. There are federal agents here looking for Jordan, so I'm feeling better about things."

"The agents came to your house?"

"Yeah. I told them about Sam Howser and they wanted to check things out themselves."

"Do you think Jordan had anything to do with Howser's death?" Carter's voice was charged with urgency and Val immediately regretted telling him. She climbed in her car and started the engine to get the A/C running, balancing the need to conserve gas when money was tight with her need to not show up at a job interview looking like she'd been sweating in a tin can.

"I don't know. But Carter, please don't say anything. I'm talking to you as a friend, not as a reporter. It's up to them to decide how to involve the media, but I can't handle that kind of publicity right now."

Carter blew out a breath. "I get it. I just…wow. You've had a wild ride."

"You can stay that again. Thanks for checking in on me, Carter. You're a good friend."

"No problem. Let me know if there's anything else I can do." But he sounded distracted and Val hoped she hadn't made a mistake in telling him as much as she did. She almost called him back to make him swear he wouldn't put it on the news, but she only had a few minutes until her interview.

As she drove the few blocks down Main Street, thoughts of Carter gave way to memories of Joel. The feel of his arms around her the night before. The way his dark eyes made her melt when he smiled. The promise of seeing him again.

That thought gave her a fresh jolt of confidence, and she faced her interview without any of the earlier embarrassment she'd felt when applying for the job. Maddie was formal and professionally distant during the interview with the bank manager. But she hugged Val before she left and whispered in her ear, "You rocked it."

For the first time in a long time, Val allowed herself to hope that things were going to get better.

As Val left the bank, a warm wind whipped her hair. In the distance, thick white clouds were boiling up over the hills, their underbellies dark and heavily shadowed. By the time she got back to the station, they had doubled in size.

"It looks like there's a storm brewing," she said as she came in to gather Abby.

"Oh, that would be nice," Kathy said. "As long as it brings rain and not just lightning. Those poor firefighters need all the help they can get."

Abby was happily occupied at a table in the interrogation room, noisily sorting through the box of Legos. Joel crouched at her elbow, handing her long skinny pieces.

"Mom! Do you like my spaceship?" she asked, holding up a fragile construction that looked like a Cubist tree.

"That looks amazing. Are you ready to go?"

"Now? But Kathy said she was going to get donuts!"

Joel stood and stretched. "Abby can stay, if you want."

Abby looked at him sharply.

"Sorry! Abigail. I'd be happy to bring *Abigail* home when I'm finished here. I know things are chaotic at your place."

"Hmm…tempting. Honestly, I could really use a nap. I wonder if I could get one with those marshals beating the bushes."

"So, what do you say? You want to leave her here and go get some rest?"

Val turned to Abby. "What do you think? Do you want to stay or come home with me now?"

Abby cocked her head incredulously. "I want donuts."

"Well, that's settled, if you're sure you don't mind."

"Absolutely. It'll be no trouble." Joel's response was casually neutral, but she caught a gleam in his eyes and knew he was glad for the excuse to come over as much as she was. "I'll walk you out."

He held the door open for her, and she felt heat rise in her neck as she walked past him, near enough to smell his aftershave and sense the warmth of his body. He followed her out, and as soon as they were out of sight of the door, his fingers brushed hers. She took his hand, the small touch making her heart skip. It felt so surreal to be affectionate with him after all their years of friendship, but also like the most natural thing in the world.

"Do you want to stay for dinner tonight?" she offered. "I've been promising Abby a blackberry cobbler for days, but we keep getting thwarted. The bushes at the pump house are so loaded they're practically obscene."

"That sounds amazing. But I was actually wondering if you wanted to come to my place this evening. Get out from underneath the investigators."

"Really?" Val realized she didn't even know where he lived. The idea of seeing his home excited and terrified her.

"What is it? What's that look for?"

"I'm trying to guess if your house looks the same as Lacey left it or if you've let it go all bachelor pad like a college kid."

Joel laughed. "I'd like to think I have some standards. I'll make sure to pick up the pizza boxes and video games before you get there."

"Save a slice of pepperoni for me first," she said, giving him a quick kiss on the cheek. She didn't know who might be watching from the office windows and didn't want to embarrass Joel in front of his colleagues. But as she drove away, the sensation of his hand on her back lingered pleasantly in her thoughts.

The clouds in the west were darker now and had filled nearly half the sky, casting the world in an ethereal contrast of light and shadow. Colors seemed both muted and vibrant at once, and the rays of remaining light shone in dramatic shafts against the gathering gloom.

If the dark clouds unleashed all the moisture they were amassing, it could be a great boon to containing the wildfires. But if they held back and brought only lightning, setting off dozens or even hundreds of new fires, it could be catastrophic.

Val followed a pickup truck with bales of hay stacked in the T-shaped pattern that always reminded

Abby of George Washington's signature hairstyle. Little bits of chaff blew at her in the truck's wake, glittering in the fading light like autumn leaves.

It really is a gift to live in a place like this, she thought. Maybe when the property sold she and Abby would stay in the area, at least until things were resolved with Jordan. No one here knew what he'd done. And even if they found out, she had a better chance of finding support here than anywhere else. It was her hometown. They'd give her the benefit of the doubt, wouldn't they?

Thinking of it all made her stomach clench uncomfortably. She was going to have to tell Abby what the investigators were doing there, otherwise, Abby was bound to overhear something. The longer Val waited to tell her, the more confused and betrayed Abby would feel. She was old enough now that she was starting to understand that the world was complex, and people weren't always what they seemed. But Val didn't relish destroying her image of her father.

Making a cobbler suddenly seemed more important than ever. It was such a small thing, but the kind of gesture that might show Abby she could count on Val, that some things in life could be depended on no matter what. No matter how many false starts, unexpected interruptions, or even significant sacrifices it required, Val would be there for her.

A black van was parked outside her house when she arrived, and Val saw more federal agents crossing her yard than had been there that morning.

Bines greeted her as she exited the car. "I wish we'd been first on the scene," she said. "It's hard to come in after the locals and do a proper job of it."

Val objected to the derisive use of the word 'locals.' "Maybe if we'd known two weeks ago that Jordan had come through Seattle, we could have told you sooner what was going on here."

"Yeah, that was our fault," Bines said matter-of-factly. "Breakdown in communication. We didn't find out until yesterday. Should have detained him the second he hit Border Patrol."

Bines was a brisk, no-nonsense woman. Val could imagine her dominating the volleyball court when she was young, slamming the ball down in a powerful spike as her opponents cowered. Val had no question Bines could get the job done. But she was eager to have an excuse to leave the house tonight and leave her to her work.

Val changed quickly out of her interviewing clothes and grabbed a bucket—an old ice cream tub with a crack near the lip where the handle connected to the base. She thought about telling Bines where she was going, but worried the woman would insist on sending an agent with her. And Val really didn't want someone standing around impatiently, waiting for her to finish picking blackberries.

Val slipped out the back door while Bines was busy at the van. She pulled her hair into a ponytail as she walked to keep it from blowing into her face. She hoped for rain to break the oppressive heat, but not until after she'd finished. With her back to the farmhouse, her thoughts filled with Joel and the evening ahead. It was just her and the wide fields and the air thick with the promise of rain. Val couldn't remember the last time she'd felt so alive.

Joel had a message waiting for him when he returned from saying goodbye to Val. It was Roxy Nickels, manager at Sherm's Hardware Store. She said she remembered Eliza well and would be happy to talk to him anytime and how glad she was that the police were still investigating her disappearance all these years later because it was really horrible that her mother had never gotten closure and if there was anything she could do to help, she would.

Joel glanced at his notes. He didn't know for sure if Sam Howser's death was connected with the teenager's disappearance, and the only real evidence linking the two were the *Robert Apocalypse* drawings. But now he had two additional persons of interest who didn't have any relationship to the webcomic—Paul Sheen and Jordan Fisher.

And then there was the question of Bryson Gottschalk. Not exactly a person of interest, but Joel still felt compelled to dig a little further. His fan site for *Robert Apocalypse* had posts dating all the way back to 2008, nearly six months before Eliza disappeared. Could he have been the one who introduced her to it? At a time when no one else in the area even knew it existed, was it possible the two early fans knew each other?

Joel rubbed a hand against the back of his neck, thinking. With federal agents looking for him, there wasn't much he could do about Jordan Fisher. But he could talk to Roxy and find out if she remembered Paul

Sheen being friendly with Eliza when she worked at the hardware store.

Grabbing the copies of the drawings and a six-pack of photos, Joel told Kathy and Abby his plans. It was no more than a three minute drive to the hardware store with its weathered plank siding and rusted tin roof. As he parked, he thought of the new buildings he'd seen in Pineview that had intentionally been constructed to look old and run-down. What had Lacey called it? Rustic chic? By comparison, he appreciated that the hardware store was genuine, not contrived. Though in this case it was all rustic, no chic.

Some of the photos he'd chosen were residents of Owl Creek, Paul Sheen included. He didn't feel comfortable putting any unwarranted pressure on Sheen until he knew if he had a connection with Eliza Bellingham, so Joel was careful to keep his questions to Roxy neutral.

He laid the photographs on the counter in the break room.

"Did any of these men frequent the hardware store while Eliza worked here? Do you recognize any of them as being regular customers?"

Roxy peered carefully at the photographs, her long red hair falling over her shoulder. She had the voice and stained fingers of a smoker. "Him, him, maybe him. I can't tell with that mustache. But this one was here a lot to see Eliza. They'd sit in the back on her smoke break. Sat in his truck during the winter when it was too cold to be outside."

Joel perked up. "Interesting. Did you tell the deputies this when she disappeared?"

"They didn't ask. And I hadn't seen him around in a long time. Besides, I knew they were looking at that Moyer kid. I figured they had a good reason for it."

"Did you think this man and Eliza were involved romantically?"

"I don't know. Ryan was Eliza's boyfriend. But she didn't seem the type to be happy with just one guy. She really liked the attention, you know? Sweet girl, though. I didn't want her to get in trouble."

"Did you worry she'd get in trouble with him?"

"Well, the age difference concerned me, obviously. But sometimes I wondered if she was doing more with him than just smoking, you know?"

"I'm not sure I do. Can you explain?"

"She didn't always seem happy to see him. I don't know if she felt guilty about cheating on Ryan or if she owed him money or what. But it seemed like it was getting to be too much for her. I tried to get her to talk about it once, to see if she was in some sort of trouble. But she brushed me off. Said he was more mild than menacing anyway."

Joel started. "Can you repeat that?"

"Just what I said. She laughed at me and said, 'Roxy, you don't need to worry about me. No matter what he says, he's more mild than menacing anyway.'"

"You're sure she said that exactly? Menacing?"

"Yeah. She always liked using big words. Smart girl in some ways, but so stupid in others."

"Thank you, Roxy, you've been very helpful." Joel couldn't get to his car fast enough. He tossed the photos on the passenger seat, Carter's picture staring at him from the top of the pile.

22

The wind turned cool as Val followed the rutted road along the perimeter of the field to the old pump house. From this angle, the shack looked like it was leaning against the weight of the encroaching bushes. The blackberries were profuse and plump, especially the deeper into the bushes she reached. Old vines had died off, leaving space where she could worm her way between the younger bushes, tamping down canes as she went. Soon she was almost surrounded.

There was something peaceful about being surrounded in a thicket of blackberries, Val decided. From there she couldn't hear the distant sounds of cars on the highway or the chatter of the federal agents on their radios. Across the valley, thunder rumbled, and the wind gusted steadily. She had just finished filling her bucket and turned to leave when her foot caught on a vine.

Val cried out as she stumbled, dropping the bucket. She fell to her knees, her skin tearing on sharp barbs.

But even worse was the carnage of berries now spilling among the trampled canes and dead grass. She sucked at a bloody spot on her finger and hurried to pick up as many of the berries as she could without gathering too much dead grass with them.

Val shook her head. This was just as much a part of the process as the sweet cobbler with cold vanilla ice cream. Some of the berries were gone for good. Sighing in exasperation, she went to stand, but noticed something under the layers of trampled canes beneath her feet. It was red and boxy. She carefully moved aside the canes wide enough to slip her fingers through. A thorn pricked her as she pulled it out.

It was a red flip phone, an old style she hadn't seen in years. It had obviously been out here for a long time, overgrown as the area was by blackberries. Its paint was faded and the seams were caked with dirt.

She flipped it over to see if it still held a SIM card and stopped. On the back, centered over the battery cover, was a decal sticker of a symbol she'd become very familiar with in recent weeks. The Grover-C.

No, not the Grover-C.

She'd read enough *Robert Apocalypse* now to see the difference. This was the O.Blivion.

The same symbol Sam Howser had drawn on himself before he died.

The symbol of Doctor Menace. Villain and possible namesake for Eliza's mysterious Dr. M.

Police thought Eliza hadn't texted anyone for help the night she broke down. But maybe she had. Was Val holding the secret phone Eliza had used to contact her enigmatic Dr. M?

A chill crept down Val's neck. Daylight dimmed as dark clouds rolled in front of the sun. The thunder was getting closer.

Thorns scratching at her bare ankles, Val left her bucket and charged out of the blackberry bushes, phone in hand. She held it between her thumb and forefinger, afraid to touch it. She knew it was stupid, but the thought that the phone may have been connected to a girl's disappearance—and possible death—made her feel like she was holding a snake.

When a man appeared from around the pump house, she yelped in surprise.

"Carter! What are you doing here?"

Carter looked just as surprised to see her. "Val! I…I was looking for you. The marshals didn't know where you were so I thought I'd try our old hangout spot."

"I wanted to pick blackberries before the storm hit. But look, you'll never believe what I found."

She thrust the phone at him, but he fumbled it, dropping it to the ground.

"Where did you get that?" His voice sounded accusing.

Val picked it up again. "I found it in the blackberries just now. I think it could be Eliza Bellingham's missing phone. Look, it has Doctor Menace's symbol."

She flipped it over to show him the sticker. "I think Ryan was right. Dr. M—whoever he was—was responsible for Eliza's disappearance. I think this was a phone he gave her so she could keep their relationship a secret. He had to get rid of it when he killed her—and I'm sure he killed her, or why get rid of the phone?"

She looked at Carter, expecting him to whoop in delight at the great clue she'd uncovered.

Instead, he looked deathly pale and very still.

"Carter?" she asked hesitantly. Then, the pieces fell into place. Carter, who had a tattoo of the same symbol. Carter, who had sounded so urgent when she told him about marshals on her property.

He grabbed her so fast she couldn't react. He twisted her arm behind her painfully and his hand covered her mouth, tasting of salty sweat.

"You've always been too smart for your own good, Val. I really, really wish you hadn't found that phone."

Joel called the university from the hardware store parking lot. It was an agonizing wait to get past the phone tree and get to a live person, then escalate his request to someone who could do something about it. He tapped his steering wheel, jittery with the need to act and unable to do anything but wait.

Carter had lied. He'd looked Joel right in the eye and lied to him about knowing Eliza Bellingham. What else was he hiding?

At last, he talked to a registrar with the authority to tell him what he wanted to know.

"Carter Millston was not enrolled during spring term of 2009."

"And he wasn't doing an internship or study abroad or anything like that?"

"Not enrolled means not enrolled, including in any of our special credit-earning programs."

"Would you have record of where he was living at the time?"

"Only if he were living on campus, which he could only do if he were enrolled." The registrar was getting impatient.

Despite the dark clouds amassing overhead, Joel's car was getting stuffy. He turned on the engine and air conditioning and reached for his radio.

"Larry, I need you to get started on a warrant affidavit to search Carter Millston's residence. Specifically electronics—any device that would connect to the internet."

"Carter Millston, the reporter? You're kidding me."

"I wish. I'll fill you in when I get back."

He texted Carter from his personal phone next, trying to keep his tone light.

Hey, how'd your date go last night?

Carter didn't respond.

That wasn't much bait. He went for something more scintillating.

Did you hear about Val's husband? Crazy story. Need to chat.

Still no response.

There was no reason to worry. Carter had hidden his involvement with Eliza for seven years. There'd be no reason for him to think anything had changed as long as Joel played it cool.

Except Joel had already told him too much about Eliza's suspected connection to Dr. M.

He texted Val.

I'm going to have to postpone tonight. I'll explain later. So sorry. I'll make it up to you, I promise.

By the time he got back to the office, Carter still hadn't responded. Val, too, was quiet.

She was probably just napping like she'd planned. No need to get worked up about it. But Joel still felt a tension he couldn't shake.

Val struggled against Carter as he pushed the pump house door open and muscled her inside. He was strong, and her skin chafed painfully where he held her. When he released her, she staggered and caught herself against the old pump, looking down at the damp particle board screwed over the top of the old well.

Carter looped an old length of baling twine through the door latch and back, wrapping it tight around itself to hold the door closed. It wasn't secure, but would stop her from making a quick escape. He stood in front of the door, shaking his head.

"I can't believe this. I never meant for you to get mixed up in all this."

"What's going on?" Val demanded, trying to hide the fear in her voice. "What have you done?"

"Stop. Don't talk to me. I've gotta figure this out. This wasn't supposed to happen. None of it, I swear."

"So *you* are Eliza's Dr. M?" Val asked.

Carter didn't answer. He moved around the room,

kicking at debris and picking up scraps of wood and concrete, hefting them.

"What are you doing?" Panic surged from her stomach to her chest. "Are you looking for…do you plan to kill me?"

"Shut-up, Val! This isn't what I want, I promise."

"Then don't do it! You're a good man, Carter! Whatever happened with Eliza, you don't have to make the same mistake!"

"I didn't kill Eliza," he snapped.

"Then what happened to her?"

He ran a hand through his hair, making it stand on end. "She texted me that night to pick her up after her car broke down. We went up the mountain to try out some new stuff. Speed balls. They were messed up. I don't know if it was dirty or what, but she started, like, foaming at the mouth and thrashing around. I was going to call 911 but it happened too fast. And then it was over, and she was dead."

Lightning flashed ominously outside. Thunder rumbled on its heels.

"Why didn't you call the police?"

"I panicked. She was underage, and I didn't want to go to jail. I was halfway through college and would lose everything. And for what? None of it would bring her back." His eyes were anguished, and his hands shook as another rumble of thunder sounded.

"So you did...what?" Val wasn't sure she wanted to hear the rest of the story.

"I remembered this place where we used to hang out. I knew no one would think to look for her here."

In horror, Val looked at the boarded up well and

backed away until her back hit the wall. She recognized the dank smell in the pump house as rotting wood, but knowing a corpse lay beneath her feet was a hard image to shake.

"I'm sorry, Val. I didn't mean to!" Carter said miserably. "That stuff, it was seriously messed up. I never touched it again after that. It scared me so bad. I never meant for anyone to get hurt."

"Then explain everything. This isn't you. Don't make things worse by..." Something outrageous clicked together in her mind and truth flooded her mind. Sickening, horrible truth. "You were here the night Howser was killed," she said, the words coming faster than she could stop them. "I don't know why I didn't think—you stayed here in the house, keeping an eye on things. But that's not all you did, is it?"

"That was his own fault," Carter growled. "I wanted to find him, see if it would make a good news story. But he had your dad's old baseball bat. Turns out he saw me change my shirt the day I did the story on the fire camp. He recognized my tattoo and decided I was Dr. M. The man was crazy. Took a couple of swings at me with the bat. He would have killed me if I hadn't gotten it from him."

Val's jaw dropped. "How did I—where is it now?"

"Long gone. I washed it up and stuck it in those boxes I cleaned up for you. You didn't want to go through them, remember?"

Val felt woozy thinking of the loads she'd taken to the donation center, never knowing she was getting rid of murder evidence.

"And what about me? If you kill me now, how will you convince yourself it's not your fault?"

Another strobing flash of lightning, and this time the thunder cracked almost at the same time, a sound like the earth being torn in two.

Carter looked panicked. "I can't go to prison, Val. They won't understand. They'll think I meant to kill her, but it was an accident. Howser too, I was just trying to protect myself but—"

"*This* isn't an accident!" Val shrieked. "Let me go and we can work it out. But if you do this now, there's no going back. How many people do you think you can kill before it catches up to you?"

Carter looked for a moment as if he was considering it. Then his eyes hardened. "No. This is the only way."

Wind blew dust across the road as Joel pulled up to the station. In the distance, lightning was sparking against the hills, a firefighter's worst nightmare.

He checked the time. With any luck he'd reach Pineview with affidavit in hand so he could catch the judge before he left for the day. Hurrying toward the building, he pulled out his personal phone. Still no response from Val.

He paused, deliberating, then called. Thunder echoed across the valley as he waited. After four rings it went to voicemail.

That wasn't reassuring.

He knew he was probably overreacting. There were

federal marshals swarming her property. She was safer than she'd been in weeks. But still he felt anxious.

Maybe it was because he was still reeling from learning that Carter had lied to him. That Carter was probably a murderer. For now, he could set his personal feelings aside to do his job, but it made the world seem like a darker place.

Maybe it was thinking about how familiar Carter had been with Val lately. Coming to her home, offering to help, even staying overnight to—

Joel stopped. He checked his calendar to be sure. The night Carter had stayed at Val's fit within the time the medical examiner thought Sam Howser had been killed.

Carter wasn't just a one-time murderer. He'd killed again. And recently.

23

"You don't have to do this," Val pleaded. "We can find another way."

Carter ignored her. He'd abandoned his search and was leaning against the door, staring up at the ceiling.

In the corner, she saw a length of rusted pipe. Could she reach it before he stopped her? The last thing she wanted to do was trigger his desperation. She needed to appeal to his rational mind. Keep him thinking, not feeling.

"You know me, Carter. Can you really look me in the eyes and kill me? You're not a bad person. But if you do this—if you choose to kill a friend in cold blood—then you're the worst kind of monster."

There was a small window—broken, with bits of jagged glass clinging to the frame. But it was too high to climb through without something to stand on. Lightning continued outside, the thunder rising and falling like a tide.

Val continued her pleading. "Think about what this

will do to Abby. Losing both of her parents? How can you do that to her?"

At this, he looked at her. Pink splotches darkened his cheeks, and his eyes looked wild. "I don't want to hurt Abby. I don't want to hurt you either."

His eyes fell on the boarded up well. He looked back at Val, considering.

The blood drained from her face as she imagined being thrown into the abandoned well and left to die with the remains of Eliza Bellingham.

"Don't you dare. I'd rather you killed me outright. You can't seriously think—"

"Shut up, Val. I'm not…I'm not a violent man."

Val bolted for the pipe, and he rushed after her. She grabbed it and swung it at his head, but he easily dodged and caught her wrist. She kicked against his shin, and he grunted, but he grabbed her other hand and twisted her last two fingers so hard she screamed.

She dropped the pipe, panting and blinking back tears. Lightning and thunder cracked overhead, shaking the pump house.

"I know you, Carter. Eliza might have been an accident, but if you kill me, you'll never be able to live with yourself."

A look of pain flashed in his eyes, but he clenched his jaw defiantly.

"I've lived with myself this long. I'll manage."

Joel raced to Val's as fast as he could, the Charger bottoming out with every rut as the road wound closer to the Rockwell house. Trees whipped in the wind and lightning shot out of the sky, but still the clouds held back rain. Joel hoped he was overreacting. He hoped he was worried for nothing.

But then he saw it. Carter's Lexus was pulled off the road onto a little turnout, an abandoned road that had long since overgrown. It wasn't the sight of the car that alarmed him. It was that Carter was clearly trying to keep it hidden from view of the house.

Joel accelerated up the hill and as he rounded the final bend a new worry erupted. Flickering orange light, like that of a bonfire, was growing behind the farmhouse. Val's car was out front, and he offered a silent prayer that she was one of the shapes silhouetted against the light.

Please be okay.

He ran across the yard and found Marshal Bines behind the house with a hose, spraying the fence and grass. On the other side of the gate, fire chased up the hillside, black smoke billowing from the burning grass, radiating heat.

Two other agents were dousing the grass near the house with buckets of water from a spigot near the garage.

Joel shielded his face from the heat of the fire. "Is Val here? Have you seen her?" he shouted to Bines over the low roar of the burning hillside.

"Don't know," Bines barked. "More to the point, where's the fire department? This blaze has doubled in the past five minutes."

He waved away her question and ran up the porch steps, throwing open the screen door. "Val?" The only sound was the snapping of brush igniting behind him. The house was still.

Joel ran up the stairs, calling, "Val? It's me." If she were sleeping or in the bathroom, he didn't want to startle her. He'd give anything for her to be sleeping or in the bathroom.

Her bedroom door stood open, clothes tossed on the bed. He recognized the gray slacks and ruffled black blouse she'd worn earlier to the interview. He closed off the part of him that told him he was infringing on her privacy and let the policeman take over. The bathroom was empty. No sign that she'd showered. Where would she have gone that required changing clothes?

Then he remembered.

The air in the pump house was thick with the smell of ozone and an electric charge raised the hair on the back of Val's neck. Thunder boomed overhead, thrumming through her spine, and wind buffeted the shack.

A faint orange glow flickered on the inside edge of the window trim. Somewhere nearby lightning had ignited the tinder-dry grass and drought-weakened trees.

Was the farmhouse burning? Was fire racing to the pump house?

Panic tasted metallic in Val's mouth.

"We have to get out of here, Carter. Fire is coming. Abby will be so scared. Let me go to her. Let me save my daughter."

Her voice was barely above a whisper. She wasn't

even sure he could hear her above the wind and sky-ripping thunder.

In his eyes she saw only fear. He stepped toward her, hefting the pipe in one hand.

Val lunged for a board resting against the far wall. Carter pushed after her, knocking her to the concrete floor. She hit hard, feeling a sharp pain in her elbow, but she ignored it and twisted, aiming for his face. She connected with a thud.

He roared, reeling back, holding his eye. Only then did she see the bent nail sticking out of the end of the board.

"I'll fight you, Carter." She breathed heavily as she pulled herself to her feet. "I'll fight you and give you bruises and scratches so that when I go missing, you'll be the first person they suspect. Joel will figure it out, and you will have killed me for nothing."

Carter pulled his hand away. A line of blood welled up from a deep cut near his eye. He blinked and wiped his hand on his pants.

"This is your fault, Val. You should have left it alone."

He barreled toward her and she jumped out of the way, but tripped over the pump and fell hard against the particle board covering the well. With a sickening crack, it splintered beneath her.

Val yelped and scrambled off before it completely gave way. She huddled against the wall, looking in horror at the split cover. The well loomed black beneath.

Carter smiled.

Joel ran out the back door and bounded down the porch steps just as the first raindrops fell. Big, fat drops that spread larger than a coin where they hit the steps. It pattered on the roof, forming a high chorus to the deeper roar of the forest in flames.

As he reached Bines, a fir tree exploded high on the mountain, engulfing it in a fireball. Joel ducked as sparks showered down, drifting on the wind toward the house.

"Did you find her?" Bines asked, her mouth set in a grim line. Her eyes were fixed on the mountainside, the hose trained on the fence and surrounding grass. Nearby an agent tossed water on the grass this side of the fence, forming a wet firebreak to keep the blaze from coming closer.

"No, but I think I know where she is. Can I borrow one of your agents? She might be in danger."

Bines swore under her breath and glanced at the sky. "God help us if the wind sends this blaze our way. Ten minutes. I won't risk my men if this turns ugly."

As if in answer, a loud clap of thunder rocked the sky and reverberated off the hills.

Bines turned to the man with the bucket. "Glenn, go with Ramirez. Help him find Mrs. Fisher."

Joel jogged to the edge of the yard, reaching for his phone. He called Kathy, telling her to send a fire tanker to the Rockwell property.

The wind was blowing sheets of rain across the yard. Joel blinked against the water running into his eyes, trying to see through the gray haze. It felt like twilight, not late afternoon. Lighting flashed overhead, followed by a thunderous roar. Glenn eyed the wide open field warily.

"Are you sure about this? It isn't safe out in the open."

"I've got to find Val. Something's wrong. I can't leave her out here."

The ground was so dry the rain was puddling quickly, struggling to seep in past the summer crust. Joel led Glenn along the track that led to the old pump house. In the fading light, he searched for signs of either Val or Carter, but could see nothing.

As they approached the pump house, he slowed. Lightning streaked across the sky, giving it a decidedly haunted feeling. Joel scanned the surrounding blackberries and stopped. A white bucket sat on the ground like a flag of surrender, almost glowing in the early twilight. It was tipped over, spilling blackberries onto the ground. Cast aside. Forgotten.

Dread swelled in the pit of his stomach. Val had been here. Where was she now?

Carefully, he approached the pump house. Glenn rounded the other side, where Joel knew there was a window. He stopped at the door. The outer lock was missing, but when he tried to pull it open, it was jammed. He yanked at it, but it wouldn't give way.

Then, from inside the pump house, he heard a sound that sent a chill down his spine.

Val screamed as Carter lunged for her. She tried to dodge but he was too fast, grabbing her and wrestling her toward the broken cover. One misstep and the remnants would fall free. She would be lost.

Fear exploded through her. She twisted and fought, looking for any exposed skin to bite or claw her way free. Carter grunted with the effort of holding onto her, but he was so much stronger. Little by little, he inched her closer to the hole.

Lightning and thunder ripped above their heads. The smell of smoke was stronger now and the inside of the pump house was lit a sickly orange.

A gunshot split the air, reverberating inside the shack. Val looked to the window where shapes were silhouetted against the glowing sky, hard to make out in the dimness.

"Let her go, Carter!"

Joel.

Val's heart leaped into her throat.

Carter swore. "Leave us alone or I swear I'll kill her! Back away, all of you!"

"Just let her go, and I promise we'll work this out. You don't want to do this. I know you care about Val. You'll never forgive yourself if you do this. Let me help you."

Joel's voice was calm, but carried a note of authority.

"Listen to him," Val begged. "He's your friend. He can help."

In answer, Carter tightened his grip. He shouted above the rain. "Leave me alone and I'll let her go!"

"You know we can't do that. First you let her go,

and then we'll talk about it. I can help you if you'll let me."

"It's not my fault." Carter's voice cracked in desperation. "None of it was supposed to happen. I shouldn't have to go to prison."

"Of course. I understand. We'll talk about that later. But first you have to let go of Val."

Lightning and thunder struck together, shaking the earth with an ear-splitting boom. Carter stumbled, and Val reached for the soft part of his underarm, pinching as hard as she could.

Carter yelled and loosened his grip. Val pushed against him and shook free, running to the window.

"Get down!" Joel shouted.

She dropped to a crouch below the sill, hugging the wall.

Two shots fired and Val screamed, covering her head.

Carter staggered back, stepping onto the rotting well cover. One leg fell through, but the other caught on the outer rim. He lay there, body propped up by the last pieces of splintered wood, his breathing labored. A dark stain spread across his shirt.

Ears ringing, Val ran to the door, tugging at the knots in the baling twine with shaking hands. Turning her back to Carter made her pulse throb in her head, terrified that any moment she would feel his hands on her again.

At last, the twine came free, and she exhaled in panicked relief, pushing the door open. Joel caught her as she fell out of the pump house.

"It's okay. You're all right."

But she didn't feel safe. Not with Carter so near.

A deputy marshal pushed past her into the shack and called for Joel.

"Ramirez. You'd better come here."

He stepped into the shack with one arm wrapped protectively around Val.

Carter was gone. The last of the wood covering had given way. All that was left was a yawning black hole.

24

Lightning strobed in the roiling clouds above as Joel walked Val back to the house. A siren droned in the distance. Rain ran into his eyes and soaked his shirt, and Val's hair clung limply to her shoulders. They didn't speak, and not only because it was hard to hear each other above the pounding rain and rolling thunder. What was there to say? Joel had seen the horror in Val's eyes as she'd looked at the broken well cover. If she didn't want to talk about what she was feeling, he couldn't blame her.

He wasn't ready to talk about it either. If shooting Austin Wilson had nearly wrecked him, how would he survive killing his friend? A deep pain swelled inside and he pushed it away. There would be plenty of time to feel what he'd done later. For now, numbness was safer.

The siren stopped abruptly and Joel mentally praised Owl Creek's volunteer firefighters for responding so quickly. He held Val's hand firmly, even as the rain made their fingers slippery. He wouldn't let her go until he had to. When he thought of how close he'd come to losing her, it filled him with panic. If she hadn't fought to get free when she did, Val would have been the one they were calling in a recovery team for.

It made his heart race just thinking about it.

As the farmhouse came into view, Val gasped.

"It wasn't the house on fire. I thought…"

Joel squeezed her hand. He didn't mention how close it had been. She would see for herself.

The hillside behind the house was smoking now under the deluge, but bright orange patches still glowed with angry heat. A large green tanker truck was parked next to the apple trees, and firefighters were running lengths of hose to the hill.

Marshal Bines was on her phone as they approached.

"Hold on, Glenn," she said and turned her attention to Joel and Val. "You all right, Mrs. Fisher?"

Val nodded but kept her eyes on the house as if she couldn't believe it was still standing.

"Sweetzer, Jefferson, come with me," Bines called to the other agents watching the smoldering mountain. "How is it still burning? It's like a monsoon out here. Don't go far, Mrs. Fisher. I'm going to need to talk to you."

"Not now," Joel said. "Anything you have to say can wait."

Val flashed him a grateful look.

"Ramirez," Bines said sharply. "This is a federal investigation. While I appreciate your assistance, it's clear your involvement at this point is verging on inappropriate." Her eyes flickered to their hands.

"We'll be at the house. You know where to find us." Joel turned his back and continued walking.

"Are you going to get in trouble?" Val asked, holding up their hands. "For this?"

In answer, Joel kissed her hand and held it tightly against his chest. The truth was, he didn't know who had jurisdiction over the case now. But he did know he wasn't going to allow Bines to bully them about it.

When they got back to the house, Val got him a towel to dry his face and hair, then disappeared upstairs to change. Alone in the kitchen, Joel placed a call to his boss. His wet clothes clung to his skin and dripped onto the floor.

When he explained what had happened, Lieutenant Cooper was incredulous.

"You're sure he didn't fall into the well when you shot him?"

"I'm sure. I saw him hit the floor. But when the marshal went in, he was gone."

"How do you explain that? Did the structure fail afterward?"

Joel paused. "I can't say for sure, sir. He may have intentionally fallen."

Cooper swore softly on the other end of the line. "I'll send out a recovery team. Any chance he survived the fall?"

"I don't know. With the deputy marshal on scene, I focused on getting the hostage to safety."

"And by hostage you mean Valerie Fisher, whose husband is the fugitive the feds are hunting for? Jeez, Joel, what kind of a mess did you get yourself into?"

"I'm not sure, but I'm trying to figure it out."

"Eliza Bellingham is in that well." Val had entered the kitchen so softly that Joel hadn't noticed she was there. She was leaning against the door jamb wearing a light sweater and jeans, and combing through her wet hair. A small duffle bag sat at her feet.

"Are you sure about that?" he asked.

Val nodded. "Carter said he hid her body there. He must have lost her phone, though. I'm sure he meant to throw it in the well too. I found it in the blackberries. That's why…that's when he…" She shuddered.

Joel repeated what she'd said to Cooper.

This time, Cooper was silent. "Ramirez, I'm getting the sheriff and coming down there. You stay put. Get as much information as you can from Mrs. Fisher. We'll be there in an hour."

Joel hung up and sighed. His clothes hung clammy against his skin, and he was feeling chilled. But he was more worried about Val. Her skin was pale, and she struggled to meet his eyes.

"They're on their way. He's asked me to get a statement from you. Do you mind? You could wait and talk to him directly if you want. Or would you rather talk to the marshals?"

Val grimaced. "I'd rather talk to you. Where's Abby? Did you leave her at the station?"

"She's fine. Kathy ordered pizza and will bring her to my house later."

She flashed him a grateful look. "I'm so glad she wasn't here for all this. To think that if you hadn't offered to keep her…" Val shook her head as she started a pot of coffee. When it was percolating, she sat across the table from him and sighed.

"This is really hard for me," she admitted. "The only other times I've been interrogated were when the feds investigated Jordan. I didn't know if they'd believe me. I didn't even know what they were talking about."

Joel reached across the table and placed his hand on hers. "Hey, this is me. You're telling me what happened, that's all. Just tell me what we're dealing with."

By the time Val finished her story, the rain had stopped and clouds were clearing in the west. A shaft of golden sunlight cut through the room, landing on the table between them. Val blinked, looking outside at the sunset.

"What time is it?" she said, suddenly alert. "I need to get Abby. I can't believe I left her there all day. Poor thing." She grabbed her purse and keys from the counter and reached for the duffle bag.

Joel followed her outside, where Cooper and Sheriff Larson were engaged in a warm discussion with Bines about jurisdiction.

"With all due respect," Larson was saying, "this has nothing to do with your search for Jordan Fisher. In fact, with Carter Millston now the primary suspect in Samuel Howser's death, there's no legitimate reason for you to be here."

Bines was not impressed. "We'll stay as long as we need to, Sheriff. Don't worry, we'll deliver your suspect to you when we recover his body. But Jordan Fisher has ruined far more lives than your little attempted murderer, and if there's even a chance he's been here, we're not leaving."

"We have reason to believe the body of a missing

girl is in that well. That's my investigation, and you're interfering."

"Let's go," Joel murmured to Val.

"Mrs. Fisher!" Bines' voice cracked out. "Where are you going?"

Val stopped and turned, fire in her eyes. "I'm picking up my daughter, Ms. Bines. And then I'm going to sleep at a friend's house so you can continue your investigation without us being a part of it. I don't think my seven-year-old needs to be here when two corpses are pulled out of the well, do you? If you need to get a hold of me, you can reach me through Joel."

Bines opened her mouth to protest, but Sheriff Larson spoke first.

"Thank you for your cooperation, Mrs. Fisher. We'll be in touch."

Joel hid a smile as he followed Val to her car. But she growled when she saw the Sheriff's car had boxed hers in.

"Let's take mine," Joel offered.

Once inside, she slammed the door angrily and turned to him. "You know you're the friend we're staying with, right?"

"Oh." He hadn't realized. "Okay."

She nodded curtly. "Thanks."

They drove in silence down the hill, until he turned onto the highway.

"How did you know?" she asked. "About Carter?"

"I didn't. I was pursuing a lead on Paul Sheen and got lucky."

Val shook her head. "I can't believe I trusted him. I

let him sleep in my house. I let him play with Abby. Will I never learn?"

Joel looked at her profile, barely visible in the fading light. "I could say there was no way you could have known. That he deceived all of us, including me. But it won't make you feel better, any more than it makes me feel better."

Out of the corner of his eye, he saw her watching him. "Thank you for coming for me today," she said softly.

"Always," he said, then worried that it sounded too cheesy. But she fell into a thoughtful silence, so maybe it was exactly what she needed to hear.

25

Val and Abby slept at Joel's for two nights. Val couldn't bring herself to tell Abby the truth, and said they were having a slumber party to get away from the marshals. Joel had a spare bedroom, and Abby was more than happy to share the full-sized bed with Val, though Val didn't care for Abby's sharp elbows and knees jabbing her during the night.

She worried Joel would think she was trying to force a commitment too soon. But he was thoughtful and solicitous and never acted like they were more than just house guests. She'd expected him to be in the thick of the investigation, but his boss wanted him kept out of it. Joel said it was typical to be placed on administrative leave until the agency finished their own investigation of events.

"You mean they're investigating you now?" Val was appalled.

"It's a necessary protocol. I don't have anything to

hide, but if I did, they wouldn't want me muddying the waters, would they?"

"But he was going to kill me! You saved my life!"

"Maybe. Until they examine his body, we won't know whether it was mine or Glenn's shot that stopped him. Or both."

But she wouldn't be distracted from her point. "It was the right thing to do, and you know it."

"Yeah, and I would do it again. But they have to be thorough. Nine times out of ten, in a situation like this, the cop made the right call. But that tenth time, you've gotta make sure you find out what went wrong."

Val felt awkward that first day, hanging around in a strange place with a man she was just getting to know again. At least there weren't any lingering signs of Lacey to add to her discomfort. The furnishings were sensible, and the flooring and cabinets had been recently updated. It was clear that Joel had been serious about making a fresh start, a thought which comforted her.

She also gained a new appreciation for who her friend had become in adulthood. She learned that he kept things neat but not fastidiously so. He'd learned to play the guitar after he and Lacey split up, and after some good-natured teasing, Val and Abby enjoyed looking up songs on his tablet for him to play so they could sing along.

She also learned that he didn't sleep well. Both nights, she noticed his light on in the early hours of the morning.

"It started after Stan's," he explained when she

asked him about it that first morning over a bagel and coffee. "Some nights it's worse than others."

"You did the right thing," Val said automatically, then regretted it. His silence served as a palpable disagreement.

After a few minutes, he spoke without meeting her eyes. "Austin Wilson."

"Who?"

"He was supposed to graduate that spring. I came in through the loading dock and he was standing there next to the chip rack. I thought he had a gun, but it turned out to be a cell phone. Witnesses claimed he wanted to surrender, but I never gave him a chance."

Val didn't know what to say. She reached across the table and took Joel's hand. His fingers were dry and warm in hers, the bronze of his skin making her own look a dusty pink. She knew what it was like to not be able to sleep from the nightmares keeping her awake: knew enough of pain to know she couldn't reach his no matter how much she wanted to.

The second evening, before putting Abby to bed, she looked up a yoga routine online and invited Joel to join them. Together they moved the coffee table out of the way and took up positions on the thick rug. Val was out of shape, Abby was uncoordinated, and Joel had no balance, so the three of them laughed through the workout together. When it was finished, Val felt strong. It was a small thing, but it was a start.

Carter's body was retrieved the day after the storm, but it took longer to find the remains of Eliza Bellingham. When Joel told Val they'd found her, there was a note of subdued triumph in his voice. Val felt only acute sadness. So much life wasted: from Eliza to Ryan to Sam Howser. Add to that the ruined lives of those who'd loved them, who were devastated by their deaths.

She only watched the late night news, so she didn't risk Abby seeing their house on TV. But she checked online articles almost obsessively, weighing them with a healthy dose of skepticism and cataloguing which of the details she knew were wrong. The discovery of Eliza's body—and the fact that her killer had died at the same place where he'd hidden her—qualified for almost a full twenty-four hours of national attention, with headlines shared on social media for days afterward.

Val spent hours on the phone with Gina going over what had happened and talking her out of jumping on a plane to come see for herself that Val was okay. A part of Val couldn't wait to get home and settle back into a routine, but another part of her dreaded it. It no longer felt like the sanctuary she'd been looking for when she'd moved back to Owl Creek.

On the second morning, Marshal Bines called. "You'll be happy to know that Jordan Fisher was taken into custody last night in Denver." Bines was tough as nails, but she'd respected her request to not call Jordan her husband. Val appreciated her for that.

"Thank you," Val said, feeling a release of some of the tension she'd been carrying since Bines's first call three days earlier. "So he didn't come here after all?"

"Can't say for sure, but it appears not."

That was a relief. "Now what?"

"He'll be taken back to Illinois to stand trial. I won't lie, Mrs. Fisher. It's going to get ugly."

"I know."

"If you want my advice, stay as far away from it as you can. You don't have to testify against him, and you've got your daughter to think about. And if you don't mind my saying so, you've got Ramirez who's hotter than a hot plate set to sizzle."

Val's face burned, and she stuttered over a response.

But the marshal wasn't finished. "It's not over yet, but when it is, I hope you can put this all behind you and enjoy a new life."

"Thank you, Ms. Bines."

When Joel took Val and Abby home, it was oddly quiet without all the police vans and federal agents. He and Larry had come earlier to clean up police tape and debris from the investigation, an unexpected courtesy. With the wildfires nearly forty percent contained due to the recent rainfall, the skies were clear and startlingly blue, aside from a column of brown-tinged smoke in the distance. Only the scarred mountainside behind the house showed remnants of what had transpired, with charred trees skeletal against blackened grass.

All was still, but Val felt unsettled. Abby bounded up the porch steps, screen door slamming as she ran into the house. Val hesitated before going inside.

"I don't know how I'll tell her the truth."

"About Jordan?"

"About Jordan. Carter. What almost happened to me. What happened to Eliza. She's bound to hear about it eventually, and I'd rather she heard it from me first."

Joel put his arm around her waist and pulled her close. She leaned in to him, reveling in his nearness.

"If you want to talk to someone, I can get you the

name of a good therapist in Pineview. She specializes in trauma and helped me a lot after Stan's. She might be able to help you and Abby too."

Val pulled away to look at him. "You continue to amaze me, Joel Ramirez. The hero sheriff's detective who sees a shrink?"

Joel smiled. "Doesn't fit the mold?"

"Actually," she said, considering, "it's exactly what I should have expected. You're too smart not to get help when you need it."

She kissed him gently, enjoying the feeling of his arms around her, his lips moving against hers, the sharp brush of whisker where he hadn't shaved. When she pulled away, it was with a small sigh. After all she'd been through, and all that still lay ahead, there was this. She had Joel and Abby, and as long as they were together, she had reason to hope.

"We're going to be okay, right?" she asked, even though she already knew the answer.

"Yes. We're going to be okay."

Then he kissed her back.

THANK YOU FOR READING!

If you enjoyed *Smoke Over Owl Creek*, please consider leaving a review on Amazon, Goodreads, or BookBub. (Or all three for you overachievers!) Thanks for helping get my work into the hands of other readers like you.

As a special thank you, I'm delighted to share an exclusive glimpse of the Robert Apocalypse comic. One episode of this fictional webcomic has been produced in full color for your indulgence.

Find the exclusive episode at **robertapocalypse.com** (or use the QR code here).

THE STORY CONTINUES IN
HUNT AT OWL CREEK

"Nonstop suspense with shocking twists I never saw coming!"

"…from start to finish I could hardly put it down…"

"Captivating and mysterious with a nail biting ending!"

EVIL IS DARKEST IN THE SHADOWS

"...a page-turner that you better not start at bedtime..."

"...a rollercoaster mystery that keeps you guessing at every turn and leaves you wanting to ride it again!"

"...an engaging and suspenseful story that will keep readers hooked until the very last page."

CAN JUSTICE BE SERVED FROM BEYOND THE GRAVE?

"deliciously suspenseful"

"had me hooked from the beginning"

"a few twists to keep the reader on their toes and a final chapter that brought me to tears"

What do a high-octane mommy blogger, a Wild West romance, and a [possibly] possessed antique doll have in common?

You can find them all in my FREE collection of short stories. Visit carenhahn.com to download your copy!

ACKNOWLEDGMENTS

In some ways, this book is a bittersweet homage to my hometown, a rural logging town in Southern Oregon which inspired Owl Creek. Though not all my memories are cozy and idyllic, I will forever be indebted to teachers, coaches, and church youth leaders who did their best to preserve the joy of childhood, including a school librarian who allowed a shy girl who hated crowds to spend my recess time finding adventure in books.

A shout-out goes to all who saw *Smoke Over Owl Creek* when it was so fresh and green I swear its pores were dripping with sap. Some of you may remember it when I shared my daily first drafts in November 2019 as part of National Novel Writing Month (NaNoWriMo). Your excitement was the best payoff I could have hoped for.

Credit goes to members of the All Day All Write writing camp where Robert Apocalypse's namesake was born, and my readers on Facebook who helped generate names for Amy Geddon and the O.Blivion.

Thanks to those who helped shape this novel into something that doesn't require an apology every time I share it. Some who provided helpful feedback and editing support include Crystal Brinkerhoff, Jenny Hahn, Kristin South, and Emily Poole of Midnight

Owl Editors. Riley Brinkerhoff deserves special mention for generously having a scary cougar encounter and living to tell the tale. Thanks for letting me interrogate you about it later, and also for not dying.

There's nothing more nerve-wracking than having your fictional law enforcement characters critiqued by a professional. Special appreciation goes to Detective Todd Spingath, who not only provided invaluable feedback, but did so with grace and generosity. Any mistakes are my own, but I promise there are a lot fewer because of him.

This book is dedicated to my parents, Joan and Dennis Schofield, whom I credit for introducing me to the world of fiction. My earliest memories are of raiding my older siblings' backpacks as a preschooler, looking for the newest *Three Investigators* books. "You're not old enough" is a phrase I never heard, even when I transitioned to adult fiction before I'd even hit my teens.

As always, I couldn't have done this without Andrew, who never complains when drafting a new manuscript takes over my life and supports me as a marketing partner, cover designer, campaign planner, cheerleader, and most importantly, loving husband and friend.

ABOUT THE AUTHOR

Caren Hahn grew up in a tiny logging community with more than its fair share of tragedy and violent crime, giving her early exposure to the dark side of small town life. She writes relationship dramas in a variety of genres featuring empathetic characters who are exquisitely flawed—the stuff of great book group discussions. Caren is blessed to live in the most beautiful place on the planet (i.e. the Pacific Northwest), with her husband and six children.

Sign up to get updates at carenhahn.com and receive a free collection of short stories. Follow her on social media to learn more about her upcoming projects.

Made in the USA
Middletown, DE
14 July 2024